Borrowed
Time

ALSO BY KELLY COCHRAN

THE ASPEN MOORE SERIES
Buying Time

For more information about this series, visit
www.AspenMoore.com

Borrowed Time

An Aspen Moore Novel

Kelly Cochran

 BOOKRISE
Austin, Texas

ISBN 978-0-9840026-2-7

Library of Congress Control Number: 2016955595

DEDICATION

For My Mother —
People say diamonds are a girl's
best friend. You are my diamond.

1

GUILT. It was the main reason I was standing in my apartment holding a dog dressed like a devil.

My dog PJ was the offspring of my landlady's dog Sassy and a boastful Bichon Frise named Mr. Personality, aka Mr. P. Mr. P belonged to one of my clients. As a personal concierge, I spent most of my time taking care of things my clients didn't have time to do, but on the day of PJ's conception my landlady, Mrs. Rippetoe, had been my pinch hitter. She had watched Mr. P while I'd tended to the important task of saving my tail after discovering someone was after it. A few months later PJ was born. He was the runt of the litter and quickly became the king of my life.

I adjusted PJ's red horns and pointy tail. I tied a pitchfork to his collar to complete his costume, though some might argue it was more like a uniform since PJ hadn't exactly graduated with honors from obedience training class. The two of us were going to attend the Mardi Gras pet parade in Soulard with my landlady and her dog Sassy. I gathered my stuff and headed downstairs to her apartment.

I knocked on her door. "You ready Mrs. Rippetoe?"

"Oh hun, she doesn't mind the halo, but I can't get her angel wings to stay upright. See for yourself." She opened the door wide.

Sassy turned in circles as she bit the wings on her back. Her halo hovered above.

"Come on, Sassy," I said, bribing her with a treat. I removed the wings and handed them to Mrs. Rippetoe. "We'll put these on her at the parade."

We walked out to what had once been my dream car – a midnight blue, platinum trimmed Jeep. Lately, it had lost its sexy. The windows were slobber covered, the leather passenger seat scratched, and the carpet sprouted little white hairs.

I loaded the dogs into the back, closed the hatch and walked around to help Mrs. Rippetoe into the car. On the brink of seventy, she took care of herself, but I always felt obligated to assist.

"Watch your halo," I said.

Mrs. Rippetoe insisted on dressing herself and Sassy alike. She wore a white African kaftan with gold embroidery down the front. When she raised her arms they reminded me of angel wings. Unfortunately, she didn't have the face to match. Her large nose and bulging left eye lacked the necessary beauty, but her heart, well, it was definitely of angel caliber.

"Where are your devil horns?"

I looked at Peter Parker standing in the open window of his apartment, which sat directly below mine. Our platonic friendship was strong, but our flirty banter always kept us on the edge. A naughty reply lingered on the tip of my tongue, but Mrs. Rippetoe's eyes were on me. "Only room for one devil in this relationship. Sure you don't want to join us?"

"Sorry. I'm taking Madeline to the airport."

"She's heading back to L.A. already?"

"It is Sunday."

Peter's girlfriend Madeline landed a part in a soap opera a few months ago. Now a bi-stater, she lived her weekends in Missouri and her weekdays in California. I didn't like talking about Madeline too much because it only reminded me that Peter was taken. Even worse, that one day he might move to California and be gone from my life forever.

I hopped into the Jeep, lowered the window and waved goodbye. By the time I took the turn onto Gravois Road, the snorting and panting in the back of the Jeep had reached a frenetic level.

"Do you mind if I make a quick call?" I asked, picking up my cell phone from the center console.

"Hun, don't you ever take time off?"

"I'm taking time off today. I just need to give Stephanie a quick call." I pushed the call button and waited for her to answer.

"Stephanie? Oh, geez, you know I hate voice mail. Mr. Q's still out of town and I wanted you to run by and feed Mr. P. I'll try...well, darn, who knows when you'll get this message. I'm going to run by and take care of it. I'll call you when—" *Beep*.

Crap.

Stephanie, my assistant, often made my life easier, but not often enough.

Mrs. Rippetoe turned to look at the dogs. "Hear that, PJ? You're going see your daddy."

Mrs. Rippetoe had been convinced Mr. P and Sassy had been playing that fateful day. It wasn't until I brought Mr. P over to her apartment and sat PJ beside him that she finally accepted her Sassy had engaged in a one-night stand.

We made our way into Soulard, a trendy community in St. Louis and home to the second largest Mardi Gras party in the United States.

I put the car in park. "Why don't you wait here and keep an eye on the dogs."

"Oh no. I think Sassy should see her lover."

I stifled a chuckle. "Okay."

We took Sassy and PJ to the side yard and let them do their business. Mrs. Rippetoe held the dog leads while I dug through my purse for Mr. Q's house key.

"Son of a bitch," Mrs. Rippetoe said as we walked through the door.

I was shocked. I'd never heard words like those come out of her mouth. More shocking, however, was the sight of Mr. Q's townhouse. The place was a mess. I spotted Mr. P squeezed between the large leather chair and ottoman.

"It's okay, buddy." I patted my thigh, hoping to draw him out of hiding. He ran to my side by the time I reached for the phone on the kitchen wall.

"Don't touch that! The police might need to process it for fingerprints. They always do on TV," Mrs. Rippetoe said.

"I'm not going to call the police."

"What kind of crazy talk is that?"

"It's at my client's request. Besides, he probably had a wild party."

"Didn't you tell Stephanie he was out of town?"

4

Though Mrs. Rippetoe was often forgetful, she had her strokes of astuteness.

"Yes, well, perhaps he let someone else hold a party. He's a private man and I figure it's not my business."

"Mr. P, looky here. It's your son." Mrs. Rippetoe kicked a few items out of her way as she made a path toward the couch.

I walked into the kitchen putting some distance between me and Mrs. Rippetoe. I dialed Mr. Q, questioning why I'd ever signed his confidentiality agreement. It required me to refrain from calling the police for any reason. In my heart I knew the answer – the lucrative contract with my personal concierge business, Moore Time.

"Mr. Q? It's Aspen. Everything's a mess here. If you didn't give permission for a friend to host a wild party, then someone's broken in to your place."

"Is Mr. Personality okay?" he asked.

I knew he was concerned because he only used Mr. P's full name when the dog was in trouble or in danger. "He's fine. A little afraid, but unhurt."

"The kitchen. What's the kitchen like?"

"There are pots and pans and utensils all over the floor along with a bunch of boxed foods."

"What about the counters and walls?"

An odd question, but Mr. Q was odd. "They're fine."

"Please take care of cleaning up. I'll throw in a bonus."

Bonus. I've always liked the sound of the word. "No problem. Are you still coming back Wednesday?"

"Can you have it done by then?"

"Sure thing." I hung up the phone.

Last time I stumbled upon a mess like this was in my own apartment. The experience hadn't been a good one and

I imagined this wasn't good either. With Mr. Q, I knew not to ask.

"I'll take care of this tomorrow. We have a parade to attend," I said as I walked back out to the living room.

"You sure you still want to go?" Mrs. Rippetoe asked.

"Yes. We'll take Mr. P too." I ran upstairs, collected his vaccination records and a bright colored t-shirt out of the top drawer of Mr. P's special dresser.

We locked up, piled into the Jeep and drove several blocks to a parking lot located near the street where the parade registration took place. I pulled into the last vacant space in the lot.

"You ready for some fun?"

Mrs. Rippetoe smiled, lighting up my insides. "Yes, we are."

I snatched Sassy from the back of the Jeep and placed her on the ground. "Okay, hold steady and I'll get your wings adjusted. Good girl!"

Sassy perked up, but still walked calmly by Mrs. Rippetoe's side, wearing her wings proudly as if she'd just been sent down from heaven. PJ, on the other hand, was like a whirling dervish, incessantly twirling, as Mr. P stood by with a blank stare.

At the registration table, I filled out paperwork while PJ twirled. Halfway through the registration process he stopped moving. I turned to praise him for finally settling down, but he was busy introducing himself to the hind end of a Pug disguised as a pirate.

We left the registration area and found ourselves surrounded by thousands of dogs, with personalities as varied as their owners. But mostly, they were all happy.

I checked out the crowd on our way to the parade's starting point. Two Great Danes charged past us and PJ took off like the devil he was, his lead slipping out of my hand. I tried to stop him by stepping on his lead, but missed. PJ ran amok, becoming the life of the party. Half the crowd laughed as the other half looked on in horror.

"PJ! Get back here!"

I handed Mr. P's leash to Mrs. Rippetoe. "Keep walking, I'll be back to find you."

Dogs in purple, yellow, and green costumes blocked my view, but I parted the crowd, running in the direction I thought PJ had gone. I came across a little pitchfork lying on the ground and bent to pick it up. Halfway to an upright position, I was delighted at the sight of PJ's bushy little face in someone's arms. I followed the arms as I continued upward and was greeted by a set of tequila gold eyes I knew all too well. The eyes of Jack Arbon.

"You didn't mention you were coming to the parade," he said, handing PJ back to me.

Jack was... my something. We hadn't quite figured it out yet. A couple of days ago he sneaked out of my apartment in the middle of the night without saying goodbye – no kiss, no note.

"Remember, we don't tell each other everything, like why we leave in the middle of the night without a word. Thanks for catching PJ."

"Is that why you've been avoiding my calls?"

"I haven't been avoiding anything, I've been busy."

"Right. Dinner tonight?"

"Didn't you hear me? I'm busy."

I turned and walked in the opposite direction, hoping to find Mrs. Rippetoe somewhere in the crowd.

"At least you could give me a chance to explain," Jack shouted.

I lifted my hand and waved without turning around. No need to piss him off entirely, especially since he and Peter were old friends.

"Hun? Aspen?"

I heard Mrs. Rippetoe's voice, but couldn't see her.

"Aspen. I'm here."

I turned around and saw Mrs. Rippetoe holding Sassy in one arm and the angel wings in the other, while Mr. P walked around her legs.

"Here, let me put those back on."

She gave me Sassy and I re-strapped the wings. "Good girl," I squealed. Once she perked up, I handed her back to Mrs. Rippetoe. I secured Mr. P and PJ's leads around my wrist and the five of us got in step with the procession and strolled uneventfully to the end of the parade route.

"Lord, there's one of my old students. We'll be back in a minute." Mrs. Rippetoe adjusted her halo and sauntered off into the crowd with Sassy.

I didn't bother going with her because I knew she'd be back before the coronation ceremony started. She hoped Sassy would be crowned queen. I didn't have the heart to tell her Sassy's chances were slim because twenty-five percent of the score centered around how well the Mardi Gras colors were represented and Sassy wore nothing but white and gold.

I scanned the crowd wondering if I knew anyone else braving the cold weather. I didn't recognize anyone. A brisk breeze shot past me and I prayed Mrs. Rippetoe would hurry back because I needed to go to the bathroom. I fidgeted, trying to stop myself from peeing. So far it was helping, but I didn't know for how long. I eyed the crowd. They all seemed nice, but I needed someone trustworthy. I headed toward a guy with a purple poodle.

"Excuse me. Could you watch my dogs for a second while I go to the bathroom?"

I tossed PJ and Mr. P's leads in his direction. He caught them, his eyes wide and mouth agape. I darted toward the portable toilets, turning my head back and yelling, "I'll be right back."

Leaving the dogs with a stranger was risky, but he looked honest. Besides, negotiating a portable toilet was difficult enough without trying to hold a dog or two. If I accidentally dropped one into the blue goo, I wasn't so sure I'd be willing to reach in to get him out.

The line was longer than it had appeared from a distance. I danced around, crossing my legs.

"I really gotta go. Could I please cut in front of you?" I asked a short-haired brunette standing at the front of the line.

"Are you kidding me? No way! I've been waiting for over ten minutes." She glared at me through her dark-rimmed glasses.

Ten minutes? I eyed the bench where I'd left the dogs. PJ was safely twirling around at the feet of the guy with the purple poodle. I took off toward the restaurant across the street. I'd buy anything just to use their restroom.

I burst through the door and threw my wallet at the hostess. "Burger, well done, double pickles, no onion, lettuce, tomato, and...oh, god." I dashed into the bathroom and the door closed behind me.

An overwhelming sense of relief came over me as I flushed the toilet, having averted spending the rest of the day in wet jeans. I scrubbed my hands. My nose involuntarily scrunched as I walked toward the paper towel dispenser. *Dog poop?*

I didn't see anything around my feet. I turned to leave, stopping as soon as I noticed brown footprints at the bathroom door. They continued toward the stalls, getting fainter before they disappeared in front of the stall I'd recently exited. *Crap. Literally.*

I checked my shoes, wincing at the sight of brown spots on the side of one. I lifted my foot, removed my red sneaker and hobbled over to the sink, slipping it back on only when the crevices were clean. Had I not thrown my wallet into the restaurant's clutches, I would have sneaked out the back. I reluctantly left the bathroom and walked toward the front door.

"I'm sorry," I said to the young girl mopping the floor.

"Yeah, well—"

"I mean it. I'm really sorry, I wouldn't have come—"

"Lady, I need to get this mess cleaned up before the parade crowd realizes their hungry."

I walked away without another word, stopping at the bar. "I'd like my, uh. Uh."

"Burger?" the bartender offered.

My face was the color of my sneakers. I didn't have to see it. I felt it. My earlier run in with Jack made the hot looking bartender seem even hotter. Dark curly hair, Caribbean blue eyes, and biceps I was sure could dance if I sang the right tune.

"Uh, yes. Please."

He handed me my wallet. I paid and left the restaurant even more convinced I'd be forever socially challenged. I shook off the embarrassment and headed back to PJ.

The man with the purple poodle was right where I'd left him, still holding the leads of PJ and Mr. P. I jotted a quick note on the back of one of my business cards. "Thanks. I appreciate it. By the way, what's your name?"

"Albert."

"Please take my card, Albert. I made a note on the back. It's good for two free hours of service."

He took the card and stood for a minute reading the front. "Anything?"

My company slogan, *'We'll do just about anything, for just about anybody'*, seemed clever when I wrote it, but it created more questions than business. "Let's just say it's subject to approval. A list of services not offered can be found on our website."

"Thanks. If I can't use it, I'm sure my partner can. You probably saw him when you went into the restaurant. He's the bartender."

Once again I'd been attracted to an 'unavailable'. Gay, married or commitment-phobe, it didn't matter. They were simply unavailable and the only men I gravitated towards. "Yeah, I did. He is handsome."

"He is, isn't he?"

Albert's expression was the same one I'd had at the beginning of my encounters with Jack. Funny how time changes things.

"I need to run, but please take one of my cards too. I just opened a catering business, so if you know of anyone that needs one."

"Thanks again for watching the dogs," I said, taking the card.

He waved goodbye and I settled on the bench to share my burger with PJ and Mr. P. We split it equally, though I ate all the pickles and onions.

From the sea of dachshunds, it was clear the wiener dog derby was about to begin, which meant the King and Queen would soon be announced. I stood on the bench. It was way too crowded, even to spot an angel.

PJ began barking. I looked to my left and saw Sassy running straight for us, her wings sliding from side to side.

"Hey, Sassy. Where's your mommy?" I grabbed her lead.

I tossed the burger bag into the garbage can, and then unhooked the other dog leads from the bench. "Come on you three."

We walked in the direction from where Sassy had come. Mrs. Rippetoe was probably frantic. Sassy was her baby.

"Have you seen a woman in an angel costume?" I asked every person I passed. And each time they shook their head.

The constant rumble of the crowd grew into a loud and excited chant as I neared the derby race area. The dachshunds were running for their lives, mostly in different directions, except number eight, who appeared to be tending to an itch in his ear.

I made my way to the area where the King and Queen would be announced. Mrs. Rippetoe wasn't there. I worked my way back to the portable toilets, figuring nature may have called her. The lines were much shorter and didn't include a single angel. I went back to the bench assuming she'd return.

"Where's your festive parade face?"

I raised my head and found Jack, holding a miniature dachshund. He seemed uncomfortable and so did the dog.

"I'm waiting for Mrs. Rippetoe. She went off to talk to someone, but only Sassy came back."

"I wouldn't worry. She probably went to report Sassy missing." Jack craned his neck, looking back toward the portable toilets.

"Whose dog?"

"Belongs to a friend."

"If Mrs. Rippetoe reported Sassy missing, wouldn't they make an announcement or something?"

Jack craned his neck again and shifted his stance when a skinny brunette with tight fitting clothes walked in our direction. "You should go check with someone."

"I'm not sure who—"

"I need to run. I'll call you later," Jack said, walking away before I could say goodbye. He headed in the direction of the skinny brunette.

Jack's interaction with the woman caused a knocking noise inside my head. The jealousy door opened. I worked hard to slam it shut. We'd never talked about dating exclusively, heck, we'd never talked about our relationship, period. I made myself look away, turned around and headed in the opposite direction. I hit the speed dial on my phone. "Peter? I'm at the parade and I've lost Mrs. Rippetoe."

"When did you see her last?"

"Around one-thirty. She saw a former student and walked off, but Sassy came running back alone."

"It's probably nothing. Maybe she went back to your car because she couldn't find you."

"You're probably right." I felt much better. Peter had a way of making everything okay.

"I'm just heading back from the airport. If she's not at your car, give me a call back."

I scanned the thinning crowd one more time, but didn't see a single halo. She wasn't a real angel, so I knew she couldn't simply disappear into thin air.

After a few minutes, I made my way back to the parking lot. Only a handful of cars remained. When I reached my Jeep, Mrs. Rippetoe wasn't anywhere near it. I opened the hatch and placed the dogs inside. This wasn't good. My heartbeat was rapid. I dialed Peter.

"She's not here."

"Calm down. Maybe she couldn't find you and her student gave her a ride."

I walked around to the front of the Jeep and jumped inside. "Maybe you're right. I'll call her place."

"Okay, and call me back if you do—"

"Wait! There's something on my windshield."

I pulled a plastic baggy from under the windshield wiper.

"This is weird. Someone left a flash drive on my car."

"Is there a logo or anything on it?" Peter asked.

I opened the baggy and took out the drive, turning it over, trying to find some sort of label, or logo, or notation of any kind. "Nothing."

"Might be some sort of guerilla marketing campaign."

"What's wrong with using a flyer?"

"People are trying to find new ways to get your attention. If they'd left a flyer you probably would have wadded it up and thrown it away."

"Yeah, well, I don't have time for this. I need to find Mrs. Rippetoe." I opened the door and tossed the baggy with the flash drive onto the passenger seat.

"Did you try her cell phone?"

"She doesn't have one, Peter. You know that."

"I thought you got her one."

"No, she said she wasn't important enough to be needing a phone you carry around. I'm going to drive back to where the parade ended and search again. I'll call you later."

I drove a few blocks and parked the car closer to where the parade ended. It was cold, but I cracked the windows, locked the doors, and told the three musketeers to be good before heading out in search of Mrs. Rippetoe.

The coronation ceremony came to a close. As I expected Sassy was not a contender. I passed by the stage, eyeing the St. Bernard who'd been crowned king. He wore a fake Mardi Gras king cake with a life size naked baby on top. Next to him was the queen – a miniature schnauzer dressed like a parade float. They appeared uncomfortable, but sat obediently by their owners.

I had to believe Mrs. Rippetoe found a ride home, because I didn't want to think about the possibility of her wandering around lost. I hated to head home without her, but I couldn't leave the dogs in the back of the SUV much longer. I wasn't worried about them so much as I was worried about my Jeep.

Another quick scan of the crowd turned up everything but an angel, so I went back to my car. It was still intact, though the windows had accumulated a little more slobber. Ecstatic to enter a car that didn't smell like poop or pee, I praised them all, "Good boys and girl! You're such good doggieeeees!"

Mr. P and Sassy jumped around and wagged their tails while PJ mysteriously kept to himself in the back of the Jeep. The mischievous twinkle in his eyes left me wondering whether I wanted to solve the mystery.

I chose to ignore him and backed out of the parking space, slamming on my brakes when a motorcycle zoomed behind me. Something rolled out from under the passenger seat. I pulled back into the space and stuck the Jeep in park.

"That's where that went!" I said to the dogs while I bent over the console to retrieve a slightly dented can of Red Bull peppered with tiny teeth marks.

Staring at PJ in the rearview mirror, I caught sight of a small reddish-brown colored patch of fur under his chin. "PJ!" He didn't move an inch. He stood panting and wagging his tail. Had the can been empty I might have been alarmed, but it was just shy of being completely full. Still, I mentally prepared myself for what might become PJ's wild caffeine-infused evening.

———

I opened the door to my building and hustled the dogs inside. I knocked on Mrs. Rippetoe's door. She didn't answer so I dragged the four of us upstairs to my apartment. My two four-legged guests would be staying the evening since Mr. Q's place remained a mess and Mrs. Rippetoe's whereabouts were unknown.

As I fixed myself microwavable mac-n-cheese, Mr. P and Sassy laid quietly on the sofa while PJ's Red Bull buzz awakened his Bichon genes. He skillfully executed the Bichon Blitz, running down the hall to the bedroom and back again, then circling the coffee table, and running back down the hall, over and over again. I licked the last piece of elbow macaroni off the spoon and set my dish in the sink. When I turned around, PJ stood in the kitchen panting.

"I hope that Red Bull was worth it, little man." PJ's ears perked.

I took a couple of bowls from the cabinet and poured some dry kibble. When the pups finished snacking, I took them for a walk.

The temperature was falling and I worried Mrs. Rippetoe was wandering the streets cold, perhaps too afraid to knock on someone's door or too stubborn. I didn't know how long she had to be gone before being considered missing, but I knew if she wasn't back tomorrow I'd have to report it.

I knocked on her door when we returned from our walk. Nothing. I tugged on the dogs' leads and headed back upstairs. My worry would escalate if I sat around my apartment for the rest of the night, so I gated the three musketeers in the kitchen, grabbed my jacket and briefcase, and headed for my office.

The sky edged its way into darkness as I drove. The clouds were no longer white and fluffy instead the entire sky was one gray cloud.

I parked in front of my office, located next to Peter's store. Both our storefronts were dark, except for his lighted sign, Parker Security. Officially, the business was a security and surveillance company, but to me it screamed spy shop. He not only sold security cameras and alarm systems, but cool stuff too, like tie-clip microphones, baseball cap cameras, and bug detectors.

The flash drive that had been left on my windshield earlier fell onto the floorboard when I picked up my briefcase. I was surprised and thankful that PJ hadn't eaten it as a snack. I tossed it inside my purse. It wouldn't hurt to see what product or service they were selling.

I made my way to my desk behind a Plexiglas wall in the rear of the store and plugged the drive into the USB port. It contained a single file. I crossed my fingers, hoping it didn't contain some highly aggressive computer virus, then double-clicked on the file.

I rubbed my eyes and looked at the document again. There it was, my name, Aspen Moore in bolded text, centered, and underlined. It was a PDF document of a slide presentation. I scrolled through the document, the pit of my stomach filling with dread. Whoever put together the presentation knew a lot about me and that was alarming. Even worse, they wanted me to steal a diamond.

2

THE DOCUMENT didn't actually state, "Aspen we want you to steal a diamond," but it suggested my obtaining the diamond was a matter of life or death. Compensation wasn't offered, so the suspicious part of my brain worried the return of Mrs. Rippetoe might somehow be the payment. Whoever wanted the diamond needed a way of motivating me to get it. Either way, a job request or a ransom request, getting it in presentation form on an unmarked USB flash drive, deposited on my windshield, was bizarre.

It was all very cloak and dagger. There were no instructions identifying the whereabouts of the diamond or what to do with the diamond once I had it in my possession. Half the document demonstrated knowledge of my current life and the other half referenced a blue diamond worth millions. But it was the last page that stood out. It did what any last page should do in a presentation. It made an impact. It gave me a call to action. Literally, it gave me a number to call.

The call to action would go unanswered, at least in the immediate future, because I knew not to jump into a pot of water without first knowing if I'd scald myself. The more I could find out about the diamond and its owner, the better.

The only clue pointed to the diamond being in St. Louis. I wondered if it belonged to one of my clients. Why else would they choose me?

My client Oliver Lott was a contender. A super rich software company owner, he made millions creating turnkey automated solutions for the pharmaceutical industry. He lived in the wealthy town of Ladue, was intelligent, but arrogant, and a lover of expensive things. When he spoke to me, he dumbed things down, having no idea I once held the title Vice President of Technology. I mentally put him on my list of possible blue diamond owners, but below Mr. Q whose place had been torn apart.

I viewed the images included in the presentation. The photos were small and fuzzy, but even so, I could tell the diamond was gorgeous. My limited diamond education revolved around the four C's – cut, clarity, color and carat. Something I learned as a result of my engagement. My ring had been beautiful, but when my fiancé became my ex-fiancé then my dead fiancé all on the same day, I ended up in the Witness Protection Program, ringless and living my life as Aspen Moore.

A familiar sadness descended on me. I shook it off focusing on the diamond. I knew nothing about blue diamonds, but a jeweler would know. Varriano's Jewelry, the family-owned store located at the opposite end of our building, had been open when I pulled up to my office. I'd never stepped inside it for fear of temptation, but now it almost seemed like a requirement.

I walked past Peter's place, then the empty storefront next to his, before reaching Varriano's. I stepped inside and began surveying the display cases. "Hello?"

There wasn't much inside. Perhaps they were getting ready to close for the night. "Hello?" I called again.

A man popped up from behind the counter. He looked more like a construction worker than a jeweler, with his dark tan and white tee shirt. "We're closed."

"I'm Aspen Moore. I own Moore Time at the other end." I pointed over my shoulder with my thumb while I offered him my other hand.

"I know," he said, not bothering to shake.

"Have we met?" He was a large man with a head full of dusty brown hair. A single dark gray strip ran down the left side – a feature I would not have forgotten since he wasn't an older man.

"No. Name's Carmine. You knew a friend of mine. Plus, I read about you in the paper."

"You did? What's your friend's name?"

"Rocco."

A shiver made its way down my neck. I was speechless. Rocco was currently incarcerated. The day he went to live in the big house was the day the world moved that much closer to being a safer place. Rocco and his boss were not nice people, which made me think Carmine might be just as unfriendly.

The black curtain separating the showroom from the back moved slightly. It freaked me out. Perhaps it was my imagination, but I wasn't taking a chance. I swallowed involuntarily and tried to keep the sweat from breaking out on my forehead. I needed to get out.

"I'm sorry about your friend. It was a pleasure meeting you." I turned to walk out the door.

"Wait."

I turned back, hoping I wasn't making a big mistake.

"What did you want?" he asked.

"Oh, uh, nothing important. I was thinking about getting my niece a pair of earrings." The sentence popped out of my mouth without assistance from any logical thought. I didn't even have a niece. In reality my only sibling, my brother Birch, was another lucky winner of a life in the Witness Protection Program.

"I'll come back another time." I turned and walked out the door.

Nearing my office, I saw Peter at the reception desk. He was talking to someone on my office phone.

"What's wrong with the phone in your store?" I asked, after entering my office.

"Where the hell have you been?" Peter hung up the phone. "I saw your Jeep then found your office unlocked and empty. I thought someone snatched you."

"You were worried about me?" I smiled.

"I'm always worried about you because you always seem to get yourself into trouble. So, where were you?"

"Always is a little exaggerated, isn't it? I mean it's not like every hour of every day I'm in trouble."

Peter stood there like he was calculating exactly how often I did get in trouble. "So, where were you?"

"I went down to the jewelers, but they were closing." I left out the part about Carmine. I didn't want to give him the satisfaction of knowing my next date with trouble might be at the other end of the shopping strip.

Scooting back to my desk, I reached for the phone, hoping there would be a message from Mrs. Rippetoe.

I checked the voicemail. "Hi Ms. Moore. This is Harry Corbitt. I want to talk to you about planning my wedding."

Déjà vu. Mr. Corbitt was creepy. He'd asked me once before to plan his wedding but it didn't quite work out. I pressed number two on the phone to save the message, postponing my decision on whether to call him back or not.

"What did you buy at the jewelers?" Peter asked when I hung up.

"Nothing. I went to ask them about blue diamonds."

"What for?"

"That USB flash drive I found on my windshield. Check it out." I clicked the left button on the trackball.

Peter watched as I scrolled through the presentation. He jotted down information in the black Moleskine journal I'd gotten him for Christmas. He carried it everywhere.

"Security Guard?" Peter said, after seeing his name mentioned.

"Peter. Focus. Who cares if they called you a security guard. The point is everyone closest to me is on the list."

"Did you call the phone number?"

"Not yet. I don't want them knowing I've seen this until we figure out what to do."

"Aren't you a personal concierge?"

"I'm not answering that stupid question because you know I am."

"Isn't finding things one of the services you offer people?"

"Aaargh. Get to the point."

"Call the number. They probably want to talk to you about the details of what they want."

"But why did they list everything about me? Why didn't they just call me up and ask me? Why are they being so secretive and leaving it on my windshield?"

"Are you done with your questions?"

"Yep."

"They probably want to remain anonymous, which is why they haven't called you or come to see you. Listing that information is one way to show you how easy it is to find it, expecting you'd understand and respect their need for anonymity."

"You got all that from the stupid document?"

"I'm trying to think out of the box."

"If you're right, then why did they give me their phone number? I can track down who it belongs to or I mean, you could track it down."

"Could be one of those burner phones that can't be traced would be my guess."

"I totally went the other direction. I mean, you're the one that thinks me and trouble are soul mates. Why wouldn't you think someone kidnapped Mrs. Rippetoe to get me to steal the diamond? Because that's what I'm thinking."

"Not me. I think Mrs. Rippetoe disappearing is a coincidence. I think you're dealing with an eccentric person here, like that damn Mr. Q."

Peter wasn't a fan of Mr. Q because he'd put my loyalty to the test when I first started working for him. Ever since, Peter didn't trust him.

"No. He's out of town."

"If you want to figure out who it is, then call the number."

"No. They'll call me if it's legitimate work. I'd rather go home and see if Mrs. Rippetoe has returned."

"At least try to remember if anyone followed you today. Someone knew where to find you."

"I don't remember seeing anyone."

"Think back. Did anything seem out of the ordinary?"

"I don't think so." I wanted to tell him about Mr. Q's ransacked townhouse, but I wasn't at liberty to disclose the information.

"As I said, it's most likely some ploy to hire you."

"If they are going to all this trouble to hire me then they must believe I'm in contact with the blue diamond's owner. I mean it's clear they didn't pick me out of the yellow pages. They didn't even tell me who has the diamond." I rolled my trackball to wake up my computer and pointed to the screen.

"Your reputation alone is enough to make any man want to choose you."

"Man? What makes you think it's a man?" I asked, refusing to get derailed by the hidden nuance I'd extracted from his words.

"It's in the way the presentation comes across. It's very matter of fact. No emotions. Straight and to the point. A woman would include graphics, be more forthcoming, even toss a little emotion in the mix. You should go through your client list."

"Oh, and what am I supposed to do? Call them up?"

"That's what I suggested earlier and it's a great idea."

"This is crazy. Is this person trying to hire me or coerce me? And, I feel especially awful about Mrs. Rippetoe. What if her disappearance is related? Maybe we should call the police."

Peter, well acquainted with my aversion to police, raised his brows. "You must feel awful if you want to call the police."

He had no idea of the real reason I shied away from the men and women in blue and I wouldn't tell him. In the entire St. Louis metro area, only Marshal Anthony Cutter knew the entire truth.

Cutter's job was to make sure I stayed safe. Last time I was in a terrible predicament, he'd been pissed that I hadn't reached out to him. I'd promised never to do that again. But, I'd have to break that promise because I was sitting on the precipice of a diamond heist with me as the felony perpetrator.

"I'm worried about her," I said.

"Worrying doesn't solve anything. Nothing criminal has taken place. Mrs. Rippetoe probably went off with her student. You know how she can be sometimes. Right now I need to get going and you should go home. We'll talk in the morning."

The jingle of the bell on my office door caused us both to turn around.

"Hey. I was in the neighborhood and thought you all might be up for some Chinese," Jack said.

Peter crossed his arms over his chest. "We've got some work we need to do."

I glanced at Peter. We didn't have any work to do and didn't he just say he had to go?

"Sorry. The dogs are waiting for me at home," I said.

"Take out?" Jack persisted.

My stomach grumbled.

"Not for me," Peter said.

"Sure," I answered.

Peter flashed me a look or perhaps it was a warning. He hadn't been happy about me dating Jack. They'd been college roommates and Peter possessed more stories about Jack than he cared to share.

"I'll take a Mongolian beef, egg roll, and a hot and sour soup, please."

"You got it. I'll meet you at your place."

"I thought you two stopped dating," Peter said, after Jack left.

"Not exactly."

"Aspen, you told me that you were tired of—"

"I know, I know. It's not easy meeting people when you're older. And, well, a woman has needs."

Peter laughed. If I didn't know him well, I'd have smacked him in the face. Instead I fought back with words. "So, does this mean you'll step up to the challenge?"

"Tempting, but I think Madeline might be a little upset, don't you? Now, if she ever breaks up with me then I'm your man."

I wasn't about to dig myself any deeper. Whenever he mentioned Madeline, our flirt sessions ended, which was for the best anyway. "Guess we should go."

"Yep," he said, smiling that damn smile that caused my heart to sing a slow vibrato.

I cleared my throat. "So you following me?"

"No. I've got some things to take care of." Peter walked me to my Jeep and waited for me to belt myself in before ducking inside his store.

The drive to the fourplex didn't take long, even so, the temperature had dropped. I braved the cold air as I walked the block to my apartment. What I once thought would be rain had become snow. My skin melted the large flakes, instantly sending cold water running down my face.

The lights were off inside Mrs. Rippetoe's apartment when I walked up to the building's door. It made my heart ache. I had a strong urge to knock, but I heard the dogs whining so I ran upstairs to take them outside before Jack arrived.

Saddling up three dogs was much harder than saddling up one. They jumped, barked, and twirled, creating something weirdly similar to a Jacob's ladder with their leads. I untangled them and headed down the stairs.

The dogs pulled me out the door and I ran into Jack. Regardless of Peter's opinion, Jack was hard to resist. He wore a full-length grey cashmere coat and even with the snowflakes covering his hair and balancing on his lashes, he was corporate sexy. Just the kind of guy I fell for in my previous life. The kind of guy who thrived in the world I left behind.

"I asked them for special fortune cookies," Jack said, holding the brown bag in the air.

Jack and I stood outside waiting for the pups to finish. We finally dragged them inside and up the stairs. Jack placed the bag on the counter. I grabbed a dishtowel and began brushing the snowflakes off me, Jack, and then the dogs. I tossed the towel into the hamper and stepped back into the living room as Jack hung his coat in the closet.

"No kiss?" he asked.

"Nope. I'm placing you on probation."

"I'm a lawyer, remember? I'll get the probation overturned in no time."

Damn him. I needed to double up on my armor if I had any hope of kicking him out before bedtime.

"Court's closed so you're stuck on probation until it reopens. Here, have an egg roll." I passed Jack the bag and a paper plate I'd retrieved from the cabinet.

As we ate, I told him about the disappearance of Mrs. Rippetoe, leaving out the details about Mr. Q and the blue diamond. Jack listened, asking only a few questions.

He poured the fortune cookies out of the bag and onto the coffee table where we'd been eating dinner. He handed one to me.

"Unless this says Mrs. Rippetoe will be returned alive and kicking, I won't be impressed." I cracked it open.

Jack lifted himself off the floor and onto the couch. "Well? Read it out loud."

"Fine. A satisfied lawyer is a happy lawyer."

"And?"

"And what?"

"You forgot to add the ending you always use."

I tried hard not to laugh. "In be—"

"Oh, no. Start from the beginning."

I held back a laugh and squeaked out the words, "A satisfied lawyer is a happy lawyer, in bed."

I wiped the tears from my cheek after I stopped laughing. "Where'd you get that?"

"The Internet."

"What did they insert in yours?"

"Nope, mine's the real deal. Straight from the restaurant." He bit into his and pulled the paper from his mouth. He held it up and almost choked.

"Are you okay?" I asked, genuinely concerned.

"It's blank."

"No way."

I plucked it from his hand and stifled the giggle working its way out of my mouth. The poor guy. It wasn't the first time he'd gotten a blank fortune. What were the odds?

"So, you know..." Jack leaned forward and pulled me up onto the couch. "I am sorry for the other night." He completed the apology with his moist lips, causing the skin on my neck to tingle.

"Yeah, bu...bu...but," I whimpered, catching my breath, as he worked his way down the front of my neck.

"Really, Aspen, do you want to stay mad at me?" He stopped his seduction attempt only briefly to look me in the eyes.

When he came back in for a kiss, I became the weakest strong woman this side of the Mississippi. I kissed him back.

We dropped our clothes behind us like breadcrumbs, as we made our way to my bedroom. A few minutes later, I didn't care if I ever found my way back.

Almost an hour later, Jack was sound asleep. With him no longer distracting my thoughts, I was wide awake worrying about everything. I slipped out of bed and threw on my big St. Louis Rams shirt. I'd been meaning to get rid of it since the Rams abandoned St. Louis, but it was just too darn comfortable. I snuck out of the bedroom and into the living room where I could occupy my mind with the Internet.

While my laptop booted, I cleaned up the leftover Chinese food, throwing Jack's specially made fortune into my memory drawer located in my antique roll top desk. It held only memories of my life in St. Louis. Anything prior lived in my head, except for a few mementos I kept hidden in a box.

My Internet search yielded basic information about blue diamonds. Rare and expensive, the Hope diamond was among the most famous blues. A few more taps on the keyboard and I came across an article about a blue diamond called the Blue Monkey. Unlike the fictitious Blue Monkey diamond in the "Looney Tunes: Back in Action" movie I watched years ago, this one wasn't embedded in any statue and didn't possess the ability to transform someone into a monkey. But it wasn't without its mystery.

The article went into the history of the diamond, explaining how a Vervet monkey in South Africa threw the diamond at a man. When the man bent over to pick it up he missed being hit by an errant bullet, sparing his life. The diamond reportedly brought good fortune to its owner as long as the person told the truth and lived an honest life. The man eventually succumbed to a horrendous virus he picked up after traveling to North Africa to sell someone a fake Blue Monkey diamond. Upon his death, the legend was born.

I continued reading about the diamond and its juju and found the most intriguing part of the article toward the end. The diamond had been recently auctioned off in Denmark. The final tally, three-million-dollars, sold to an unidentified American from St. Louis, Missouri.

——

Last night's instant gratification turned into morning turmoil. *What happened to my willpower? Why didn't I demand Jack explain the presence of the skinny brunette?* At least I had the good sense to kick him out last night. I walked into the bathroom and washed my face. I looked into the mirror, but could barely make out my reflection. Instead my mind filled with the images of Mrs. Rippetoe and her halo.

After the dogs finished eating, I snapped on their leads, and trotted down the stairs, crossing my fingers before knocking on Mrs. Rippetoe's door. No luck. I headed out to the front yard.

The dogs turned in circles, each one eventually stopping to take care of business. When they were done, I sat down on the stoop. They sniffed the ground, the bushes, each other and then finally lined up before me. The three of them stared at me as if judging my intelligence, wondering what type of woman would keep having sex with a guy who flitted in and out of her life on his own schedule. Or more likely what type of idiot would stay out in the cold when they could be up in a warm apartment napping. I figured it was the latter and quickly herded them up the steps.

I glanced at the pendulum clock on my wall and added an hour to adjust to east coast time before picking up my phone and calling Mr. Q. He was in New York to promote his syndicated radio show.

"This might sound like an odd question," I said after he picked up. "Do you know anything about a blue diamond?"

"Mr. Q? Are you still there?"

"Yes. I'm here."

"Did you hear me?"

"Yes. Why?"

"I'm only interested in a specific blue diamond. If I'm not being too nosy, do you own one?"

I waited for his response.

"Mr. Q?"

"Yes. Yes. I'm here. Hold on a second."

Muffled voices came from the phone.

"I'm sorry, Aspen, can you call me later?"

"Sure, but could you answer my question first?"

I waited.

"Hello?"

The call had ended.

Mr. Q's oddness could mean something or nothing at all. I checked the calendar on my cell phone and found a note I'd made on the date that corresponded to the auction. Mr. Q had been out of town, but the note didn't say where he went. Maybe he'd been visiting Denmark that day.

I picked up Mr. P, my briefcase, and the bags of poop I'd left outside my door then headed down the steps. I tied Mr. P's lead to the handrail, dropped my briefcase and trotted down three small steps to the back door to dispose of the bags.

When I came back inside, Mr. P was yelping. I called out to him as I closed the door behind me. "What are you so excited about, Mr. P?"

"Aspen, hun? Is that you?"

"Mrs. Rippetoe? Oh my God! What happened?"

Dirt clung to her white kaftan and her lipstick was smudged. Her sphagnum moss colored hair, perfect when I last saw her, now appeared flat on one side and curly on the other.

"Where's my Sassafras?"

"Don't worry about her. She's upstairs. Are you okay?"

"Oh honey, I'm fine. After I finished talking to my old student, a nice couple came up to play with Sassy. She accidentally got loose and ran off. They tried to catch her but couldn't. Then somebody called them on their cell phone saying they found her. They took me in their car to go get her, but she wasn't there."

That sounded strange. "Why were you gone so long?"

"We waited at their office for someone to bring Sassy, but nobody came. They said I could stay there and they would go get her. Put me in a room with a bed and everything. Never heard of anyone with a bed in their office, but it was real nice. Guess they must work overnight or something. Had a comfortable chair and even one of them little refrigerators."

Mrs. Rippetoe had a way of meandering through the woods as she told a story, taking the longest path to the destination. I listened patiently.

"I didn't see a phone. They must have gotten lost or something because they were gone a long time. I took a little nap, I think, but it got too warm. I tried to go out the door to get some air, but they must have forgotten about me because the door was locked. I—"

"How'd you get out?"

"Well, I pushed a chair to the window and climbed out, of course!"

"Don't you think you should call the police?"

"Heavens no. I've got my little Sassafras."

"I mean don't you think you should call the police about the couple holding you against your will?"

"They didn't hold me against my will."

"But you said they locked you in a room."

"I'm sure they didn't realize how long they'd been gone. They're probably still looking for Sassy. I feel bad for not leaving them a note. They were so friendly."

She wasn't going to budge. "What did they look like?"

"A young white couple about your age, maybe a little younger. She was pretty with dark hair, but she didn't talk much. Her man friend did all the talking."

"How'd you get home?"

"I started walking and found a kind man in a cab. Oh, my goodness, I forgot the man. Hold on." She turned, walked to her apartment and unlocked the door with a key she must have had hidden in her bra.

When she didn't reappear after a few minutes, I went inside, catching a glimpse of the taxi cab waiting on the street. "Mrs. Rippetoe?"

She sat in her kitchen chair, crying. Her money jar sat on the table with the lid removed.

"Oh Mrs. Rippetoe. I'm sorry. Did you forget your jar was empty?"

The money jar had been pilfered a while back and the money never replaced. It broke my heart that the sight of the empty jar brought back her bad memories.

She stopped crying. "How am I supposed to pay the taxi man? I don't have enough money on me."

Mr. P's excited yelping turned into an irritated whine. "I've got you covered. You get yourself cleaned up. I'll bring Sassy down."

I ran upstairs, ignoring the noise coming from Mr. P. Sassy was lying on the couch and PJ was bouncing around like a nut job. "Down PJ!" I grabbed Sassy, ran downstairs and deposited her into Mrs. Rippetoe's lap before untying Mr. P and racing out the door to pay the driver.

"Sorry about that, sir."

"Quite alright, miss. That'll be thirty-seven fifty."

I was pretty sure the gasp I let out was only in my head, but by the expression on his face it might have been audible. "You mind my asking where you picked up my landlady?"

"I didn't overcharge you miss. I've been sitting out here quite a while waiting."

"No. No. I'm not contesting the amount." Although it did sound high. "I am just wondering where she's been."

"I found her wandering the streets in East St. Louis near the river. She didn't look like she belonged, with her dress looking like angel wings and all."

"I can't thank you enough for making sure she got home safe." I paid the man fifty dollars and bid him farewell.

East St. Louis was not in St. Louis at all. It wasn't even in Missouri. It was located across the Mississippi river in

Illinois. Once a recipient of the All-America City Award, it was now sadly blighted, with large sections of overgrown vacant property, empty buildings, and strip clubs. Efforts were underway to rebuild the city, but they had a long way to go. Mrs. Rippetoe was lucky the cab driver crossed her path before it was crossed by an unscrupulous criminal.

3

AS MR. P AND I WALKED to my car, I scanned the 'to do' list inside my head. The closer I got to my Jeep, the clearer it became that I no longer had time to tidy up the mess at Mr. Q's townhouse before going to the office. I tucked Mr. P under my arm and walked back inside my building.

I knocked several times on Mrs. Rippetoe's door. "Are you there?" I asked through the closed door. When she opened the door, I was relieved to see her hair combed and face washed.

"Hey, hun. I thought you were leaving."

"I am, but I hoped you could watch Mr. P for a little while."

"Looky here, Sassy. It's your boyfriend!" She snatched Mr. P out of my arms and placed him on the ground next to Sassy. Mrs. Rippetoe no longer had to worry that Mr. P was a boy because I'd convinced her to spay her little girl after the litter.

"Thanks so much. I'll come by later this afternoon to pick him up."

"What about PJ, hun?"

"He's upstairs. He'll be okay. He likes having his castle to himself."

"You sure?"

"Yes." I made sure she locked her door before making my way out to the street and into my Jeep. Even though she thought her new acquaintances were harmless, I didn't.

"Stephanie?" I spoke into my cell phone and buckled my seatbelt at the same time. "Stephanie?"

"Yeah, sorry, I'm slipping on my boots."

"Are you still at home?"

"No."

The 'Stephanie Alarm' went off in my head as it did every time she sounded as though she might be in trouble. "Tell me you're just switching into your boots after getting to the office."

"Well, no. You see, there's a new bar that opened up Saturday night and I met this guy. He is so awesome. We spent all Sunday together and—"

"Stephanie, where are you?"

"I'm at Roberto's house! Aspen he is so hot. I stayed at his place last night. It was magic. Magic, I tell you. I'm in love!"

One. Two. Three. Four. I kept my focus on the road, trying not to lose control of my Jeep or my temper. I counted silently, until I felt the heat release through my ears. "Stephanie? How long until you're at the office?"

"I was hoping you'd give me the day off. Roberto went to get us some lattes and when he gets back he wants to take me to the casino and teach me how to play the craps table."

"I'm sorry, Steph, but I can't give you the day off. Today's schedule is booked and I need you."

"But, Aspen—"

"No, Stephanie. I need you at the office by ten." I came to a stop at a red light and sat patiently waiting for Stephanie to answer.

"Fine. But, I'm going to text you his picture and then you'll change your mind. Because that's what girlfriends do."

"I'll see you at ten, Steph."

I ended the call thinking it might be time to release Stephanie from the constraints of her job. I'd need another assistant lined up before I fired her and I'd need to harden my heart a bit before dumping her without her having another job.

My phone vibrated. A text message from Stephanie. I knew she wanted me to respond telling her to take the day off, so I ignored it and made my way into the office.

Had Stephanie made it to the office on time, the coffee pot would be full, but she was in love and for that I would suffer. I made a pot of coffee, sneaking a cup before the pot completely filled, took a big swig then sat the cup down on the only clean spot I could find on my desk.

I retrieved the company voicemail. A message from Thomas Brackford suggested he was upset. Brackford, a paraplegic, had been my client for more than a year. I always wanted my customers to be happy, especially my long term ones. I deleted the message, pushed down the receiver button for a second and dialed his number.

"It's about time you called," Mr. Brackford said.

"I called as soon as I got your message. You sound upset."

"Damn right I'm upset. How long have you been working for me now?"

My clients often forgot I operated a personal concierge business and thought of me as their employee. "A little over a year. Why?"

"And don't I pay you well?"

Thomas Brackford's lucrative account had become less lucrative since his friend Belinda began running his errands. Of course it was my fault completely. I'd convinced Brackford to dine by candlelight the first time he invited Belinda over for a platonic dinner. My hope was for him to find that someone special. I never expected to lose his business.

"Of course you pay me well."

"Then why are you stealing from me?"

"Excuse me?"

"You heard me."

"Mr. Brackford. I didn't steal anything. What did you lose?"

"I can't find my sister's blue diamond necklace."

My heart skipped a few beats. I caught my breath.

"Did you say blue diamond?"

"Yes. She was wearing it the day she died. I planned to give it to Belinda, but it's not in the box."

Giving that necklace to Belinda meant things must be serious between the two of them. Thomas Brackford loved his sister. She'd been his caretaker before she died. If the blue diamond had belonged to her then it couldn't possibly be the Blue Monkey. Of course, the presentation on the USB drive hadn't specifically stated they wanted the Blue Monkey diamond.

"What does it look like?" I asked, conjuring up the fuzzy image that had been on the drive.

"It's silver. Has a bunch of blue stones in the shape of a diamond."

Not the diamond. I gathered my thoughts before speaking, relieved I wasn't going to actually be stealing something from Mr. Brackford. "I'm sure it's just been misplaced. I'll come over today and help you find it. Is that okay?"

"I suppose so. When are you coming?"

I checked my schedule. "Is three o'clock okay?"

"Can you bring my mail? Belinda is at a nursing seminar all day."

"No problem. I'll be there at three."

I checked the time on my phone. Nine-thirty. Stephanie should arrive in thirty minutes. I gulped some coffee, clicked on the thread of text messages from Stephanie and looked at the image she'd sent earlier. I held my hand to my mouth, but it didn't help. Coffee shot out of it like a geyser, splattering across my desk. She'd sent me a picture of Roberto alright, from the waist down. He was nude and now it was no secret why Stephanie thought he was awesome.

I ran to the bathroom to clean up. The office door chimed and I couldn't wait to lay into Stephanie. I focused on my shirt, patting it dry as I walked back out of the bathroom. "I spit coffee all over myself when I saw the big bonus your friend Roberto had for you."

"You don't say. So, Roberto has a big bonus, does he?"

Peter leaned against the reception desk with his arms across his chest.

My face flushed. "I thought you were Stephanie."

"Is the redhead from hell late again?"

"I wish you wouldn't call her that, but yes, she is and I really need to get going."

"Victor's at my store, so I can man your office until Stephanie arrives, if you like."

"Thanks, but I should wait for her. Hey, I'm glad you came by. Did you see Mrs. Rippetoe came home?"

"No, I left my place early. Did she say anything about where she—"

"Hello! It is such a wonderful day, isn't it?" Stephanie chirped as she danced into the office.

One quick glance at her and Peter headed for the door. "Gotta go. Call me later, Aspen."

"Wait I have some—"

Peter was out the door. He peered through the window and gave me the devil horns symbol behind Stephanie's back. I ignored him.

"Steph. I have to go too. I'm running behind. Don't forget, I need you to call the list of people with motorhomes for sale because that doctor is ready to buy."

Moore Time had been tasked with finding the perfect motorhome for a successful pediatrician, his wife and their five-year-old twins. Once we delivered, a hefty finder's fee would land in the company bank account and hopefully we'd gain a long-term client.

As I pulled out of my parking space, I saw Stephanie on her cell phone. Somehow I knew the conversation wasn't centered around motorhomes.

———

I entered the Falcon Ridge Towers and walked toward the front desk. The exclusive residential high-rise condominiums were located in the city of Clayton and were home to Mrs. Penelope Paddy. I'd met her through a man whose father once threatened my life. Luckily I hadn't declined the man's offer of introduction because he ended up being a good guy and Mrs. Paddy ended up being loaded, and in desperate need of someone to help her out every week.

I made a quick stop at the lobby desk. "Could you please ring her, Edward, and let her know I'm on my way up?"

I signed the logbook and headed to the elevators, pressing the button marked P when I stepped inside. The twenty-fifth floor housed two units. The doors opened and I took a right to Penelope's penthouse. I rang the doorbell, waited a few minutes and rang it again.

I heard a clunking sound and the door knob turned.

"Miss Moore! So glad you came today." The door banged against a walker.

"Go ahead and back up. I'll handle the door. Why do you have a walker?"

"I hurt my ankle a tiny bit when I exercised last time. Junior gave it to me to help me walk easier. But if you ask me, I think he's wishing I'll walk faster to my grave."

"Now Mrs. Paddy, I'm sure Junior is trying to make things easier for you. Your grandson loves you."

"Is that what they call fussing and fighting over everything I own? Even the receptionist at the foundation was asking me about these silk Persian rugs." She pointed to the carpet in the foyer.

Beads of perspiration formed on her forehead. "Do you want to take your coat off for a bit? We can put it back on when we're ready to go."

"No. I am ready to go now."

"Why don't we sit and talk a while?" Penelope and I usually sat in what she referred to as her parlor and talked about whatever entered her mind.

"I don't want to be late for the movie."

"We didn't discuss going to a movie this week. Are you sure you wouldn't rather sit and talk?" A movie would take more hours than I could spare. The plan had been to spend a few minutes talking before driving her to the Paddy Cake Foundation offices where she'd spend fifteen minutes greeting the employees and then we'd return to her penthouse. She was the grand dame of the Paddy Cake Foundation. Her philanthropic charity gave millions to individuals and groups who championed the rights of both children and animals.

"No. I want to go see that new foreign film playing at the Galleria. I looked it up in the newspaper. It starts at eleven."

Ugh. I could be as cultured and hip as the next person, but a foreign film on a Monday morning when my mind was already on overload. It was going to be excruciating, but whatever Penelope Paddy wanted, Penelope Paddy got. "We better leave now then or we'll be late."

"If we don't make it we can go this afternoon."

Putting off my other clients to spend an entire day with Penelope wasn't an option, regardless of her net worth. "The early show will be better."

"I'm leaving this darn walker here."

"You still have that wheelchair from when you had your hip surgery. Would you like me to get it?"

"If I don't need a walker, I sure don't need a wheelchair. Now, here, just grab my arm."

My visions of using the wheelchair to speed things along vanished. I took her arm and we meandered our way out to the elevator, down to the garage and to her car parked in the handicap space right next to the door.

"Here's the key, Miss Moore."

"Thank you."

Our agreement was that I would drive, but we had to use her car. I'd originally been fine with the arrangement until I discovered she drove a 1936 Packard Twelve

Phaeton. It was a snazzy-looking convertible worth almost two hundred thousand dollars. It had been a part of her late husband's collection, which had long been sold to fund the foundation. The car held a special place in her heart. My heart, on the other hand, nearly stopped every time I drove it.

Double and triple checking the mirrors, I pulled out of the garage and onto Forsyth Boulevard. The Galleria was less than ten minutes away, a good thing because if we were late I wasn't sure how I was going to tell Mrs. Paddy I couldn't go to a movie this afternoon.

The handicap placard allowed me to pull into a space near the door closest to the theatre. "It's just now eleven o'clock. We should make it inside in time for the movie."

"Not to worry, Miss Moore. The movie doesn't start until eleven forty-five. I wanted to make sure we didn't dawdle."

Great. Another forty-five minutes added to my day. I began calculating how much time I'd be spending with Mrs. Paddy, factoring in the visit to her office and the slow-paced walking. I could make it to Mr. Brackford's house by three o'clock as long as there were no other delays.

"Let's get going so we can do some shopping."

"Mrs. Paddy. I don't think we have time."

"Nonsense. Theater's right in the mall."

I didn't argue. I helped her out of the car and we hobbled our way inside the mall.

"I want to go to the leather store, right there." Mrs. Paddy pointed her bony finger up toward the second level.

"What do you need from there?"

"Nothing."

"Then why don't we get a soda instead, before we go in to the theatre."

"No. I need to go to the leather store." Once again Mrs. Paddy raised her arm and pointed her boney finger with laser precision. "I know exactly what I need to get."

"I thought you said you didn't need anything." My upper and lower jaws tightened.

"I don't. You do."

"Mrs. Paddy, I don't need anything."

"Yes you do and I'm going to buy it for you."

"Now, Mrs. Paddy, remember when I told you I didn't want you spending money on me. It's not right. I am working for you."

"Exactly. I always buy gifts for all my employees."

"But Mrs. Paddy, I'm not your employee. I'm, well, I'm like your doctor, your lawyer, or your—"

"Exactly. I buy them gifts too."

I could tell she wasn't going to budge, so I escorted her up to the Coach store wondering what leather product she thought I needed so badly.

"Now you stand outside the store because I am going to surprise you."

What was a ninety-year-old woman going to purchase for me? It brought back memories of old-fashioned foo-foo dresses my grandmother gave me on every birthday. At least whatever Mrs. Paddy intended to buy me would be top quality.

She slowly made her way into the store. I turned away so I wouldn't spoil the surprise. Ten minutes later I felt a tap on my shoulder.

"For you, Miss Moore." She handed me a bag with a wrapped package inside.

"Thank you very much, Mrs. Paddy. Would you like me to open it now?"

"No."

We took the escalators back downstairs. "Why don't you sit here?" I gestured toward the bench. "I'll be right back. I'm going to run this to the car."

"But it's eleven-forty." She tapped her finger on the crystal face of her white gold and diamond watch.

"It will only take me a minute."

I ran all the way to the car, put the bag in the trunk and ran all the way back only to find an empty bench. *Crap.*

I looked up and down the mall, but she was nowhere in sight. I walked up to the ticket counter. "Did a little old lady purchase a ticket and go inside?"

"No."

Just the word I didn't need to hear. I felt the palpitations begin. I lost a ninety-year-old multi-millionaire. I walked toward the middle of the mall looking for an information desk, or some place where I could page her. The desk was unmanned. I turned to walk back to the theater and spotted Mrs. Paddy coming down the escalators with a bag in her hand. I hustled to meet her.

"Where'd you go?"

"I went to the leather store to buy you a gift."

"Mrs. Paddy, you already bought me a gift. Don't you remember?"

"Of course I do. What do you think I am, senile?"

"But—"

"I knew you needed this too." She handed be another bag with a gift-wrapped box inside, smaller than the first one.

"Mrs. Paddy, you shouldn't be spending money on me like this."

"It's my money and I'll spend it any way I want to spend it. Now let's go see the movie."

After maneuvering the Packard into its space in the garage at Falcon Ridge, I opened the door to the passenger side and woke Penelope. She'd snoozed through the second half of the movie and fallen asleep again before we'd left the parking lot of the Galleria.

"You okay Mrs. Paddy?"

"Just a little tired. That was an excellent movie. Why are we back in the garage?"

"You were sleeping and I thought you might be too tired to go by your office."

"I am a bit tired." Mrs. Paddy swung her legs attempting to land her feet outside the car, but barely made it to the edge of the door.

I ran around and took hold of her legs. "Let me help you."

"I don't need help, but if you insist."

I moved her legs so they dangled over the concrete. She wiggled her body over the seat until she was able to get her feet on the ground. She raised herself up and began walking toward the elevator.

I grabbed the bags with the gifts and found my way to her side when the doors opened. We rode to the top in silence.

"Come on and bring those gifts into the parlor," Penelope said.

I didn't want to sound ungrateful, but in less than an hour I needed to be at Thomas Brackford's place to look for his dead sister's necklace. "Mrs. Paddy, I have another appointment. I really can't stay."

"Oh. Then you can open them when you get home."

The inflection in her voice reeked of disappointment. If I could only make myself not care about anything or anyone, life would be a lot less stressful. "Well, I can spare a few minutes."

We sat in the parlor and I opened the larger gift first. "Mrs. Paddy! This is way too expensive. I can't accept this."

"You didn't want to even open them up and now you tell me you don't want what I got you?"

"It's not that I don't want it, because the bag is beautiful. But, you spent way too much money."

"I'm not taking it back."

I held the cherry red tote in front of me. "It's so, me."

"I may be old, but I'm still aware of fashion. And look, pockets, pockets, pockets! Perfect to keep you organized. It's a limited edition."

Those two words let me know the bag was expensive. It would match my red briefcase perfectly. It too was an expensive limited edition I'd received as a gift. "I don't know how to thank you."

"Open the next one," she said with glee. I imagined buying gifts for a woman was a treat. She'd had four children, all boys, all having passed away in their late fifties. Her only heir was her grandson, Junior.

I quickly opened the smaller gift box. "It's perfect!"

"I thought you could use a wallet that you can wear around your wrist if you didn't want to take the big bag."

The navy and cherry red leather wallet had must have set her back another hundred or more. I felt both excited and uncomfortable receiving such expensive gifts for no reason. But the last thing I wanted to do was insult her by not accepting them.

"Thank you again, Mrs. Paddy."

"You can call me Penny if you like."

"Thank you, Penny." I cringed when I said her name. Addressing her by her first name created a tiny crack in the foundation that could cause the invisible wall between client and friend to crumble. Without that wall, we both took the risk of becoming too close. It was a risk I didn't want to take because the closer I became with my clients the more it exaggerated the fact that I was a fake, a fraud, a person no one would ever again truly know. Even worse, it reminded me that the only people who truly knew me were no longer part of my everyday life.

"See you next week, Mrs. Paddy," I said, and closed the door behind me.

I made my way through the lobby, past the desk, and out the revolving doors to my Jeep. I tossed my gifts in the back and hopped into the front. A quick check of my rearview mirror revealed no car behind me, so I backed up, preparing to pull out of the space where I'd parallel parked. As I glanced in my side mirror I got distracted by a USB flash drive on my windshield.

4

I PULLED INTO THOMAS BRACKFORD'S DRIVEWAY right on time even though I'd been tempted to cancel so I could go back to my office and review the flash drive I'd found tucked under my wiper. It looked exactly like the first one I'd received.

Whoever placed it on my windshield must have followed me. How else would someone know where to find me? Unless they knew my schedule. Obtaining that information meant they either cloned my phone or talked to Stephanie. My bet was on Stephanie.

Walking up the wheelchair ramp to Brackford's porch, I noticed signs of infestation on the evergreen plant. The leaves were brown and a funky white web-like substance wove its way from branch to branch. Months ago I would have tended to the problem immediately, but now with Belinda in the picture, I rarely stopped by Brackford's house.

"Bout time," Thomas Brackford said, opening the door before I'd even knocked.

"It's exactly three o'clock."

"No, ma'am. It is three-ten."

Where did the ten minutes go? My mind lost track of time.

"Where was the necklace last time you saw it?" I asked, bypassing any idle chit-chat.

"Back here."

Brackford wheeled his way down the hall past the bedroom containing an entire model town built for his trains. He was a model train enthusiast, an expert really. He entered the next room, which had also housed model trains until Belinda convinced him they needed a place to watch television together or read.

"See. Right here." He pointed to a wooden cigar box on a small dresser.

"Is the box kept here all the time?"

"It's been there ever since Belinda helped me clean out the closet."

"Did you see the necklace then?" I lifted the lid and looked inside the box.

"I didn't look, but it had to be. That box belonged to my father. Friend of his smuggled it out of Cuba. The day I brought my sister's necklace home from the hospital I put it in that box. Nobody else has been in this room except Belinda, you, and that employee of yours, Stephanie."

Stephanie. Crap. I didn't want to come right out and accuse her of stealing the necklace, but I didn't take it. Belinda was in love with Brackford and I couldn't imagine any reason why she would take the necklace, so that left Stephanie. Plus, her history of permanently borrowing other people's items, sort of supported my theory. Before I went any further in that direction I needed to confirm the necklace was really missing.

"Let me look around a bit just in case the necklace fell out when you and Belinda moved stuff around."

"Suit yourself. But I'm pretty sure it was stolen. If you don't find it, I'm going to stop using your services."

The amount of business from Brackford had already fallen off. Losing his remaining business wouldn't close the shop since I had Mrs. Paddy and her bottomless purse, but I didn't want him to be unhappy. Unhappy clients talked and he could damage my reputation. Besides, I'd grown fond of him.

I began by taking everything out of the closet, shaking each item. Nothing. I put everything back in the closet and then checked behind the small dresser where the box was sitting. Again, nothing. I looked in the drawers, behind the couch, under the couch, and between the cushions. The necklace was nowhere to be found.

I walked into Brackford's kitchen where he was sipping a cup of coffee. I trumpeted the one message he didn't want to hear. "Mr. Brackford, I didn't find anything."

"What are you going to do about it?"

"Give me time to think. You know I'll find a solution. I can't look through the rest of your house right now, but I will come back this week and go through the other parts of the house. Don't worry, if it's here, I'll find it."

"You need to find it fast because I have a special occasion coming up."

I couldn't resist. "Are you going to ask Belinda to marry you?"

"No. I thought about it, but then I watched a show about trains and it was followed by a segment on why people should live together first, so I'm going to ask her to move in with me."

"That's great. I hope she agrees. You seem to like her quite a bit."

"That's personal."

Brackford didn't open up much. I couldn't imagine what his relationship with Belinda was like, but he must offer her something because she'd stuck around.

"Sorry. I'll call and set a time to search your house again."

I left him in the kitchen and showed myself out. I backed out of his driveway and dialed the office.

"Hello?" Stephanie said as though she were surprised by the call.

"Stephanie. You're not supposed to answer the phone like that."

"Oh yeah. Sorry I forgot. Moore Time, how may we assist you?"

"That's more like it. Is everything okay there?"

"Yes. Fantastic. Roberto came by and he's going to take me for drinks and dinner."

"But it's only four o'clock."

"It's fine. Peter's here. He said he didn't mind manning the desk. Oh, and he said he heard I was getting a big bonus. Are you giving me a bonus?"

Oh God. Peter. I was going to kill him. "No, sorry. I'm not sure what Peter was talking about."

"Sure," Stephanie said.

Somehow I didn't think she believed me. "Honestly."

"Okay. Whatever you say."

"Seriously Stephanie, I am not giving you a bonus."

"Oh," she said, her voice trailing off like she'd just found out her ticket with the winning lottery numbers was for the wrong date.

"I'll see what I can do." What was I supposed to say? She was the saddest happiest person I knew. If I'd been standing in front of her she'd be looking at me with her puppy dog eyes and wagging her tail at the same time.

"Awesome. I'm so excited!"

"I said, I'll see. Let me talk to Peter real quick and don't leave before I talk to you again."

"Hey, sweetheart," Peter said.

"Making Stephanie think she's getting a Bonus? Not funny."

"Oh, but I think you are mistaken."

"You are so bad," I said trying to sound serious.

"So good. Isn't that what you meant?"

"I appreciate your offer to stay, but I'll have Stephanie close up early."

"You sure? You know I'd do anything for you."

"Hmm. I'll email you my 'to do' list."

"And who's being bad now?' Peter asked.

"Still you. Can you put Stephanie back on the phone?"

"I wish you had been here to meet Roberto," Stephanie said.

"I feel like I already know him with that graphic image you sent."

"What?" Stephanie asked.

"The pic of his junk."

"Oh no! I didn't mean to send that one. Sorry. But, he is great isn't he."

Stephanie giggled.

"Yeah. He's great, Steph. Hey, I need you to close the shop early and meet me at Mr. Q's to help clean up his place. There was no time this morning since you were late. With two of us it shouldn't take long. You'll have plenty of time left for drinks and dinner."

"That should work. I'll call Roberto to make sure. What time?"

"Meet me at Mr. Q's place in thirty minutes."

"Will do. And thanks for closing early. You really are the best boss ever. Roberto and I will be right on time."

"You can't br—"

Stephanie ended the call before I could tell her not to bring Roberto. She wasn't the best employee that was certain. I didn't bother calling her back because Roberto was sure to bail once he found out there was cleaning involved.

I called the on-call pet care service to run by and let PJ out. Who knew when I'd be home.

———

I took Mr. Q's key out of the key organizer Peter had given me for Christmas. Peter always knew what I needed.

The temperature had fallen dramatically, making the distance to the townhouse seem farther away. I wiggled into my jacket and dropped my keys into the pocket. My mind tried to convince me the disaster inside Mr. Q's place was trivial, but it was big. I'd made a mistake telling Stephanie the clean-up wouldn't take long.

I braced myself and opened the door. I didn't see any mess in the living room because my attention was drawn to Mr. Q on the stairs.

"What are you doing here?" we both screamed.

"I live here," he said.

I stood, my eyes fixated on the lifeless body of Mr. Q's neighbor and best friend.

Buh, bam. Buh, bam. Mr. Q continued dragging his neighbor's body down the wood steps to the landing. There were no other sounds. A few seconds later Mr. Q turned to face me. "I need your help, Aspen."

My mouth opened but no words came out. This had to be a joke. Mr. Q and his neighbor always played pranks.

"It's not what you think," he continued, "I found him like this."

My eyes skimmed the neighbor's body, stopping at his chest. No movement. Clearly this wasn't a joke.

"What...why did you come home early?" I don't know why that particular question popped out of my mouth first. I should have asked the most important question — why was he dragging his friend's body down the steps?

"When you called to tell me about my place being broken into, I knew I had to come home because Gavril might be in trouble."

"Who's Gavril?"

"He is." Mr. Q pointed at his neighbor.

"That's not Greg?" Even though his face appeared a little greenish, the guy still resembled Mr. Q's neighbor, Greg.

"Yes, he's Greg, but his real name is Gavril."

"What? I'm confused."

"I guess since he's dead I don't need to keep his secret. Greg is, I mean was in the Witness Protection Program. Gavril's his real name. He told me last week. I suppose it ate at him, being my best friend and me not knowing the truth." Mr. Q walked over to the couch and sat down. He placed his head in his hands.

I wanted to run, get in my Jeep, call Marshal Cutter and ask him why they dumped me in a virtual potter's field for witnesses. *How many others were there?* Inside my head I screamed. I wanted to yell at Cutter, tell him I was tired, tired of lying and tired of hiding. But what I wanted and what I needed were two different things. My anxiety level increased. I squashed it the best I could and re-focused on the situation. "What happened to him?"

"I don't know. I didn't see any blood or anything. Maybe he had a heart attack or something."

"But you said you thought he might be in trouble. What made you think that?"

"When you called and asked me about a blue diamond, something felt off."

"What's the blue diamond have to do with this?"

"I wanted to buy this blue diamond. Such a great history. They call it the Blue Monkey."

Mr. Q acted like we were making idle conversation though his friend's body lay less than ten feet from where he sat. "What does Greg, I mean Gavril, have to do with the blue diamond?"

"I sent Gavril to Denmark a while back to bid on the diamond for me at an auct—"

"Do you think someone tried to steal the diamond from you, but Gre...Gavril interrupted them? Eeeew, does that mean Greg was upstairs dead when I came by here Sunday?"

Feelings rushed over me almost dropping me to the ground. I'd been in similar situations, people dead or dying and me unable to take action. *What if Greg had been incapacitated, but alive on Sunday? Why didn't I see him when I went upstairs to get Mr. P's t-shirt?*

"I got home a few hours ago. The door to the room was closed. I never close that door," Mr. Q said.

A sick feeling came over me. Why hadn't I noticed the closed door?

"How long do you think he's been dead?" I asked.

"I don't know. How long do you think he's been dead? Come look." Mr. Q got up off the couch.

Was he joking? I didn't want to get anywhere near Greg. It didn't matter how many times you saw a dead body, you either had the stomach for it or you didn't. "I'll pass."

"No, seriously. Come take a look."

"Shouldn't you call the police?"

"No," he said, delivering his answer without hesitation.

"What are you going to do? Don't you want to report the diamond stolen?"

"No. I didn't win the auction. Gavril said he got distracted and missed the final bid. But get this, the person who won lives in St. Louis. Can you believe that?"

"Why would someone break into your house if you didn't have the diamond?"

"I don't know. Gavril told me when he flew back from Denmark he had a feeling he was being followed. He worried someone from his past recognized him at one of the airports or something. I told him he could stay at my house if he needed a place to hide."

How could someone just happen to see him? It seemed far-fetched. I didn't want to believe it could happen because then it could happen to me. "Did he ever tell you what landed him in the Witness Protection Program?"

"At first I didn't believe him. I mean really, the Witness Protection Program? It was like something from a movie. I mean would you believe someone if they told you that?"

I fidgeted with Mr. Q's key that I still held in my hand. "I dunno."

"He sits me down, says he testified against the Russian Mob. I almost laughed, but then he started speaking Russian. We talked a lot that night. I think it must have been like breaking out of a straitjacket for him because I could see the relief on his face after he told me. He was an interesting guy, even if he was a little quirky. I'm going to miss him."

If anyone knew anything about quirky, it was Mr. Q, the king of quirky. "I think you should call the police."

"No," Mr. Q said, his tone firm. He never wanted police involvement where his own life was concerned. I had to admit, I could relate. I wasn't a big fan of the police either. Not because I didn't respect them. But with police came lots of questions. I didn't like people asking questions and neither did Mr. Q.

It was difficult to argue with him, but I had to, the situation wasn't a simple break-in, wild party, or any other menial crime or nuisance. It could be murder. "Mr. Q, you should call the police. I mean even you said it might just be a heart attack or something."

"I don't know. The bed is messed up in the room and there are two wine glasses on the nightstand."

"See. Maybe he had a heart attack having sex and the woman got scared off."

"But, why did they mess up my place?"

"Good question. Are you thinking he didn't die of natural causes?"

"Exactly. I'm not calling the police."

"You don't have a ch--"

My heart jumped at the sound of the doorbell chiming.

5

"CRAP. What the hell do we do, Mr. Q?"

"Mister who?"

"Uh, I mean Mr. Quetzalcoatl. Never mind."

I went to the door and opened it just enough to slide my body out on to the front stoop. "Stephanie! What a surprise."

"You did say to meet you here right?"

"Right. Yes, but guess what? I'm practically finished. So, you're off the hook!"

The eyes had a way of telegraphing thoughts. In some cases, they could betray you and in others they could emphasize the good. Stephanie's eyes were emanating happiness even before the smile appeared on her face. And if they could speak they'd being saying, "Yahooo!"

"Awesome! I'll see you later."

Without hesitation she turned and headed back to the car and to the person in the driver's seat, which I assumed was Roberto.

I slipped back inside, my heart still pounding.

"I don't care what you do, but you've got to do something." My words were aimed at Mr. Q, but my eyes were aimed at Greg.

I walked over to the couch and sat down. "The right thing to do is call the police. You don't know if his death was natural or a homicide."

"Right. But, does it matter really? I mean either way he is dead. Figuring out how he died isn't going to bring him back."

He had a point. We didn't kill him. At least I know I didn't kill him. *Crap. How do I know Mr. Q didn't kill him?*

"Why don't you want to call the police?"

Mr. Q sat on the couch next to me. "I'll call them, but not right now."

"What are you going to do? Sleep here with his body? You need to call the police."

I should just walk out the door and call the police. Not look back and kiss Mr. Q's lucrative contract goodbye. But, I wasn't. *Why?*

Mr. Q stood. "Fine. So I have no choice. But I do have a choice about where they find the body."

"What?"

"Aspen, I need you to help me move Gavril's body."

Holy Crap. If I had a hard time looking at a cadaver, how the heck was I going to move one? I closed my eyes and leaned back against the cushion. Thinking. There had to be some way to get out of this. I'd agree not to say anything to the police, but I sure wasn't going to help him move the body.

"The two of us could easily get Greg out the back an--"

My eyes popped open. "No, freakin' way. Are you nuts? I'm not touching his body and neither should you."

"I'm not leaving him here." Mr. Q paced back and forth, forcing me to look at Greg's body every time he passed by it.

"Well, I'm not moving him," I said.

We were at an impasse.

"If you think about it, we really aren't doing anything wrong. We're just relocating the body."

"Not doing anything wrong? And don't say we. You'd be switching the crime scene. No, you'd be creating a secondary crime scene."

"But still, it doesn't matter. He's dead. I don't want the police poking around. They always ask so many questions. And you know, I'm a private man."

My head knew exactly what he was talking about, but still, I couldn't. "I don't want to talk about it. It's final, I won't help you move the body."

"Understood. I'll do it."

"What?"

"I know some people."

"Stop talking. I don't want to know anything more."

"I just need to ask you--"

"No, I'm not helping move him!"

"I just wanted to know if you can clean up the bedroom. I can't bear to do it. He was my friend."

I understood. I empathized. I compromised. "Fine. I'll clean it up."

––––

If I slept all day I could avoid thinking about last night's crazy moment of paranoid solidarity with Mr. Q, but PJ had other plans. He bounced, jumped, and flipped on my mattress like a confused Olympic athlete.

"I just want to sleep." I reached out and snatched PJ when one of his moves landed him within striking distance. I held him close and pulled the comforter over us, wishing my life would have turned out more like the Brady Bunch instead of The Fugitive.

PJ whined.

"Ok. Come on little man, let's get up."

I threw on some sweatpants and a tee shirt. PJ and I sneaked out the back door of my building into the crisp air. PJ took his time sniffing each blade of grass. "Hurry up," I said, tugging on his lead.

He stopped what he was doing and looked up at me as if he wanted me to repeat what I'd said. I kept my mouth shut. He finally got around to business. A few minutes later we were back upstairs in my toasty apartment.

I threw some kibble into PJ's bowl before running back to put on real clothes. There was no need for a shower, because I had signed up to do dirty work today and once I finished I'd need to clean the filth and guilt from my body.

I said goodbye to PJ, bolted down the stairs and knocked on Mrs. Rippetoe's door. She opened it wearing her robe.

"Thank you for watching Mr. P overnight. Is it possible for you to keep him until this afternoon?"

"Of course...is that PJ crying?"

The sound of PJ whining broke my heart. I felt like I'd been neglecting him. "Yes, but he'll quiet down."

"Why don't you bring him down here. He won't be a problem. I'm sure his mommy and daddy would love to spend time with him."

"I'm not sure. He's not completely trained." The word 'barely' would have been a better choice.

"He'll be fine. I insist."

With that, I ran upstairs and rescued PJ from his castle.

"Here he is." I placed him in Mrs. Rippetoe's arms while Sassy and Mr. P wagged their tails in excitement.

I walked out of our building. The air was crisper than earlier, but the sun on my face took the edge off. The stress that had been setting up camp inside me, slowly eased its way out of my body and the sides of my mouth inched upward. If I wasn't mistaken, I was starting to feel good. *Hallelujah!*

By the time I jumped inside my Jeep I was whistling. An incredible feat considering where I was headed and what I was about to do. The corners of my mouth began to droop. I struggled to keep their upward position. I thought about calling Jack, hoping it would interject some light-heartedness into a day that was sure to be depressing.

Despite his irritating habit of disappearing from my life on short notice, I did enjoy talking with him. And the sex, it was fantastic and exciting. But sometimes it felt like sex was all we had. Whenever I was with Jack, we got along great, we laughed, he was attentive, but as soon as I began to give him more or ask more of him, he backed off. It was as if I were the mouse and he the cat. Just as his paw landed on my tail, he'd sense the chase might be over and he'd run off sniffing around some other mouse hole.

I shook off the image and forced a smile. For one day, I wasn't going to care about the chase. I was going to care about being happy. Having sex with Jack made me happy. So, I wasn't going to worry about cleaning up Mr. Q's place, I would just do it. And I surely wasn't going to worry about what might be missing from my relationship with Jack. "It is what it is," I said as I dialed his cell phone. He didn't answer so I tried his office.

"Jack Arbon."

"What? Your assistant finally get tired of you?"

"No. She took a personal day. If anyone seems to have gotten tired of me it's you."

Exactly as I expected. I hadn't returned his calls so the chase was on.

"How so, counselor?"

"Don't go using that sexy law talk with me. I should call my pals at the station and have you arrested."

"For what?"

"Attempted assault on my feelings."

I wanted to ask him if he possessed any feelings because it sure didn't seem like it. Whenever I tried to move us past the casual relationship, he closed up. But I didn't want our conversation heading in that direction. "I'm sorry I didn't return your calls. Hectic day. Is there anything I can do to make it up to you?"

"You could come to my place and let me make you dinner."

Despite the length of time Jack and I had been seeing one another, I'd never received an invitation inside his home. I'd been to his front yard, his back yard, even his garage, but never inside.

"Cat got your tongue?"

No, Mister Cat not right now, but definitely tonight.
"It's a date. What time?"

"Seven?"

"See you then." I tapped the screen to end the call and tossed the phone on the front seat.

I drove a few more blocks and entered Soulard. As I turned onto Mr. Q's street, the police looked like they were actively investigating Gavril's home. As the gap between my Jeep and law enforcement narrowed, I reduced my speed, slowing just enough to check it out, without drawing their attention. It appeared Mr. Q kept his end of the deal, so now I had to keep mine.

Technically what I was about to do was wrong, but if I could find some way to help the police find Gavril's killer maybe it would make up for the sin I was about to commit. What was the harm, right?

In my rearview mirror, I watched one of the officers cross the street. I continued down the road.

My agreement to clean Mr. Q's place didn't include involuntarily getting caught up in the investigation. If no one answered the door at Mr. Q's house they couldn't go inside. It was the best thing for me and for Mr. Q.

———

When I walked into my office, it was almost noon. Stephanie sat at the reception desk talking on the phone.

"No. You hang up, Roberto," Stephanie said.

"No. You," she repeated and then laughed.

I cleared my throat.

"I'll see you in a half hour. Aspen's here." Stephanie hung up the phone and began clicking away at her keyboard as if I hadn't been privy to the personal phone call she'd made.

I didn't mind her making personal calls, but I had my suspicions that she'd been on the phone with Roberto for most of the morning. Stephanie by herself wasn't the type to go above and beyond in her job, but add Roberto into the mix and she didn't even seem to want to strive for average. "I'm glad you found someone you like Stephanie—"

"Isn't it wonderful? He is amazing."

"No Steph, that's not exactly what I'm trying to say. I am happy for you, but you seem to be spending more time focusing on Roberto than your job."

"I know, but relationships take time to build. You should spend more time with Jack and it would move a little faster. You and him move soooooo slooooooow."

"We don't need to be talking about that. It's time to work. Can you please get me the file on Harry Corbitt? I've decided to go ahead and take him on as a client again."

"Sure, but then I need to leave to meet Roberto for lunch. Do you want anything? We're going to Charlie Gitto's."

"They're not open for lunch," I said, walking back to my desk.

Stephanie followed me. "We're not going to Gitto's On The Hill, we're going to Gitto's From The Hill."

She was driving all the way to Chesterfield for a sit down lunch at a nice restaurant, which meant she planned to be gone for more than her hour lunch break.

"How about I bring you back some toasted ravioli?"

I almost lost it until she mentioned the toasted ravioli. It was one of the St. Louis born foods that I happened to love and I was pretty hungry. "Okay. But, be back by two o'clock."

Stephanie walked over to the file cabinets. "Oh I will. I'm driving up to meet Roberto because he's got a meeting afterward."

I got up from my desk and leaned on the Plexiglas wall that divided my space from the rest of the office. "You know, Gitto's is kind of expensive. What kind of work does Roberto do?"

"He's a professional gambler." Stephanie said the words like she was saying he was a civil engineer, or a teacher, or any other normal profession.

"What kind of meeting does he have?" I asked, worried Roberto might be getting ready to lose his legs.

"It's not really a meeting, I guess. He's playing in a poker tournament at the Casino in Maryland Heights."

I wanted to ask her more about Roberto, but I didn't want to encourage discussing her relationship on company time. Stephanie passed me the Corbitt file and I handed her a twenty-dollar bill.

As soon as the door closed behind her and she was out on the sidewalk, I picked up the phone and dialed Harry.

"Hello."

"Mr. Corbitt? It's Aspen Moore."

"Hello, mate."

"I'm returning your call. You're planning on getting married again?"

"Yes. I need you to plan it all."

"If you aren't in a rush perhaps you should use a wedding planner this time."

When the silence began scratching at my ears, my body tensed, and the memory of creepy Harry filled my head.

"No. You. I want you. You get me."

Get him? I didn't get him and the more we stayed on the phone the more I wanted to reverse time, un-hear the message he'd left, un-do my request for his file, and un-dial his number.

"Harry. I don't know you. I mean, we only met once and talked on the phone a few times."

Harry's breath was audible. Fast and heavy. "Harry? Are you okay?"

"You're the one."

Goose bumps popped up and a sense of doom poked at my chest. "When do you plan on getting married?"

Again, his breathing, in and out, in and out. This time fast on the intake, but slow and eerie on the exhale. I was about to hang up when he spoke.

"Sometime."

My way out. "Harry, I need to know the date if I'm going to plan your wedding. I'm afraid I won't be able to help you. I'm sorry."

"No choice."

"What?"

Harry's silence triggered my fight or flight. "I'm sorry I need to go. Goodbye."

I tried to overlook his creepiness, after all, not everyone possessed the social skills of a butterfly. But why did he surface now? The man showed up in my life at the same time my clients experienced difficulties. If there was a connection I didn't know what it was, but what I did know is that something was a little off about Harry Corbitt.

———

I spent my time surfing the Internet and dodging Harry's calls for a few hours. Moore Time always saw things through to completion and I wasn't about to change that policy now. At some point, I'd have to call Harry back, gather all the information and plan his wedding

Stephanie was late. Again. I dialed her number. "Stephanie, where are you?"

"I'm sorry, Aspen. Someone dropped Roberto off at the restaurant, so I'm giving him a ride to the casino. I'll be there soon."

I almost spit out the words, "you're fired," but remembered if I fired Stephanie I'd be replacing sporadic help for no help at all. Rush hour traffic would make Stephanie's trip back from the Casino a long one and even longer if she couldn't resist doing a little gambling herself. "You know Stephanie, go ahead and take the rest of the day off. I'm closing early."

"But, what about your toasted ravioli?"

"Go ahead and keep them for your dinner." My stomach growled in protest.

"Thank you. I'm sorry. I am, really. I know I let you down. I will make it up to you."

I found my perfect opening. "You know how you could make it up to me? I've got a special date with Jack and I'm going to wear this great blue top, but I don't have the right necklace to wear. You always have such great jewelry. Can I stop by your place and pick something out for tonight?"

"Oh that is fantastic. Yes, of course, girl!"

"Three-Thirty good?"

"Sure. I should be back to my place by then."

"Don't be late, please. I want to make sure I have plenty of time to get myself ready for my date."

She promised to be on time. I hoped Stephanie would let me look through all her jewelry. If I found the blue diamond-shaped necklace, I could permanently borrow it. If I ended up finding the necklace at Brackford's place this afternoon, I'd just tell Stephanie I changed my mind.

I locked up my shop and headed over to Peter's store to borrow a metal detecting gadget. I owned a metal detector, but it was the big long kind with the disc on the end. The type you could swing back and forth while walking the beach in hopes of finding a diamond wedding ring some poor bride let slip off her finger after too many beers. It was much too big to be swinging it around Brackford's house.

"Is Peter here?" I walked up to the counter behind which Peter's employee, Victor, stood. He was the type of employee who was pro-active and always on time. Not that I was jealous of Peter's excellent employee or anything.

"Yeah. Go on back."

Peter's store was larger than mine. Instead of a Plexiglas divider, he had an office with actual walls. I knocked on the office door. "Peter?"

"Come on in."

He sat at his desk, his head down, reading some type of manual. The fluorescent lights bounced off his head. The only bit of hair on his entire head was the soul patch on his chin. Along with his height and muscles, his look could fulfill any woman's bad boy fantasy.

Peter looked up. "What are you looking at?"

"Nothing." I felt my face heat up.

Peter smiled. He knew damn well I'd been checking him out. I was crazy about him and he was crazy about Madeline. Him knowing how I felt made our relationship uncomfortable at times. The worst part was that his faithfulness made him even sexier.

"You are so darn cute. What's on your mind?"

"Oh stop, Peter. Cute's for kittens. Cute's for teddy bears. Cute's for—"

"For people like you who are irresistible." He winked.

Why did I embrace his flirtatiousness when I knew it would go nowhere? "Irresistible as long as no one else is in the picture." *Ugh. Madeline. I brought her up again.*

In person Madeline looked as though she'd been modified with Photoshop, that's how darn beautiful she was. I was definitely average in comparison. No wonder

Peter turned down my intoxicated advance when I'd first met him. Our relationship was defined that night when I tried to kiss him. He instantaneously went from being an exciting possibility to plain old friend.

Peter feigned being hurt, clutching his chest. "Oh. Low blow."

"I only speak the truth. Besides, I've got Jack."

"Oh. Another low blow."

"Stop." This time the word was devoid of playfulness.

He got up from his chair. "You know I'm kidding. He's my friend. He has lots of good qualities. It's just his bad qualities I worry about."

"I can handle him."

"I bet you are pretty good at it," he said, wiggling his eyebrows up and down.

"Oh gross. Enough of that. I came here to borrow some of your spy stuff."

"Security equipment?"

"Yeah, that. I need some kind of small metal detector."

"No problem. Follow me."

He led me to the front of the store to the shelves against the wall.

"Will this do?" He gave me a small box. "It's a hand-held detector."

"Wow. It's like the size of a flashlight."

"In fact, it has a flashlight built in."

"Don't you have a used one. I don't want to take a new one out of the box."

"It's okay. Once you're done I'll use it as a display. Let me show you how it works."

Peter opened the box and took out a short black wand. I followed him to the counter where he grabbed a 9-volt battery. "The entire bottom half of the wand detects, three hundred and sixty degrees. LED light's here. What do you need to find?"

"Brackford lost a necklace that belonged to his sister. I told him I'd look for it in his house. He thinks I took it, but I didn't. Probably been misplaced."

"This should work then. Just remember there are a lot of metal things in a house you don't see, so you'll most likely get some false positives."

"Thanks." I took the hand-held detector and placed it into my briefcase.

"Why don't I treat you to dinner and you can return it then."

"Jack's cooking dinner for me at his house."

"He's finally letting you see the inside of his house?"

"Can you believe it?"

"Why don't you drop it by my apartment when you get home after dinner."

"Uh. I uh—"

"Oh. Right."

6

THE SEARCH OF BRACKFORD'S HOUSE was a flop, unless sixty-nine cents, a nail, and an old cuff link counted as a measure of success. I drove to Stephanie's place, the whole time trying to figure out how to question her about the necklace without accusing her of stealing the thing.

Stephanie was sensitive about her problem. I understood because a friend in my old life struggled with alcoholism. Their problems were different, but the challenges the same. My friend was always at risk of falling off the wagon while Stephanie was at risk of stealing one. An alcoholic or kleptomaniac, one thing was certain, neither wanted to be reminded of their disease every minute of every day.

I walked through the courtyard and into the building to the front door of Stephanie's condominium. It was perplexing how she could afford the place while working for me. She'd once hinted it didn't cost her much, though the fees had to be high. But, her cost of living wasn't my concern as long as she wasn't stealing from my clients to pay her bills.

Stephanie opened the door after the first knock. I almost fainted because I hadn't expected her to be on time.

"Come on in."

"I appreciate you letting me borrow a necklace."

"No problem. I laid out a few on the coffee table."

Several necklaces formed a neat row on the table in front of the sofa, some with matching earrings. I scanned them quickly not finding Brackford's necklace. The exclusion didn't mean anything. The necklace could be stashed away in her jewelry box. "Nothing quite strikes me as being the one. Can I peek in your jewelry box?"

"There's nothing else that would go with the shirt you described."

"But what if you didn't think I would like something and it turns out to be perfect for me?"

"Honest. I don't have anything else."

Her resistance heightened my suspicion that Brackford's necklace was tucked inside the jewelry box. And that would mean Stephanie had ripped off a client. "Why don't you let me be the judge. You are always wearing different necklaces and I can tell they aren't all on the table."

"Aspen. There isn't anything else." She stormed off down the hall.

Stunned, I stood for a moment not sure what to do. Then I thought better of it and jogged down the hallway sliding in to her room before she had a chance to empty the jewelry box. "Stephanie, I didn't mean to upset you, but—"

"Here. See." Stephanie grabbed the jewelry box from the top of her dresser and shoved it into my hands.

I opened the box, fully expecting to find the shiny blue diamond shaped pendant. Instead I found a single set of shiny purple Mardi Gras beads. "What happened to all your jewelry?"

"I...oh...this is embarrassing. I had to pawn most of it to help make my mortgage payment."

Perhaps I let the silence hang around a little longer than I should, but I was confused. "I thought your condo was practically paid for. What happened?"

"It's not paid for completely. I put down some inheritance money and got a loan. My payments were really low, but the interest changed on my loan. I don't remember exactly what type of loan I got. Named after a body part, I remember that. Leg loan? No. Arm. Yes, an ARM. I didn't pay attention to what I signed and now my payment's almost doubled."

Poor Stephanie. "Have you thought of refinancing to a fixed loan? The rates are pretty low."

"I'm not sure if I can. Finances aren't easy for me. Plus, I don't think I make enough now."

Being her boss made that statement sting. Was I the reason her future might include foreclosure? "I could look over your loan papers. If you want me to."

"Great. I need help figuring out what to do. You are so smart, having your own business and everything. Maybe you could give me a review too and see if I deserve a raise."

Her statement let me know finance wasn't the only thing she didn't get. I was closer to firing her than rewarding her. "Where did you pawn your jewelry? Do you have a certain time to get it back?"

"I took the necklaces to Pauperazzi on Watson Road. Used to be called John's Pawn, but he told me they're trying to make the store fancy, more like a boutique. Said my jewelry would make an excellent addition to his store. I straight out sold it to him, but he didn't give me half of what I originally paid. He did say he'd hold a few pieces back for a while if I wanted to come back and buy them. I think he felt sorry for me."

I felt sorry for her too. "I don't think I need a necklace to impress Jack. Tomorrow, bring in your mortgage papers and I'll look them over and perhaps we can maybe see about possibly giving you somewhat of a review."

How could I trample on her while she was down? She wasn't a great employee, and not even a great friend, but there were times she was there when I needed her most. I'd figure out how to give her a raise and begin the – find Stephanie another job – project.

———

The outside of the pawn shop was amazing, the Pauperazzi sign dazzled and beckoned me to enter. The inside didn't give off quite the same feeling. The store was still undergoing renovation, but I saw the vision. The back of the store was junky, dusty, reminding me of an elderly couple's basement. The front of the shop contained clean and shiny glass cases displaying collectible memorabilia and jewelry. Lots of jewelry.

"Hello?" I asked, looking around the shop.

"Hi. What can I do you for?" A burly man walked toward me. In the back of the store, he fit, like a man in his natural habitat, but the minute he crossed over into the newly renovated portion, he was like a lumberjack in a day spa.

"My friend pawned a necklace. I'd like to get it back for her."

"That's mighty nice of you. I'm John, the owner. What's the necklace look like?"

"It has a pendant shaped like a diamond with blue stones."

"Oh yeah. The nurse brought that in."

My initial shock that the necklace was actually in the pawn shop soon turned to confusion. "Nurse? What made you think she was a nurse?"

"She wore scrubs like they wear in the hospital."

I pulled up a picture of Stephanie on my phone and showed it to him. "Is this the woman?"

"No, but I remember her coming in here too. She sold me a lot of jewelry. I felt bad for her. I wanted to give her more money because she seemed down on her luck, but I am running a business."

"Can I see the diamond shaped pendant necklace?"

"Sure. Down here in the last case. The other lady's jewelry is over there." He pointed to the two cases closest to the front."

"What did the nurse look like?"

"A bigger woman, not height-wise if you know what I mean. Had short, dark hair. Nice, but seemed like she had a chip on her shoulder."

My heart broke. His description fit Belinda, except for the part about having the chip. Belinda always seemed sweet and caring. How was I going to tell Brackford that the woman he loved ripped him off?

"Yes. She's my friend too. I'd like to see the diamond shaped necklace first."

"You got a lot of friends pawning jewelry."

"Times are tough."

He walked to the case at the end and removed the blue diamond shaped necklace. Definitely not the type you'd keep in a safe. The necklace was small and not what I would call breathtaking, but it meant a lot to Brackford. Couldn't have cost over fifty bucks brand new. "I'll take it, how much?"

"Two hundred."

I worked hard to hold back the choking sound. "Are these sapphires?"

"Sure."

His answer sounded like it would have been the same had I asked if the stones were rubies. "How about one-twenty-five and I'll buy a second necklace?"

"What necklace?"

"Let me look at the necklaces in the front cases." I'd buy one of Stephanie's necklaces back. I peered through the case. A two-chain, gold necklace with a red ruby heart caught my eye. I remembered her telling me that her father had given it to her when she'd turned sixteen. "I'll take the one with the red heart."

"I can sell both necklaces for three-hundred."

"Three hundred?"

"Yes, ma'am."

I surveyed the jewelry-filled cases with barely an empty space. He couldn't have sold much. "Two-fifty and you got yourself a deal."

"I don't know. They are excellent pieces."

"I can only do two-fifty. Do we have a deal or not?" I didn't know what I would do if he said no. I didn't want to go over two hundred, but I needed the blue diamond-shaped necklace.

"You are a shrewd shopper. Deal."

"Thank you. What credit cards do you take?"

"None."

"Where's the nearest ATM?"

"Right next to us at the Circle K."

I ran to the convenience store and withdrew money, unhappily agreeing to the processing fee. The smell of hotdogs made my stomach grumble. I hadn't eaten all day, I was tempted, but I didn't want to ruin Jack's home-cooked dinner he had planned.

I scooted back to the pawn shop, exchanged the money for the jewelry and hustled out the door. My hopes of having a few hours to take a bath and pretty myself up for Jack, were now dashed.

———

I sat in my Jeep, in the dark outside Jack's home. The hour I'd spent getting ready for my date had turned into an hour thinking about the past few days of my life. The relief of having Mrs. Rippetoe return eased the pressure, but I still had to deal with Mr. Q's predicament.

I popped open the center console to retrieve my emergency lip plumper. *The flash drive. Crap.* The shock of finding Mr. Q dragging his dead neighbor down the steps had caused me to forget about the second flash drive I'd found on my windshield. Reviewing the contents, no longer seemed like an emergency. Mrs. Rippetoe was safe at home and I had a date.

I closed the lid to the console. I wasn't going to think about the drive or the mess at Mr. Q's or how I would find the words to tell Mr. Brackford he had a thief as a girlfriend. Tonight, I was going to be selfish.

The anticipation of laying my eyes on the inside of Jack's home was almost as high as the anticipation of having sex with Jack. The excitement built with every step I took.

Jack's home with its stone exterior gave way to fantasy. I imagined myself standing on the front balcony letting my tresses tumble to my shoulders while Jack kissed the landing spot of every curl. The outside of his home was beautiful, but the inside was like the inside of Jack's head, a deep, dark secret...until tonight.

Although he invited me inside his home for the first time, I had no expectations he'd also invite me inside his head. It was the precise reason why I'd been trying to turn my attention away from serious relationship sex to c'est la vie sex. The key word – trying. I calmed the fluttering in my stomach and rang the bell.

"Welcome to my abode." Jack took my hand and led me inside.

I didn't see anything deep or dark. The inside was open and airy, but man-ified. A leather sectional filled the living area, softened with a large sheepskin rug. The logs in the fireplace burned with intent and I almost giggled. I felt like I'd just walked into a romance novel.

"For you." Jack held out a glass of red wine.

"Thank you. It smells scrumptious in here. What's on the menu?"

"A friend of mine is the chef at Le Canard Chanceux. He gave me his recipe for Tarragon Chicken. It's in the oven."

The chef's French cuisine at the La Canard Chanceux resulted in hard to get reservations. I'd only eaten there once. "I can't wait to taste it."

"And neither can I." Jack pulled me close. A bit of red wine lingered on his lips and made its way inside my mouth as he kissed me. The best wine tasting I'd ever experienced.

I pushed him away. "One more of those and we'll end up having Tarragon Chicken for breakfast. Why don't you give me the tour?"

"Breakfast? What about PJ?"

"He's staying with Mrs. Rippetoe for the night."

Jack pulled me in again and my knees almost buckled. God, he was hot. He made me hot. The temperature in my pants teetered on sizzling, almost like I was on—"

"Shit. Take it off! Take your jacket off!" Jack yelled.

"Wha—"

"Smoke. You're on fire!"

I screamed. The sound of my wine glass shattering when it hit the floor, didn't even rival the noise coming from my lungs. I struggled with my jacket, finally dropping it to the floor. I shut my mouth, ended my crazy 'I'm on fire' dance, and watched as Jack stomped on the jacket until the fire was extinguished.

"How the heck did I catch fire?"

"The candle." Jack pointed to the sofa table I'd been leaning against. "Sorry."

I started laughing. I couldn't stop. Jack began laughing too. I bent over, holding my stomach. It ached.

While I gasped for air, Jack caught his breath for a second. "You should have seen your face. And the screaming and jumping." Jack resumed laughing.

"Oh my God." I gasped for another breath, wiping the tears from my face.

Jack, suddenly composed, reached to the floor and picked up my jacket. "Let me get this mess cleaned up. I'm sorry about your jacket."

"It's okay. I'm just glad my hair didn't go up in flames. I'd have hired a lawyer and sued you."

Jack walked to a small pantry closet and brought out a broom and dustpan.

"Here, I'll do it. You go tend to the food."

I rolled up my jacket. Its usefulness reduced to an excuse to go shopping. I swept the glass shards into the dust pan. "Where's your garbage can?"

"Right here."

I walked around the dark granite peninsula and dumped the glass into the trashcan housed by a specially designed cabinet, Jack had opened. He took the broom and dustpan from me and I looked around the kitchen while he put it back in the pantry. The kitchen neared gourmet status. Peter once told me Jack's place was a dump inside and the main reason Jack never invited me in. But, this place didn't look like a dump. Either Peter had never been inside Jack's place or he'd been helping out his buddy by providing an excuse.

"Your kitchen is incredible."

"I've been working on it for a while."

"How long has it been finished?"

"Not long at all."

Another example of our problematic relationship. He'd been renovating his kitchen for a while and I had no idea. What kind of man dates a woman and doesn't discuss what is going on in his home life? I knew a lot about his work, but evidently I needed some sort of top secret clearance to get any information on his personal life. Little Pop Rocks of anger exploded in my head. I took a deep breath. *C'est la vie sex. C'est la vie sex.*

"I'd love a tour of the rest of your house."

"Chicken's done. Why don't we eat first?"

I wasn't sure we needed to eat at this exact moment. It felt more like he dodged my request. But, it didn't matter because I was hungry.

Jack handed me a new glass of wine before directing me to the kitchen stool to watch him plate our dinner. He impressed me with his command of the kitchen. In fact, even Peter was impressive in the kitchen. Of course, anyone appeared more impressive in the kitchen than I did.

"Hope you don't mind if we eat at the kitchen table. I haven't gotten around to furnishing the dining room yet."

"I'm easy. Kitchen table is great."

"Excellent."

If Peter were here, he'd have jumped right on my 'I'm easy' remark. Jack never was quick on the attack, which surprised me for a lawyer. But, he was funny, interesting, and especially sexy. He had a lot of good things to offer, one of which I planned to enjoy a little later in the evening and hopefully through to the morning.

He carried our plates to the table. We ate in silence for a while. Though the lull made me uncomfortable, he seemed at ease with the lack of conversation. I wondered if he'd been raised that way. "So, do all your brother's and sister's cook too?"

"I only have a sister. I thought I mentioned her before."

"Yes, you did. I didn't know if that was your only sibling."

"She's younger. And she doesn't cook. Neither does my mother. My father was the chef of the family. Guess that's where I get it."

"The meal is excellent." I took a few bites of the carrots. "What'd you do to these? I don't usually like cooked carrots."

"Butter. Honey. Onions."

"No wonder they taste so good." I put down my fork trying to avoid onion breath. It was bad enough that I already smelled of smoke.

"You finished?" Jack reach toward my plate.

"Yes. Thank you, it was all delicious."

Jack stood up from the table, with our plates in his hands. I stood up too.

"No. You sit." He filled my wine glass to the top. I believed he intended to get me drunk.

"The least I can do is clean up."

"Not tonight. Let me pamper you."

Pamper? Did I just hear Jack Arbon say the word pamper?

"Go ahead and sit by the fire. I'll be there in a minute."

"Fire? Really?"

He smiled. "Don't sit too close."

I obeyed his orders, grabbing my glass of wine, I headed to the sofa in front of the stone fireplace. The leather felt soft and cool against my skin. I set my drink on the coffee table making sure to use a coaster instead of the Ansel Adams coffee table book.

"I didn't know you were into photography." I turned to face Jack working in the kitchen.

"I'm not."

"Oh. I saw the book on the table."

"It was gift from...uh, you allergic to strawberries?"

"I'm not allergic to any foods."

"Good. Give me another minute."

The hesitation in his voice sent small electric shocks up my arm. I took his request for another minute as a sign that he didn't want to continue our conversation. I turned to face the fire, took a sip of my wine, then leaned back and closed my eyes.

Everyone owned a past. Some more secretive than others. So, why wouldn't Jack have a past too? Maybe he didn't feel comfortable talking about it. Or whoever gave him the book wasn't a part of his past at all. Perhaps the gift giver was someone currently in his life.

My brain began a wild ride. Pictures of the skinny brunette at the dog parade flashed in my head and I didn't like where the ride was going. I willed my mind to go blank, envisioning an eraser, dragging across a white board in the shape of a brain. I wasn't succeeding. It was as if my thoughts were being written in permanent marker.

"Open your mouth. I've got something sweet for you," Jack whispered into my ear, completely short circuiting my brain.

His breath warmed the back of my neck. "Let's both take a nibble."

The touch of Jack's mouth on my neck and the feel of his teeth gently dragging across my skin heightened my arousal. I went to bite down on the chocolate covered strawberry he held to my lips. He pulled it away.

"Not so quick," he said and walked around to the front of the couch where he placed a plate full of chocolate covered strawberries onto the coffee table. He brought a strawberry to his mouth and closed his lips around it then winked at me.

"You're such a tease."

"Mmmmhmmm."

Jack sat down and held a strawberry to my mouth. I parted my lips, took a bite, and then another until it was gone. He held my chin with his hand and kissed my lips, taking in the juice that lingered. Brushing my hair behind my ear, he leaned in and nibbled at my neck. "You taste so good," he whispered.

"That strawberry is so sweet, so good. You are so good," I murmured, having a hard time speaking.

When his hand caressed my breast through my shirt, I no longer cared about chocolate covered strawberries. My only thought was about how much I wanted him.

A few more minutes of nibbling and Jack repositioned us on the sofa. The weight of his body confused my own. It was heavy, yet the pressure felt like a release. The tingling between my legs encouraged me to slip my hands in the back pocket of his jeans and pull him closer.

The sound of our breathing muffled the sound of the crackling fire, but not the sound of my cell phone ringing inside my purse. I ignored it as Jack shifted and began unbuttoning my shirt.

Two buttons undone. My phone rang and once again I ignored it. Four buttons undone. I lifted Jack's shirt over his head and tossed it on the floor. I ran my hand across his hairless chest, feeling the contour of his muscles. He remained by my side unbuttoning his way down my shirt. I anticipated the feeling of skin on skin as Jack undid the final button. He ran his tongue along the contour of my left breast.

"I think we need to get this pretty little lacy thing off you. Well maybe it's not so little." Jack winked at me then once again ran his tongue along my breast as he reached underneath my back placing his hand on the clasp of my bra.

My breath was heavy. I ignored my cell phone when it rang once again. I felt agitation spring up between each breath.

Jack's phone rang. He ignored it.

When my phone rang for a fourth time, I couldn't let it go. "I'm sorry but it's obvious someone really wants to get a hold of me. Keep that shirt off. It's just the way I like it."

I ran over to my purse and took out my phone. Peter's name dominated my missed call list.

Jack's phone rang again, but he remained on the sofa.

"Where's your bathroom?"

Jack pointed toward the hall. I went into the bathroom carrying my phone, shut the door and called Peter.

"What's the emergency? I don't care what you say, I'm still spending the night here. I know it upsets you, but underneath it all I'm sure Jack is a good guy otherwise you wouldn't be his friend. So let me hand—"

"You need to come home."

"Peter, I told you, I can handle myself. I know what I'm doing. You can't te—"

"Something is wrong at Mrs. Rippetoe's place. The dogs have been barking for almost forty-five minutes. I knocked on her door and she isn't answering. I'm going to break the door down but I need you here because of the dogs."

"I'm on my way."

7

Jack pulled up in front of my apartment and let me out before driving off in my Jeep to find a parking spot. I heard the dogs barking as I entered the building.

I banged on Peter's door. "What if she's injured? Why didn't you just break the door down?"

"And risk losing all the dogs?"

"You're afraid of them, aren't you?"

Peter had some childhood dog related trauma I didn't quite understand, because he was over six feet tall and the dogs were a little over one foot at best.

He ignored my question.

"Did you try the door?" I asked, walking across the hall. I turned the knob and Mrs. Rippetoe's door opened.

Jack entered the building. "What's going on?"

"We're checking on Mrs. Rippetoe." I swatted the bouncing balls of fur trying to keep them from shooting out the open door. PJ did the majority of the bouncing. Sassy and Mr. P half-heartedly hopped a couple of times then wandered around whining.

"Peter, Jack and I'll take the dogs up and then you can check her apartment. Can you help me Jack?"

Jack and I hustled the dogs upstairs to my apartment.

"Mrs. Rippetoe?" I heard Peter call out as Jack and I headed back down the steps. He called her name again as Jack and I entered her apartment.

"Did you search her bedroom?" I asked.

"I'll let you do that," Peter said.

"Uhm, I can't."

"What do you mean you can't?"

"What I mean is I won't because I'll freak out if she's laying in their dead. I-I-I—"

"Stay here." Peter ventured down the hall and toward her bedroom.

Jack stood in the doorway, showing no effort to help in the search. And making no attempt to comfort me.

Peter came back from the bedroom. "She's not there."

Nothing seemed to be disturbed, nothing to indicate any kind of struggle. She might be at the store. But still. "Should we call the police?"

"Probably. Her door was unlocked." Peter opened the hall closet and looked inside.

"She tends to do that. Leave her door unlocked. Especially if she's just going to the store, or up the road to her friend's home," I said, more for my own peace of mind.

Jack walked toward me and put his arm around my shoulders. "Aspen, why don't we drive to the store. Maybe she's on her way back now."

My shoulders dropped and the rest of my body relaxed. His small gesture touched me.

Peter turned toward me. "Why don't you wait here and Jack and I can go. You need to watch the dogs anyway."

"Dogs aren't like children. You can't leave them at home with a bowl of food and water you know."

"Right. But, you should be here in case she returns."

I accepted that my date with Jack was officially over. Probably for the best anyway. "Okay. Can you give Jack a lift home?"

"I sure can." Peter's grin was unmistakable.

"Aspen?" Jack's eyes locked on mine. He seemed disappointed, but why? Perhaps he realized he'd end up at home having c'est la vie sex with himself.

"Peter's right, Jack. I should be here when Mrs. Rippetoe returns. Do you have my keys?"

Jack handed them over. I said goodbye and kissed his cheek. He didn't appear to be happy about the tiny peck I planted, but it was all I could give him. Kissing Jack with any kind of sexual heat in front of Peter made me uncomfortable.

I ran back upstairs to my apartment, gave the dogs a little kibble and jotted down a note to leave in Mrs. Rippetoe's apartment. If she came home, I didn't want her to worry about Sassy.

Jack and I forgot one important exchange, the location of the Jeep. I went searching for it so I could grab the mysterious second flash drive. He couldn't have parked it too far away since it wasn't long between the time he let me off and the time he walked into the building.

On the surface, I believed Mrs. Rippetoe would come back from the market and tell me how difficult it was to find a good whole chicken. How she'd spent hours looking at each one before finally deciding none were good enough to cook for Sunday dinner. A dinner to which she intended to invite her tenants. But underneath, all I could think about was Mrs. Rippetoe's run-in with the mysterious couple and whether or not it was tied to the Blue Monkey diamond. The possibility of a real connection frightened me.

I finally located the Jeep. By the time I got back to my apartment the situation hadn't changed. Mrs. Rippetoe still wasn't home. I listened to the message Peter left letting me know his search had been unsuccessful. Jack must have wrestled the phone from Peter because the message ended with Jack wishing me sweet dreams.

I switched on my laptop and settled in on what used to be my bright, geranium red couch. It was now enveloped in a slight grayish tint. A process that began the day I brought PJ home. The couch was still comfortable and I decided there was no need for a new one until I'd properly trained my little man.

The fan on the laptop whirred. Windows appeared and all the other programs in the startup list found their appropriate place in the computer's memory. I plugged the flash drive into the USB port and once again found a single file. I opened it.

THIS IS NOT A JOKE. GET THE DIAMOND.

I was steaming. Of course it was a joke. How could I find the diamond if I didn't have any idea who owned the damn thing? And if it wasn't a joke then why was someone running around dropping off USB flash drives as if we were in some sort of covert spy game?

My finger hit the mouse button, scrolling to the next page. An image of the diamond appeared and instructions to call the number listed. *Date? Monday. Time? Eleven PM*. The remainder of the message instructed me to keep everything to myself and warned me not to involve friends, family, and especially the police.

I exhaled. If the instructions told me not to involve my family then the request to find the diamond definitely didn't pertain to my past, because contact with family was a forbidden activity when you were in the Witness Protection Program. Not that I always played by the government's rules.

The relief lasted mere seconds because I scanned the document again and realized it was Tuesday evening. I dialed the number anyway but received a 'no longer in service' message.

Shoot. I'd missed the deadline and now Mrs. Rippetoe had disappeared. Just like the first flash drive, this one didn't provide an indication of who owned the diamond or how I'd be paid once I delivered the diamond. I didn't have to be Marilyn vos Savant to figure out Mrs. Rippetoe was my compensation.

My eyelids were heavy. So tired. Nothing could be done about Mrs. Rippetoe, the blue diamond, or Mr. Q's hidden crime scene at this hour of the night. I hooked up the dogs and took them out one last time for the evening.

My breath met the cold air, making it visible. PJ ran ahead, a happy boy, extending his retractable lead to the maximum point of escape. But, Sassy and Mr. P, in their stillness, attracted my attention. They looked old and sad. Two little babies, each without the one person in their world that loved them unconditionally. I had to clean up Mr. Q's place and I had to find Mrs. Rippetoe because Mr. P and Sassy desperately needed to go home.

I brought all three of the dogs into my bedroom and threw some comfy blankets on the floor for Sassy and Mr. P. After I slipped into some flannel pajamas, I jumped into bed and PJ joined me. A good night's sleep might not solve all my problems, but it couldn't hurt.

Unfortunately, sleep eluded me. I laid in bed thinking about my life. I was surrounded by people, yet isolated. How many others lived this way?

My life was a bad piece of fiction. It had no hero, unless I counted Peter. His friends did call him Spidey since his name was Peter Parker. But, even with a super hero, my life still had no plot. I never felt like I was going from A to B, working my way to a happy ending.

———

The pressure of PJ's body snuggled against my back comforted me. I opened my eyes to darkness. I turned over to pet PJ, accidentally knocking him off the bed. He landed on his feet. I pulled the comforter up over my head and closed my eyes.

I hummed trying to drown out the sound of PJ's whining. But when Sassy and Mr. P joined in to create a chorus, I knew my day had started. I peeked out from the covers, smiling at the site of the three of them sitting in a perfect row.

"Good morning, everybody."

Their tails wagged in response. When my feet hit the floor their tails moved even faster. I glanced at my clock. *Six o'clock?* I scrounged around in my hamper for a pair of sweats, threw them on and fumbled my way through the apartment and out the back door with the dogs.

"What are we going to do?" Peter asked, when I walked back into our building. He stood in his doorway with his eyes on the dogs. He was clean, dressed, and looking like a superhero with Cynophobia. Ready to save somebody's day as soon as the dogs were gone.

I tried running my hand through my hair while keeping control of the dogs, but I failed. PJ took off toward Peter.

"Aspen! What the he—" Peter shut his door.

"I'm sorry." I grabbed PJ's lead. "You can open your door back up."

"Man, I wish you wouldn't do that."

"I didn't do it on purpose. We really need to work on your fear of dogs. I think we should schedule some PJ desensitization sessions."

"Yeah. Well, you get right on that. I'm going to report Mrs. Rippetoe missing. I kept searching for her after I dropped Jack off. Drove through the neighborhood, even checked the alleys and dumpsters."

"Oh God. Don't go there."

"I wanted to cover all the bases. And since she isn't back yet, I'm giving the police a call."

"You can't do that."

"Aspen, you need to get over your fear of police."

"As soon as you get over your fear of dogs."

"You're a bucket of chuckles this morning. Aren't you, Tonto?"

Peter's nickname for me took me by surprise. He hadn't called me that in a while.

"You can't call the police because I got another flash drive. They didn't even want me to talk to you. I think it has something to do with Mrs. Rippetoe's disappearance."

"When'd you get it?"

"Monday."

"But Mrs. Rippetoe was here Monday."

"I know. I forgot about the drive and I just reviewed it last night."

"If they kidnapped her, why would they give you something telling you they were going to kidnap her?"

"Why do you keep saying, they?"

"It's not impossible, but it is more difficult to kidnap someone by yourself especially if you're doing it for a ransom."

"True. They didn't say they were going to kidnap her. They only asked me to call another number. But, I missed their deadline and now Mrs. Rippetoe is missing. Coincidence?"

"Can I see it?"

"Yeah. Come on up."

"You go ahead. Corral the herd and I'll be up in a few minutes."

I did as instructed and gated the musketeers in my bedroom then went into the living room to power up my laptop. My cell phone rang and I ran back to the bedroom falling over the gate as I tried to jump over it.

"Aspen Moore, how can I help you?" I asked, not paying attention to the caller id.

"Aspen? Aspen, is that you?"

"Yes."

"Why are you breathing so heavy? You really must exercise. You're too young to be so out of shape."

"Mrs. Paddy? Why are you calling my cell phone? Do you have an emergency?"

"Of course I do. I told you I wouldn't call you on that phone unless I did."

"What's the matter?"

"I need you to come over today."

Mrs. Paddy's concierge account was important, especially since I might lose Thomas Brackford once I told him his girlfriend was a thief. But, I wasn't sure how I was going to fit Mrs. Paddy into today's schedule.

"Is there something specific you need? Are you sure it can't wait?"

"No. I need you to take me shopping."

"Mrs. Paddy, don't you remember? We went shopping Monday."

"Of course I remember. Why do you keep insisting I'm senile? We went to the Galleria and I purchased a beautiful tote and wallet for you."

How could I turn down her request with that reminder? "Where do you need me to take you? Do you need to go back to the Galleria or perhaps I could take you to West County Plaza?"

"I...well, I need to go to Walmart."

Interesting. Mrs. Paddy had the finest of everything. Fine linen, fine china, fine jewelry. She didn't strike me as a Walmart shopper, because I was a Walmart shopper. "Is there something specific you need?"

"Unmentionables."

"Excuse me?"

"Walmart is the only place I have found the nice cotton briefs. They fit me just right. They do the best job at absorb—"

"Okay then. I'll be at your place around ten o'clock." I hated to interrupt her but I certainly didn't want to hear any more about Mrs. Paddy and the functioning of her nether parts. I knew it would be hard enough getting that little bit of information out of my head. Besides, someone knocked on my door. "Bye."

I removed the gate instead of jumping over it, putting it back in place quickly. I limped my way to the front door.

"Are the monsters in their cage?"

"Stop. They are cute little sweethearts who love people unconditionally. I am sure once you get over your fear you'll want one too."

"Are you insane?"

"Look how cute they are?" I pulled up a picture of PJ curled up on the couch, one of the only moments he looked like an angel, and shoved my cell phone under Peter's perfect nose.

"You didn't answer my question."

I swear, if Peter weren't so handsome, funny, and everything I wanted in a man except his unavailability, I'd tell him to take his rhetorical questions to his next proctologist visit so the doc could put them back where they belong.

"No, I'm not insane."

"That's good to know." Peter tossed me a wink.

"The flash drive's already plugged into the port. Take a look while I get ready."

I gathered my clothes from the bedroom then maneuvered my way back into the hall, and into the bathroom. My claw-foot tub beckoned me, but I settled for a quick shower. The warm water magically relaxed my body. I turned it off and my epidermis called all goosebumps to assume formation.

My teeth stopped chattering once I was dressed. I blew my hair dry then threw on a little blush and eyeshadow. I didn't need to put makeup on to clean up Mr. Q's crime scene, but I wanted to look half way presentable when I met with my other clients.

"We can talk about the flash drive stuff later," I shouted, so Peter would get the message ahead of my arrival in the living room. But he never got the message because he was gone.

8

I OPENED THE DOOR to Mr. Q's place and scanned the living room. Mr. Q hadn't cleaned up any of the mess before he'd gone to stay in a hotel. I was barely over the threshold when my phone rang.

"Did you hear the news?" Mr. Q asked.

"What news?"

"Greg's death is still under investigation and at this time isn't being treated as a homicide. Isn't that fantastic?"

"Not for Greg."

"I know, that's not what I meant. What I meant was, you and I don't need to worry about the police thinking we killed him."

"What? Why would they think I killed him?"

"I didn't mean that either. I'm just saying the best outcome is for them to rule his death an accident. That's all."

"I'm still not sure I should be cleaning the room upstairs. Perhaps you should leave the room the way you found it until you find out what the police are thinking."

"Aspen. I can't leave the room the way it is. I haven't been staying at my house because my good friend died there and seeing the room like it was when I found him is just too much. Clean the room. In fact, I need you to clean the downstairs too. I'm checking out of the hotel today. I'm running into fans and even co-workers are wondering why I'm staying at a hotel."

I understood where he was coming from, people could be nosey. When you didn't want people in your business it made carrying on conversations with them difficult. "I'll see what I can do. I can at least get everything off the floor."

"That would be great. It needs to be clean enough for Mr. P too. I want him back home with me."

"I know. I'll make it happen."

I ended the call and found my brain tossing around the idea of getting drunk even though I wasn't a big drinker. The very fact that I was seriously considering it meant what I really wanted was for everything to go away even if only for a little while. I settled for coffee.

Mr. Q's expensive espresso machine was the type espresso lovers with money wouldn't be without. I checked the bean hopper, poured some milk into a cup and used the steam wand to froth the milk. I pressed the single shot button and started picking up the mess on the kitchen floor left behind by whoever rummaged through Mr. Q's house.

I carried my cup into the living room and surveyed the mess, trying to figure out where to start. In order to spend more time on the room upstairs, I decided to pick everything up downstairs and just place it on the dining room table. The minimum needed to keep the area safe for Mr. P.

Over the next hour, any evidence that Greg had ever met the one person in his world I'm positive he wished he hadn't would be removed. I'd erase any memory of Mr. Q's dead friend from his house.

The cup felt warm in my hands. I took another swig, set it down on the end table, and began picking up anything that wasn't broken. I ran back into the kitchen, grabbed a broom and dustpan and swept up a broken set of large ceramic Foo dogs. I searched the bookshelf for the empty space where they once kept watch over his home and noticed something I'd never noticed before. Mr. Q was superstitious. Almost every item displayed on the shelves represented protection, good luck, or fortune. There were horseshoes mounted upward, elephants with raised trunks, pigs, a single ladybug dish, a framed set of four leaf clovers, even a bowl of antique rabbit's feet. No wonder he wanted to get his hands on the Blue Monkey diamond.

The mess seemed endless, but I persevered picking up items and stacking them on the table. I passed the shelves full of good luck charms and couldn't shake the sense that Mr. Q was obsessed. I wondered how far he'd go to obtain the object of his obsession. I freaked out. What if he'd been angry at Greg for losing the auction? Was it possible I didn't really know him? I surprised myself that I even thought he might be capable of killing his own friend. But, reality could be harsh and the reality was – no one really knew what another human being was capable of doing.

My brain continued turning the gears, ramping up my suspicious side. Mr. Q seemed overjoyed the police were not yet ruling Greg's death a homicide. I questioned his relationship with his neighbor. Maybe they weren't even that good of friends.

As I put the broom and dustpan back into the kitchen pantry, I had a revelation. If I was going to hide a possible crime scene from the investigators, I should at least do a little investigation of my own or at the minimum collect any evidence. I gathered a few sandwich bags, corn starch, and a black paper shopping bag I found on the bottom shelf. I snatched a roll of shipping tape from the desk drawer. I dug through my purse in search of the soft bristle brush Stephanie had given me as a gift when she politely told me I looked better with makeup.

Score.

I tossed the items into a plastic grocery bag along with my Owl Lite credit card sized magnifier and a pair of tweezers. I carried the cleaning supplies and my homemade CSI kit up the stairs.

At the top landing, I glanced into the room, then hesitated. Would I find Blood? Urine? Other bodily fluids? I didn't see anything on Greg, but I didn't get that close to him. My heart palpitated causing my breath to catch. My reaction stemmed from my past. Who wouldn't react like this if they'd once hid in a closet and watched their ex-fiancé get shot to death? I shuddered at the thought of that life altering day.

The horrific experience landed me in the Witness Protection Program. The program gave me a new life, a fresh start. But still, I struggled. My former self, Amelia Millhauser, would never have agreed to make a potential crime scene disappear. It was clear I was no longer that woman.

I flipped the light switch and stepped into the room. The bed was still unmade. I didn't see blood anywhere in the room and the two wine glasses Mr. Q told me about were gone. There'd been no wine glasses in the kitchen sink. It seemed peculiar for Mr. Q to take the glasses downstairs, clean them and put them away, but not clean up anything else in the room. It made me wonder if he had gotten rid of evidence implicating him in the death of his friend.

"Hello," Mr. Q said after answering my call.

"I'm curious. What happened to the wine glasses?"

"Greg took them home."

"What?"

"They're at Greg's house. I figured they might be important to find, so I took them over when I, uh, escorted Greg home."

"Oh. That's smart."

Our conversation ended and I suddenly wondered how Mr. Q had managed to move the body and the wine glasses without being seen. I decided it was probably better that I didn't know. The important thing was I hadn't been involved in moving the body.

I scanned the room again. Besides the messy bed, not much else seemed out of place. I turned off the lights and unplugged an emergency flashlight from the outlet. I had no idea what I was doing, but I figured I'd do exactly what the actors did on almost every episode of CSI. I turned the flashlight on.

The floor appeared dusty. Near the sliding door to the balcony I found a long hair. Mr. Q didn't have long hair, though it could be mine. I grabbed it with the tweezers and placed it inside a baggy. I crouched down and inspected underneath the bed, finding two small diamonds. I bagged them. On the bottom sheet I found a couple of curly hairs. I grimaced, snatched them and put them into a baggy. Nothing else on the floor seemed worthy of bagging, so I put the flashlight back and turned on the lights to the room.

I took my homemade CSI kit over to the sliding door. The oil-rubbed bronze door handle was almost black. I poured cornstarch into a baggy, then inserted my makeup brush. I dusted the door handle trying to uncover fingerprints. Nothing. I then dusted the handle on the door to the room. Nothing. That was odd. I should have at least found prints for Mr. Q. because he'd said the door was closed when he got home. Of course I was using a makeup brush and cornstarch, not a professional fingerprinting kit. I moved on to the headboard, just in case. I began dusting upward, hoping to obtain even a partial print of a thumb, a palm, anything. I thrust my makeup brush back into the bag of cornstarch sending it to the floor. White dust flew everywhere.

The scene was contaminated, at least that's what the police probably would have said had they been in the room. What if there were important fibers I should have bagged? At that thought, I called it quits. I was acting ridiculous. I wasn't a forensic expert. What was I going to do with what I found anyway?

It was time to stop and clean up my mess. I walked into the hall bath and pulled a towel from the towel bar. When I reentered the room, I spotted it. Some of the dust had settled on the dark hardwood floor and highlighted a hand print. I was excited. Sure, the print could belong to Mr. Q, but then again, it might belong to the person responsible for Greg's death.

I ran downstairs, got my phone and took pictures, which I should have thought of long before bagging evidence. I pressed tape over each fingerprint then carefully lifted each piece of tape and placed it on the black paper shopping bag. Reviewing each one with the magnifying card, I only found two prints where I could see the detail of the ridges.

My continued search uncovered nothing else interesting enough to consider evidence. I finished cleaning Mr. Q's place then headed back to my office.

———

I left all the evidence in my jeep and ducked into Peter's store. "Peter, why'd you take off before I got out of the shower this morning?"

Victor raised his brows.

I looked at Victor. "It's not what you think."

He lowered his eyes to the catalog he'd been perusing.

Peter motioned to the rear of the store. "Let's talk in my office."

I sat down in his guest chair and crossed my legs. "I wanted to talk this morning about Mrs. Rippetoe or at least plan a time to talk about it, but you were gone and so was the flash drive!"

"Would you have let me take it?"

"No, but we could have talked about it."

"I left because I wanted to see if I could find any identifying information."

"I could have tried to find the information if you'd asked me."

"Really? You could have done that?"

I backpedaled. "Well, if you had told me how. So, how do you do it?"

"It's technical and I don't want to confuse you. I was looking for information hidden in the document, anything that might identify who created the presentation."

My blood heated up on its way to a full-fledged boil. I'd worked my way up to VP of Technology in my old life. I wanted to rattle off the programming languages I'd once used, talk about bits and bytes, and hex dumps. I wanted him to know that deep down I was a nerd, and a damn good one. Instead, I played my role well. "Wow. You are so good at the technical stuff. Did you find anything?"

"No."

"So where does that leave us?"

"Here's what we know. Someone wants you to get a hold of a valuable diamond."

I waited for him to tell me what else we knew, but he sat in silence.

"That's not all," I said, breaking the thick wall of nothingness. "We know Mrs. Rippetoe's been kidnapped!"

"No, Aspen, we don't. We know she's hasn't been heard from and we should call the police."

"I'm using my God given intuition. If we call the police, we're putting her in danger. She was lucky to escape the first time they kidnapped her, but what are the odds—"

"What do you mean, the first time? She was kidnapped and you didn't tell me?"

"I tried to tell you at my office the other day, but you were too busy trying to escape Stephanie."

"Don't you think that was important enough to call me later?"

"I didn't think it was a big deal because she escaped and she was fine. The danger was over."

"Obviously it's not over."

"I've been trying to tell you that, but you don't listen to what I say." I pushed my hair away from my face and exhaled.

"We don't need to be arguing about this. We need to figure out what we're going to do."

I wanted Peter and I to put together a plan, work out what steps we needed to take in order to uncover the truth, but more importantly to rescue Mrs. Rippetoe. But, my customers were taxing my grit, making requests above and beyond my normal offerings. If I didn't take care of them I might not be in a position to help Mrs. Rippetoe at all.

"I'm going to my office then I have some appointments I need to keep. I mean I could cancel the appointments, but I hate to lose the business."

"No, don't do that. I have a couple of appointments myself. In the meantime, I'll see what I can come up with. Did she tell you anything about where she was when they took her?"

"East St. Louis."

"Good lord. How'd she get out of there?"

"She climbed through a window and took a taxi home. Sometimes she amazes me."

"Write down everything you remember about what she told you. It might give us a lead. Though I doubt they'd take her to the same place."

Peter got up from his chair and walked over to mine, putting his arm on my shoulder as he knelt. "Is that a tear in your eye?"

Crying was not something I was very good at containing no matter how hard I tried. And with Peter's soft inquiry and gentle hand, the flood gates opened and it pissed me off. "Stop...being...so nice to me. You know it...makes me cry."

"Hey, it's going to be okay. We are going to get this situation under control."

The tears only got worse and I only got more upset that he was being nice. I disliked being unable to control my feelings.

"I'll call you later," he said, standing up. He placed a box of tissues in my lap before he opened the door.

107

"Thanks."

Peter winked at me. "It's all going to be okay. Take your time, just close the door when you leave."

More tears fell. I slowly composed myself, blew my nose, and headed up to the front of the store and out the door before Victor could get a good look at my face. My tears would give him the wrong impression, making him think I was upset about Peter leaving when I was in the shower.

The few steps I walked to my store were enough to help me regain control of my emotions. From this point forward, at least for the rest of the day, I'd only acknowledge happy thoughts. I walked into my store and instantly knew I was facing an incredible challenge because Harry Corbitt was sitting in my office in the guest chair.

"Stephanie. Why'd you sit him in my office?" I mumbled under my breath.

"He's not that bad. All he wants is a nice wedding," Stephanie responded loud enough to cause Harry to glance over at the reception area.

"Ms. Moore! I'm confused as to why you hung up on me the other day."

I shot Stephanie a glance that was intended to let her know not only was her raise in jeopardy, but her job as well. She smiled, letting me know she didn't get the message.

"Mr. Corbitt. I didn't hang up on you. I told you I was busy. And I am busy right now. Why don't you make an appointment with Stephanie for later this week?"

"No."

"Excuse me?"

"I said, no."

"Of course, I understand if you want to hire someone else to do your wedding."

"No."

My patience was wearing thin for creepy Harry and his one syllable answers.

"What do you want to do then?" I sat down at my desk.

Harry held my gaze, but didn't say a thing.

"Mr. Corbitt. I don't have time to try to figure out what you want. You need to tell me."

"I want to meet with you about my wedding, now."

"I explained to you that I don't have time right now and for you to make an appointment for later in the week."

"And I said, no."

Proof was before me as to how even a minor decision, like returning a phone call, could change things dramatically. I wished I'd never returned his call. "Mr. Corbitt, could you please leave?"

"No."

"I'm no longer asking you, I'm telling you that you need to leave right now."

"What are you going to do call the police?"

He had a point. What was I going to do?

"I just might do that."

"No you won't."

"How do you know I won't?"

"You don't like the police."

Now he'd gone from creepy to scary. My mind approached each of my memories like it was speed dating. Trying to determine which memory was the right one, the one that could provide the answer as to how Harry Corbitt knew about my aversion to the police.

I didn't have time for his shenanigans. There was a conflict in my schedule and it meant I was already heading for an unpleasant encounter with Mrs. Paddy. The more time I spent arguing with him the less time I'd have to gently convince Mrs. Paddy to let me pick up the underwear for her instead escorting her to Walmart.

"Mr. Corbitt. If you want to stay here, be my guest, but you must wait in one of the reception chairs. I'm sure Stephanie would be happy to get you a cup of coffee."

With that I turned and walked to the reception desk, whispered instructions to Stephanie to keep an eye on him and to call me if there was trouble. I wasn't going to let him bamboozle me. My life was already heading in a disturbing direction

9

THE THIRD TIME I RANG Penelope Paddy's doorbell and she didn't answer, I panicked. Unfortunately, in my experience, when my customers know I'm coming and they don't answer their door it usually means they're dead or dying.

Edward, the front desk guy, knew me so he'd waved me past without notifying Mrs. Paddy. Now, I wished I'd asked him to call her first. The penthouse had no windows in the hall through which I could peek, which in a small way was a relief.

I put my ear to the door expecting to hear her working out to her Richard Simmons' Sweatin' to the Oldies DVD. When I didn't hear anything, I took the elevator back down to the lobby.

"Edward?"

He glanced up from the security monitors. "Yes."

"Are you sure Mrs. Paddy didn't leave with someone?"

"Nobody's been here. She called me this morning to tell me you would be coming."

"She's not answering."

Edward picked up the phone and dialed some numbers. He waited a few minutes and hung up. "I normally don't do this, but I'm waiting for an important call here at the desk."

He unlocked a cabinet in his mahogany and marble command station. "Here's the key."

I preferred to wait for him so he could escort me, but Penelope might be lying on the floor in need of help. I cupped the key in my hand and hopped back in the elevator. With each floor I passed, my heart doubled the pace of its beat. When the doors opened on floor twenty-five, it was beating so fast I thought I might throw up.

Finding Mrs. Paddy dead was not what I had planned for my day. Even though she was ninety, finding her lifeless body on the floor would be the worst possible scenario. I did the sign of the cross and inserted the key into the lock.

I turned the knob and pushed the door open. "Mrs. Paddy? It's Aspen."

When I passed through the foyer and into the living area I realized there might be an even worse scenario. The place was a mess. Her once pristine, museum-like, parlor looked like a trailer park yard sale.

"Mrs. Paddy!"

Still no answer. I walked down the hall and realized it wasn't just messy, it was rifled through. On a scale of one to ten, it was a three. I estimated there was less damage then there had been at Mr. Q's place. Two of my clients, each with a ransacked home. It made me wonder if philanthropists like Penelope were fond of diamonds too, blue ones to be exact.

All the material stuff wasn't important. What mattered was Penelope Paddy. I opened the door to her bedroom and it too was messed up and she was nowhere in sight. As I got closer to the bathroom I heard a small whimper. I turned the corner and found Penelope sitting on the toilet, fully clothed, tied to the handicap railing, her mouth covered with duct tape.

"Are you okay?" I asked, pulling off the duct tape.

"Ouch."

"Sorry, Mrs. Paddy."

"Young lady, if you had been on time you might have been able to stop this."

The fallout from Harry Corbitt's unexpected visit had begun. Of course, had I been on time I might be gagged and laying in her walk-in tub. I untied Penelope and walked her over to her bed so she could lie down.

"Call the police, please."

And there it was, the even worse scenario had somehow worsened, but I still hoped I could recover my good day. "You know, Mrs. Paddy, I think you should call them yourself because I have no knowledge of anything. They may need a lot of questions answered."

"Are you not capable of calling nine-one-one? I guess I'm going to need to hire a new concierge."

She normally wasn't this nasty, maybe she'd gotten hit on the head. "Of course. I was just thinking th—"

"Exactly the problem. You are thinking and not listening."

She'd turned into a nonagenarian Godzilla. "I'll make the call right away."

My survival instincts kicked in. "Unfortunately, I won't be able to wait for the police, but I will ask Edward to come up."

"I won't be paying you for the day if you leave."

One more little white lie wouldn't hurt. "No problem, Mrs. Paddy. I tried to call you to let you know I wasn't going to be able to come by today and take you to Walmart, but you didn't answer. I just stopped by to make sure you were okay."

"You are lying. My phone never rang."

Caught off guard, I paused for a moment. I swallowed before I spoke, my Adam's apple the size of a Red Delicious. "Perhaps your phone was knocked off the hook." I picked up the handset on the desk across the room, pressed the button and heard the dial tone. "Yes, that's the problem."

"Give me that ph—"

"Just a minute. I'll go find out which phone is the problem." I ran out of the room with the handset before she could throw another belittling sentence my way. I walked around the rooms pretending to search for the problem phone. When I passed her small, but spectacular library, I noticed the picture over the fireplace was partially away from the wall. I walked through the doorway just enough to confirm the painting hung on hinges and had been hiding a safe. Luckily the door was still closed.

"Got a dial tone now," I said as I walked back into her bedroom.

"Then call the police. What are you waiting for?"

My mind visualized my hand slapping the duct tape back over Mrs. Paddy's mouth. I truly appreciated my brain's effort to stick up for me, but its Cerebellum could get a little trigger happy every now and then. I couldn't afford to act on my thoughts no matter how good it might feel, so I dialed nine-one-one.

"Hi. We need the police at the penthouse in the Falcon Ridge Towers."

"What's the emergency?" The nine-one-one operator asked.

"There's been a break-in."

"Who am I talking to?"

I walked out of the bedroom and into the hall. "I'm sorry the phone battery is about to go dead. My name is Miss—" I pushed the off button on the handset.

"Ok, Mrs. Paddy. The police are on their way. I'll send Edward up and call you tomorrow," I shouted from the hallway as I headed to the front door.

I thought I heard a sound coming from the master bedroom as I walked into the hall, but there was no time to see what Mrs. Paddy wanted. I needed to leave before the police came in order to double the odds of me not getting caught up in this mess.

When I stepped off the elevator into the lobby, I immediately walked up to Edward. "Did you finally get that call?" I asked, not wanting him to use it as an excuse to make me stay.

"Sure did. Did Mrs. Paddy have her TV up too loud to hear the doorbell?"

"Actually, there was a problem."

"What happened?"

"Looks like someone broke into her place."

"I'll call the police. Go ahead back up and wait with her."

"Not sure how they did it unless you weren't at the front desk," I said trusting he'd feel guilty or at the minimum worried about his job. "She's okay. I already called the police. You'll need to escort them up when they arrive."

"It would be best for you to go back up and for me to stay here in the lobby."

"I would stay, but I have a very important, umm, female related doctor's appointment. If I cancel I'll have to wait months to get another one," I said, knowing most men would do anything not to talk about female related medical problems and everyone could relate to the hassle of rescheduling a doctor appointment.

"I'm sorry but I can't leave my desk. You'll have to stay."

Obviously Edward was a healthy person and comfortable with his feminine side. I didn't respond immediately, thinking he might change his mind and tell me to go ahead. When I saw the police coming up the walkway and only steps from entering, I knew exactly what I was going to say to Edward. Nothing.

The first officer entered the building's revolving door, so I brought my cell phone to my ear even though it hadn't made a sound. "The dress is Faaaabulous. Oh, yes, those shoes will look great won't they?"

I jabbered away about a non-existent dress, excitedly telling no one about how beautiful it was and how I couldn't wait to wear it on my non-existent hot date. I popped into the wheel of freedom and watched as the revolving door deposited the final two officers into the lobby while depositing me onto the walkway outside. Once clear, I waved at Edward and high-tailed it down the block.

As soon as I jumped into my Jeep I had an urge to call Peter to tell him about the break-in, but like Mr. Q, Mrs. Paddy also required a confidentiality agreement. It was one of the many constraints placed upon me when I worked with the rich and famous.

———

The light turned green and I made a left onto Warson road. I was less than a mile from the estate of Oliver Lott when my phone rang.

"This is Aspen Moore. How can I help you?"

"Miss Moore, I had to change Show Me's Grand Ambition's grooming appointment to tomorrow. Sorry."

Another kink in my already screwed up day. Show Me's Grand Ambition was Oliver Lott's Champion Airedale, and the next thing on my 'to do' list.

"No, problem," I said, even though it was a problem. I'd now have to rearrange my schedule for today and tomorrow? The Lott's business with Moore Time had been on the upswing and I needed to keep that momentum going, especially if I ended up having to remove Mr. Q from my client list.

"Same time tomorrow. Goodbye, Miss Moore."

I didn't bother putting down my phone because I had some quick juggling to do.

"Mr. Brackford, "I said, when he answered.

"Who else would answer my phone?"

"I had a break in my schedule and wondered if I could come by now and look for the necklace again."

"Sure. I'm not busy. Not like I can't change my schedule at the drop of a hat, now is it?"

Something must be in the air. I looked for a digital sign on the side of the road proclaiming today a Red Air day. Seemed everyone was cranky. "I'm sorry to change the schedule, but if it wouldn't be an inconvenience."

"No. Come on over. I'm sitting here by myself anyway."

"See you soon."

I was relieved he would be alone. Telling him about Belinda wasn't going to be easy. I didn't want to break his heart. Meeting women wasn't a simple task with his reclusive tendency. And being in a wheelchair probably made it even more difficult to find someone special who could see him first and not his disability.

Thinking about Brackford's relationship with Belinda made me think of my relationship with Jack. I wondered if he would be the kind of person to stick around if a tragic accident like Brackford's befell me.

I dialed Jack's number.

"Sorry about last night," I said, when he answered.

"You can make it up to me tonight."

"I'd love to." I meant every word. My life needed tending to at the moment, but wasn't Jack part of my life? Besides, thinking about my problems would be tough with Jack nibbling his way around my body.

"My place at seven. Oh, and don't tell Peter where you're going and leave your cell phone in the car. I want to make sure we finish what we start."

"Yes, sir."

We chatted for a few more minutes then said our goodbyes. Once we were off the phone I realized he never asked about Mrs. Rippetoe. I guess I shouldn't have expected him to since she wasn't his landlady. Besides, maybe he assumed status quo since I hadn't mentioned her to him.

I saw Belinda's car when I pulled up to Brackford's house. I wondered how much worse my day could get. Thomas Brackford was one of the few clients who had sneaked into my heart when I wasn't looking. I owed him the truth.

"Belinda?"

Brackford said he was alone when I called. I was surprised because instead of having feelings of anger, I felt sad. He'd been so happy since Belinda came into his life.

"Whose there?" Thomas bellowed from inside the house.

"Aspen," Belinda shouted, then lowered her voice, "What do you need?"

"Actually, I need to ask you something and I hope I don't offend you."

I knew it wasn't the best way to set up the conversation because now she'd probably be offended, but I wasn't sure how else to go about it.

"Okay."

"I went to a pawn shop and saw a necklace that looked exactly like one Mr. Brackford told me he couldn't find. The store owner said a nurse sold it to him. Did you take Thomas's necklace and sell it?"

Belinda's eyes diverted from mine, making her appear guilty. Her posture didn't exude shiftiness as much as embarrassment.

"I need to know, Belinda."

"Yes. I found the necklace when I was cleaning. I got jealous. I love him. And I'm afraid he's seeing someone else. Is he seeing someone else? You can tell me. I mean I love him, but I'm not crazy. I'm not going to stand in his way. He's just been the most wonderful—"

"Belinda!" I couldn't let her go on.

"What?"

Discovering she was simply a woman afraid of being scorned and not a con-woman making her mark, felt liberating. "It belonged to his sister."

"What do you mean belonged?"

"He didn't tell you?"

"Tell me what?"

"His sister died and when he went to collect her belongings, he found the necklace."

"He never told me he had a sister who died. Why didn't he tell me? I feel terrible. I'm an awful person. I'm no good for him—"

"Stop! I've never seen him so happy, and it's all because of you."

"Really?"

"Yes, really."

I caught a glimpse of panic in her eyes.

"You. You aren't going to tell him are you?"

"Of course not. He's been having me search for the necklace, so that is what I am going to do. I bought the necklace from Pauperazzi, so now I'm going to go inside and continue searching and this time I'm going to find it."

"Thank you, Aspen. Let me know how much they charged you so I can pay you back. And, If you ever need my help with anything please ask. I'm so grateful to you. I know about you making our first date special."

I smiled not wanting to admit I'd had my hand in that occasion. "Shall we go inside?"

Belinda opened the door and I followed her.

"He's in the back den."

I walked down the hall.

"You think you're going to find it?" he asked.

Fishing inside my head for a tiny white lie, I pulled out one I thought would do the trick. "I was cleaning out my closet once and found something hidden in between the carpet and wall. It made me think I should take a second look in your closet."

"Be my guest, but I thought you used some magic metal detecting thing."

"I did, but I never used it in the closet because there was nothing on the closet floor."

"Guess its best you're a personal concierge instead of a detective."

I opened the closet door and got down on my knees. I thought about whether or not I should eat dinner before going to Jack's place. He didn't say whether he would be cooking again. I thought about the chocolate covered strawberries he'd fed me, and the heat of his hands as he unbuttoned my shir—"

"You okay in there?" Brackford asked.

"Sure, just looking along the carpet line."

"Wasn't sure, you were moaning kind of loud."

Moaning? Oh my God.

I hoped the moan had sounded more like an Its-hard-to-crawl-around-on-the-floor moan instead of a do-me-now moan. "I'm a little out of shape."

"Did you find anything?"

"Not yet."

I waited a few more minutes for the flush on my face to cool. "I found it! I can't believe I found the necklace!"

"You did? I knew I should have had them remove that carpet in the closet when they put in the hardwood floors."

I crawled out of the closet and grabbed a hold of the edge of the dresser to pull myself up. As soon as I was upright, I dangled the necklace in front of Mr. Brackford.

"Give me that thing. I don't want Belinda to see. I'm going to ask her tonight."

"I hope she says yes, Mr. Brackford."

"You know you can call me Thomas. I don't mind."

"I'm kind of partial to Mr. Brackford because I've been calling you that for so long."

"Thank you for finding the necklace. Awfully strange. Not sure how the thing found its way out of the box and onto the floor."

"Yes. Yes, very strange."

"Neither here nor there. Sorry I accused you of stealing it. Wasn't very nice of me was it?"

"As you said, neither here nor there."

I left Brackford in the room holding his sister's necklace and waved goodbye to Belinda before letting myself out.

My cell phone pinged announcing the arrival of a text message. I tapped the phone. The message came from Jack: "Can't wait to start another fire with you tonight."

I found his text sexy and funny and most likely the cause of the tingling sensations in certain parts of my body. I keyed a response and hit send.

Damn autocorrect.

I typed the correction, 'match not math.'

He responded to my first text. 'I'm no Pascal, but if u want math, I'll give u math + a few other things. '

'C u 2night,' I texted back.

Jack rarely sent text messages. He was probably in court and couldn't call. It meant he was thinking about me and gave me hope. Perhaps I'd been driving myself crazy thinking about our relationship when there was nothing to be worried about. Tonight might be the night we get more than our physical needs met, the night we enter a new phase.

I started the Jeep and then called the office before putting the SUV in drive.

"Hey Steph, the Lott's rescheduled for tomorrow, can you change the calendar? Also I just left Brackford's house and am heading home to let the dogs out before I come back into the office, unless you have something urgent." I switched the phone to my other hand so I could make a right turn.

"Nope. We're good here."

We? "Who's there?"

"Roberto just left, but Mr. Corbitt is still here."

"Corbitt? Can you see if you can get him to leave? Just tell him I won't be back in the office today."

"I don't like ly—"

"Steph, please? Just tell him I'm done for the day."

"Fine. But, I don't like it."

———

If I didn't love PJ so much, I would have killed him. Sassy and Mr. P were up on the sofa cheering as PJ dragged around a silk blouse I'd left in a bag sitting next to my closet. My plan to return it to Macy's when I found the time was no longer an issue. The spittle covered blouse had a great big rip down the front.

"Bad boy!" I screamed and lunged for the shirt.

PJ thought a game was afoot and took off running for the bedroom, dragging along the shirt three times his length.

"Come back here!" I stomped on the shirt, stopping PJ in his tracks.

My action only further demonstrated to PJ that it was time to play. He backed up with his teeth clamped on the sleeve and swung his head from side to side. "Grrrr."

No match for me. I reeled him in like a fish.

When I got him into my arms, he let go of the shirt and began licking my face. I looked at the tag on the shirt – $34.99. The most expensive toy I'd ever purchased for PJ. I sighed and tossed it in the trash.

I took the three of them outside. I made it a quick trip because I hadn't planned on playing catch the shirt with PJ. I checked the water bowls, packed up Mr. P and his belongings and locked the door behind me. PJ whined behind the closed door as I descended the stairs. I wondered who he missed most, me or his dad.

Mr. P curled up on the passenger seat, most likely glad for the peace and quiet. I headed down Gravois toward Mr. Q's house. An older woman sat on a bench at a bus stop and she looked exactly like Mrs. Rippetoe. I looked in my rearview mirror.

I continued to the next road, and took a quick left, so I could circle back around to Gravois. As I neared the location, the bus pulled away from the curb and the woman was no longer on the bench. It sure looked like Mrs. Rippetoe, but maybe I was seeing what I wanted to see and not the truth.

I turned the Jeep around to head back in the direction of Mr. Q's place, answering my cell when Jack's name popped up. "Hi, Jack."

"Aspen. Look, I'm sorry, but I'm going to have to cancel. Can we reschedule for tomorrow night?"

The time between Jack's sexy text message and his phone call had been dampened by the site of a Mrs. Rippetoe look-a-like. I wasn't up for a frivolous night with Jack any longer anyway, so I didn't even question his reason. "Sure."

"I'll call you tomorrow," he said, and then hung up.

Mr. P perked up as we drew closer to his home. Dogs possessed such a good sense. I had a pretty good sense of my own. But, when it came to Jack it often got clouded. Now, I wondered why he canceled and wished I had asked.

"Come on big man." I grabbed Mr. P and deposited him inside his home. I topped off his water bowl and gave him a big kiss goodbye.

"Your dad'll be home tonight," I said, locking the front door.

I started my car, then turned on the radio catching the tail end of 'Hit the Road Jack' before it segued into a commercial. I couldn't help but think the song might be a sign. Maybe it was time to end my relationship with Jack instead of define it.

The commercial ended and the news began.

"Radio Host Christopher Quetzalcoatl is being questioned in the death of his neighbor Greg Goodman. Goodman's body was found yesterday in his home. Cause of death is still under investigation."

My thoughts about Jack were replaced with thoughts of Mr. Q. So much for his excitement this morning about the police brushing off Greg's death. I knew he hoped he wouldn't be embroiled in this situation, otherwise, why would he have moved the body? Unless there was a different reason he moved it. Maybe the police knew something I didn't.

A good personal concierge might make the effort to call their client to see if they needed anything, but most concierges didn't live a secret life. I'd have to trust that Mr. Q would call if he needed something and right now, I hoped he didn't.

When I entered my office, I was glad to see Harry Corbitt had vacated the premise. "When did Mr. Corbitt leave?"

"Oh, he's not gone, he's in the bathroom." Stephanie held her compact mirror as she applied lip gloss.

"He's been here the entire time? I thought I asked you to get rid of him?"

"I know. But, he's so nice. He watched the office while I went to get lunch."

Suddenly I understood why some people snapped. It was time. I had to let Stephanie go. I had to. I hated to make her life more challenging for her, but if I could handle being plucked out of my old life, deposited into a strange Midwestern town, and left to deal with the craziness that plagued me, surely she could handle unemployment.

"Stephanie, we need to talk about your job."

"I'm so excited. I knew you'd come through with a raise. You are the best friend anyone could have."

Sigh.

"So can we talk about my wedding plans now?"

I turned to face Harry. "No. We cannot talk. About. Your. Wedding. Plans! I am up to here with everyone's problems. Want, want, want. Everyone wants!"

10

INSTEAD OF HAVING WILD, CRAZY, MONKEY SEX with Jack last night, I shoveled an entire pint of Ben and Jerry's Chunky Monkey ice cream into my mouth. I picked it up on my way home after going all bad ass on Harry Corbitt.

The scene hadn't phased Harry because he still wanted to use my services. I didn't know how to shake him. He was like some kind of demon spirit. The first time he showed up in my life it took a nose dive and almost crash landed. Ultimately, I'd survived. Now, Harry's presence was once again suspiciously linked to my life's slow motion implosion. I was tempted to ask Peter to do a background check, but I didn't want to risk him stumbling across something that might tie me to my old life.

After getting PJ and Sassy settled, I headed out. I got a late start because I'd overslept and spent extra time petting Sassy, feeling guilty and wondering how I was going to keep her from becoming an orphan.

Mrs. Rippetoe's apartment appeared quiet, but I knocked just in case she somehow had once again escaped her captors. My knock went unanswered, so I crossed the hall to Peter's place. I wanted to make a decision on how to proceed with the case of Mrs. Rippetoe's disappearance, but he wasn't home either.

When I got in my Jeep, I called him.

"Peter Parker—"

"Peter, we need—"

"Leave a message and I'll call you back." *Beep.*

"Peter we need to do something about Mrs. Rippetoe. Call me."

I spent the remainder of my drive running my schedule through my head trying to figure out how to get it all done. Stephanie spent most of her time answering the phone and taking care of the office, but in times of desperation I'd have her take care of a few clients.

Approaching my office, my attention was drawn to the reception desk where Stephanie sat talking on the phone. She didn't pause when I walked in the door. I caught bits and pieces of terms relating to recreational motorhomes which reinforced she was doing her job.

I went back to my desk. The minute Stephanie finished her call I'd spring it on her that despite her silk blouse, short skirt, and high heels, she'd be taking a sixty-pound dog to the groomer.

"Stephanie? Can you come back here?"

Stephanie flipped her hair behind her shoulders exposing her open collar that framed her bare neck. I remembered her necklace I'd rescued from the pawn shop. I was going to give it to her now hoping it would soften my request for her to do a job requiring a little dirty work.

"What's up boss?"

"I got something for you." I pulled her necklace with the ruby heart from my briefcase. "I happened to find this the other day."

"Aspen, you shouldn't have," she said, immediately grabbing the necklace from my hand.

"It's nothing really. I thought you might want it..."

A small tear escaped her right eye and I realized that Stephanie, despite her flaws, was still a human being with feelings. If I couldn't find a way to make it work with her in my business, I'd definitely get her set up with a job before I fired her. "...I'm sorry I couldn't buy all your necklaces back for you."

"This was the only necklace that made me cry when I handed it over to the pawn shop guy."

"I'm glad I chose that one then. It is such a beautiful necklace. Sorry but I have to ask you to—"

"Oh, that reminds me. Mr. Lott called and said he needs you to buy a gift for his wife's birthday. The money will be there when you pick up Grand Ambition. What did you want?"

"I forgot what I was going to say." Trusting Stephanie to pick up money, shop for and deliver the gift along with any change to Oliver Lott, seemed irresponsible. I'd have to take care of the Lott's myself. "Are you going to lunch with Roberto again today?" I asked, changing the subject.

"No. He and his partners are working on a project."

"I thought you said he worked as a professional gambler."

"He does, but he's also a business owner."

"Really? What kind of business?"

"Uhm. I'm not sure. I never asked. They run it out of his partner's garage."

I'm sure a lot of entrepreneurs started their businesses in garages. I just hoped it was legitimate and not some sort of methamphetamine operation.

"Interesting. Well, since you aren't going out, can you work through lunch? I'll bring something back for you."

"Sure. You don't need to bring anything back for me though. Roberto and I have been eating out so much, I bet I could fit in your jeans now. You'd think all the sex we have would burn up those extra calories."

Smack. Her words hit me hard. Sure, I'd let my gym membership lapse. And yes, I'd been eating a few extra sweets here and there, but I didn't think I was that much larger than Stephanie. And hitting me with the double whammy, I'm-getting-so-much-sex punch, was enough to make me scream. I decided against lunch and worked in the office until it was time to pick up Grand Ambition.

———

The Lotts were blessed with material possessions and I envied them, but not their life. Constantly traveling, more for business than pleasure, created a hectic schedule that left little time for twin teenage boys who were future mug shots in the making. I pulled into the circle drive trying to avoid the twins' Land Rovers which had been haphazardly parked on the driveway instead of housing them in the Lott's four car garage.

Bella, the housekeeper-slash-nanny, opened the door when I rang the bell. "Good morning, Aspen."

Young, tall, blonde, and a recent import, she was everything I had dreamed I would be when I was a little girl. Only later in life did I discover the truth – not everyone's dreams come true.

"Are the twins behaving for you?" I asked, following her into the living room. I was delighted to see the Lott's home was immaculate and hadn't been ransacked. One more client with a home in upheaval would be three too many.

"They are good when they are being watched and bad whenever eyes are taken off of them."

"Is Grand Ambition ready to go?"

"Yes. But first, Mr. Lott gave you this envelope. I will show you Mrs. Lott's jewelry, so you can see what she likes."

"Why do you need to show me her jewelry?"

"Mr. Lott says you are to buy Mrs. Lott a birthday gift."

"I know, but did he say to buy jewelry?"

"No, but Mrs. Lott loves jewelry."

How could I argue with the opportunity to look at Mrs. Lott's jewelry? It was like getting my own gift. Practically an invitation to investigate whether Mrs. Lott owned the Blue Monkey diamond.

Bella held out a small manila envelope with my name handwritten on the front. "You follow."

Her English wasn't perfect and at times the choppiness coupled with her Nordic accent made me want to giggle because of the cuteness factor. I followed her up the winding staircase, past several bedrooms, and finally through a double door into the master suite.

Bella opened a door to a closet with a cause. It could have been used as a lab for a professional organizer's school. Shelves, drawers, baskets, boxes, hangers, typed labels, photographs, and color-coding.

I was speechless and extremely envious.

"Here." Bella handed me a leather binder.

I perused the multi-page index, a handy dandy guide to the inside of Mrs. Lott's closet. I located the heading marked jewelry and ran down the list using my finger. After turning the page twice, I reached the end of the list and hadn't found a single blue diamond necklace. "She owns so much jewelry. Maybe Mr. Lott doesn't know what else to get her. Perhaps I should get creative."

"No. No. Mrs. Lott loves jewelry. She has a favorite shop too. Verno. I mean Verano's."

"You mean Varriano's?"

"Yes. Yes. Some place far away."

I silently chuckled. Whatever part of St. Louis county you were in, the other part seemed far way, when in reality most things were as close as a twenty-minute drive. "Great! I know the place. Can I take a look at her earrings?"

"No. I think a necklace is better." Bella took the book from me and flipped a few pages before handing the book back. "Here."

The page was marked 'Dining Necklaces', in fancy script. "Okay. Let me see section B, shelf three, blue box number two."

Without searching, Bella immediately walked toward the back of the closet while I stayed in place scanning the wall. She moved the ladder on its track, climbed up a few rungs and selected a dark blue canvas box. When she made her way back down to the floor, she turned and placed the box on the island in the middle of the closet.

I momentarily lost my train of thought when I looked inside the box. So many shiny objects, each one encased in their own see-through bag with a zipper. I took a few of the necklaces out and immediately noticed a pattern. They were all herringbone chains. Platinum, 18k yellow, or white gold. I held up a ruby butterfly necklace and fastened the clasp behind my neck. I turned to face the wall length mirror so I could gauge the length by the pendant placement. The necklace was stunning.

"I can see why she loves these. It's settled, I'll get her a necklace." I reached behind my neck. I pressed on the clasp, but it wouldn't budge. "Can you help me Bella?"

I held up my hair. Bella tugged at the necklace a couple of times but the clasp was stuck.

"Oh no. I will be in trouble. I did not have a permission to take you here, but you are so nice. I knew she would expect jewelry and it would help you."

"Bella. I'm sorry. I shouldn't have tried on the necklace."

"No worry. I will get it."

Bella worked on the necklace for several minutes until I finally felt it slip away from my neck.

"Oh thank goodness. I was worried you might get fired." A thought which I didn't altogether hate. If she were to lose her job, perhaps she'd like to take Stephanie's place.

"It is okay. This is what she wears every day. She has more expensive."

The necklaces I saw were not cheap. They had to be a minimum of six-hundred dollars each if not more, based on the karat and number of gems. I gave the box back to Bella and watched her put it away.

"More expensive, really?"

"Yes. In a safe. I will show you."

I wasn't going to argue. I followed her out of the closet. Any jewelry in a safe had to be sensational. And most likely the place someone would keep a blue diamond. It was shocking to think the Lott's had given Bella the combination. They must really trust her.

Bella stopped in the hallway. "It is here."

"The safe's in the hallway? I thought people always kept their safes behind pictures in their studies," I said, lightly laughing.

"No. Not Mr. Lott. He is a smart man," she said, apparently not getting my joke.

"Is the safe inside?" I asked, pointing to a box sitting on one of shelves of a recessed display alcove. Three wooden alcoves ran along the wall, the middle contained a box and the two on each side displayed marble statues.

"No, I told you. Mr. Lott is smart." Bella reached behind the statue on the right and before I knew it, the recessed alcove opened exposing a safe.

"Wow. I would have never known there was anything behind that. I'm so excited to see her most precious jewelry."

"I cannot show you. I don't know how to open it."

Disappointed, I wondered why she bothered showing me the safe at all. "Oh."

"I wish I could. She has even more beautiful jewelry in here. I have seen pearls, and she has a tiara, and the most special diamond, not like a regular diamond."

The words I'd been waiting to hear. "A special diamond? What makes the diamond so special, it's shape?"

"No, the beautiful blue color."

I wished Bella could open the safe. But still, there was a bright side. I now knew Mrs. Lott had a blue diamond and I could put all my effort into developing a plan to take a peek inside the safe to see if it was THE blue diamond. If it was, I'd seriously consider stealing it in order to set Mrs. Rippetoe free.

———

"Hush, Boy!" I pleaded.

"Boof. Boof. Boof. Boof." Grand Ambition barked like he was administering Chinese water torture. "Boof. Boof. Boof. Boof—"

"No! Silence!" I screamed in a deep, I'm-the-one-in-charge, tone.

As we hit Clayton Rd, Grand Ambition turned around a few times and then lay down with his head between the two front seats.

"Good Boy." I reached back and petted his head.

Grand Ambition licked my elbow when I sat my phone on the console. Even though he was a Grand Champion in the making, he was still a dog. He loved to get and give kisses and play ball. "What are you doing big boy?"

"Booroof. Booroof. Boof. Booroo. Booroof." Grand Ambition stood up and began bouncing as I made the turn into the parking lot of GlammerPoo. It didn't sound like the name of a championship groomer, but they were the most sought after groomer for show dogs in St. Louis.

The GlammerPoo facility occupied an old nineteen-forties style house wrapped in baby blue siding. The shutters were bright white, matching the background of the large sign in the front that displayed the groomer's name along with a pink poodle flashing long lashes. Inside, the living room had been converted to a reception area and dog boutique. I handed Grand Ambition over to the owner. She guaranteed I could pick him up by two-thirty, one of the perks of being a championship dog.

I trudged back to my Jeep. Mr. Q's number popped up on my cell phone. I didn't want to talk to him because I had my doubts about whether I should continue to keep him as a customer. I planned to look over my finances and my contract with Mr. Q to see if I could get out of it. I sighed before answering his call.

"Is my place ready?" he asked.

"You haven't been home? I thought you were going home last night?"

"I didn't feel like it. But I think I'm ready today. So is the place ready?"

I wanted to scream at him for changing his mind about going home last night, but, I didn't. "It's the best it's going to be at this point. Did you pick up anything in the room upstairs before I cleaned it?"

"No. Only thing I did was pick up a few big items downstairs. All the rest is what I figure I pay you for."

The feeling of being hired help had been hard to adjust to, but I took it in stride now. I was no longer a vice president of some high-tech company, but I was a business owner and I took pride in the services my company provided. "Yes. Yes, you do Mr. Quetzalcoatl."

Mr. Q cleared his throat, something I noticed he did whenever I butchered the pronunciation of his name. One of these days I'd start calling him Mr. Q to his face. He eventually accepted my calling Mr. Personality, Mr. P and even started calling him that himself.

"Is Mr. P back home?"

There was no need to tell Mr. Q he'd left his boy home all night, alone in the dark. He'd blame it on me anyway. "No. I'm going to get him now and bring him to your place in an hour or so."

"Did you get him to the groomers?"

Crap. I'd forgotten, but it wasn't my fault. The last few days had been overtaken by a dead body, missing person, and some elusive diamond. "No. I didn't."

"Can you run him by today before you bring him home."

"I'm not sure I'll have time," I said, hoping he wouldn't protest.

"I wasn't really asking."

Geez. "I'll see what I can do."

"I know you'll make it happen," he said before hanging up.

I waited until I got to a stop sign to dial GlammerPoo. It wasn't the normal place Mr. P went to get groomed, but maybe they could fit him in. "This is Aspen Moore. I just dropped off Grand Ambition. I have an incredible favor to ask. Is it possible to bring in a very small Bichon Frise for bath and grooming?"

"I don't know. We're pretty busy. Have we ever seen the dog?"

"No, but he—"

"Don't think we can do it then."

"What if I make it worth your effort to squeeze him in?"

"How much?"

"I'll pay double your rate and I'll see about making him a regular customer."

"Well, we could probably do something quick when you come to pick up Grand Ambition. Maybe not a complete blowout."

"That'll do."

Mr. Q didn't say to what extent Mr. P needed to be groomed. So what if he was a little damp when I returned him. I drove to Soulard to get Mr. P.

11

I STARED OUT THE WINDOW looking for some way to escape, but this was my life. No matter how overwhelming, I'd have to deal with it because the only other option was Marshal Cutter and the great unknown.

"Aspen?"

"Oh. I'm sorry, Stephanie. I was lost in thought."

"Are you okay?"

"Can you watch Mr. P while I run down to Varrianos."

"Jewelry. The perfect remedy for a bad day."

I ignored her comment, fetched the envelope full of cash from my briefcase, stuffed it into the front pocket of my jeans and walked out the door.

The sun beat on my face as I walked toward the jewelry store. The warmth almost made me forget it was the middle of February. *Vacation.* I needed a vacation. Someplace warm with lots of drinks containing tiny umbrellas.

I ventured over to Varrianos prepared to blow the wad of cash in my pocket. Oliver Lott had provided three-thousand dollars. A whole lot of money to me now. If my ex-fiancé hadn't cheated and if he hadn't been shot in the head sending me into witness protection, I'd be living the high life too. Married to a sexy man, fabulous jewelry, exotic vacations, fast cars, expensive restaurants, but that was a lot of ifs. In reality I now lived a life that never existed, making my home in a tiny apartment with my dog, eating mostly fast foods, driving a Jeep full of dog slobber and fur, and trying to figure out if I'd ever be able to form a real relationship and grow old with someone.

"Can I help you?" a shriveled up replica of Carmine said from behind the counter.

"I'd like to purchase a necklace. It needs to be special and not more than three grand."

If a person's eyes really could light up, his would have been in the number three position on a three-way bulb. His smile was wide and could have matched the brightness in his eyes had it not been for the layers of tar coating his teeth. "Yes. Yes. Here."

I walked over to where the old man was patting the top of a glass case. The old man was right. Everything in the case exuded luxury. My eyes immediately latched on to a gold, triple-chained necklace with dark round rubies mounted along the middle chain. The three chains were attached to a filigreed, diamond encrusted pendant, from which a large teardrop shaped ruby dangled. It was an eye catcher. "That one. I'd like to see that one."

"Yes, it is ah, lovely ah one, but is too much. The most expensive in case. Five thousand," he said, his Italian accent shining through.

Leave it to me to zero in on the most expensive item. With that knowledge, I browsed the remaining necklaces in the case trying to guess which might be right for my budget. She had a February birthday. I spied a revolving stand with birthstone earrings across the store on what must have been the poor person's side. "Just one moment."

I walked over and spun the display until I spied February. I headed back in his direction. "Do you have anything with Amethyst?"

"Here." He took a necklace from the case and placed it on a black velvet board.

The necklace possessed its own beauty, but didn't rival the ruby showpiece. The single gold chain with three square shaped stones, included a heart-shaped diamond between each Amethyst. A small gold chain dangled from one heart and then attached to the other. It wasn't like any of the necklaces in Mrs. Lott's closet, but I was sure she wouldn't be disappointed.

"How much?"

"It is ah, twenty-five hundred."

Carmine came out from behind the curtain that kept the back room out of sight. "For an additional four hundred you can add a special diamond initial drop pendant."

I bristled at the sound of his voice. "I'm not sure."

"Is it for you?"

"No. It's actually for one of your loyal customers. Mrs. Lott."

"Oh, of course." Carmine nodded his head indicating he knew exactly who she was, but the old man's face showed no sign of recognition.

I held up the necklace. "I think I'll pass on the pendant."

"I insist. I'll drop the price to three-hundred for the pendant. I promise you she'll love it."

Carmine pushed the curtain aside and disappeared to the back of the store.

"You are lucky," he shouted from the back.

I'm glad he thought so. I waited while he finished doing whatever he was doing. The black curtain parted a few minutes later and Carmine came out holding the necklace, showing off a dazzling diamond 'I', which meant he knew Mrs. Lott's first name even if the old man didn't.

"You want me to wrap?" the old man asked.

"Uh, sure." One less thing for me to do.

"Here Pops." Carmine gave the necklace to the old man who placed it inside a faux leather box. He placed that box inside a larger glossy black box, with 'Varriano' stamped in gold. Wrapping a gold satin ribbon around it, he tied the best bow I imagined he could by the looks of his bony, arthritic fingers.

Carmine took the money and quickly returned with my change and a receipt. He took the bag from the old man and handed it to me. "Thank you very much. We appreciate your business."

I waved goodbye, happy to be heading in the opposite direction of Carmine.

As I neared the door to my office, Mr. P looked through the glass. Our eyes locked. He slowly began winding up, giving his rendition of an excited bounce.

"Down, Mr. P," I commanded, but it didn't register because he was too busy being a pogo stick. I ignored him. I didn't have time to reinforce, which was probably why PJ was such a wreck.

Passing by the reception desk, I overheard Stephanie talking to a customer.

"I understand," she said, followed by a promise that we would take care of the problem.

If I wasn't in such a hurry, I'd wait until she hung up the phone to find out what client was having what problem.

But, the owner of GlammerPoo made it clear she was busy and I'd have to be on time in order to get Mr. P groomed.

I rushed around, gathering my things then gave Stephanie the 'call me' sign as I left the office with my briefcase and Mr. P in tow. I tossed both of them onto the passenger seat, put the Jeep in drive, and swatted Mr. P as he tried to make his way onto my lap. He whined, but settled down on the passenger side.

Every light had been green, until the one right before the groomer's building. I glanced at the clock in my Jeep. It was a minute fast, but still, I'd be late. When the light finally changed, I whipped into the parking lot of Glammerpoo, scooped Mr. P into my arms and ran to the front of the building.

"Here he is," I said as I pushed through the door, holding Mr. P up like an offering. When I caught a glimpse of myself in the mirrored wall, I suddenly felt like the one who needed grooming. Grungy came to mind. The cool weather hadn't stopped me from sweating. Somehow, somewhere, I'd created humidity around my head, because the condition of my hair gave me the appearance of a Komondor mop dog.

"You're late. One more minute and I wouldn't have been able to get him in."

"I owe you. I'll make sure he turns into a regular."

The owner didn't respond. She took Mr. P and vanished behind the swinging doors, leaving me to sit in a chair and wait. I thumbed through a Dog Fancy magazine and then through the latest issue of BARk magazine trying to find something helpful about training. An important tip I'd read was to keep your dog on a schedule, one goal I wasn't sure I could reach. Selling my time to others made it almost impossible to control my own.

"Baaaooof. Boof."

The desperate bark of Grand Ambition came barreling out of the grooming area.

"Boof. Baaaooof. Baaooof."

The bark became deeper and more demanding.

"Come back here!" I heard someone scream. Seconds after, Grand Ambition shot through the swinging doors, fully focused on his destination. I braced myself. I had a feeling he wasn't going to suddenly stop and gently lay his head on my lap.

"Hurrrumppf." The noise left my mouth and sounded as painful as the feeling of his big head thrusting into my abdomen.

I coughed. "Hey, boy."

"Sorry, about that. He took off before I could connect his lead," said a young girl wearing a pink apron with the Glammerpoo logo emblazoned across it.

I smiled, but didn't say a word. If I opened my mouth again in the next few minutes it would be to moan.

Grand Ambition angled his nose under my hand and flipped it onto his head. I scratched his ears as we waited.

When the owner brought Mr. P to the counter, he looked as though he owned the place, all fluffy and proud. He took after Mr. Q in that respect.

"That'll be a hundred and fifty."

"Oh, what a great surprise. That's not bad for both dogs." I reached into my purse.

"No, no. I charged Grand Ambition's services to the Lott's account. Your little Bichon was a hundred and fifty."

I pulled out my business debit card and handed it over. A small price to pay for a squeaky clean dog and a happy client.

Grand Ambition was quick to stand when I tugged on his lead. I tucked Mr. P under my arm and the three of us left the groomers with only one of us still looking like a dirty dog.

———

I dropped Mr. P off at his home and was half way to Oliver Lott's house to deposit Grand Ambition. Stephanie's name popped up on my caller id.

"Hi Steph."

"What did you want?"

"We didn't get a chance to chat before I left. What was the problem that cropped up?"

"There wasn't any problem."

"But I heard you talking to someone about something we would take care of."

"Oh. Oh yeah, I forgot. That was Mr. Q. He wanted you to bail him out of jail."

I kept my eyes on the road and drove in silence. If I opened my mouth, I'd lose control and land Grand Ambition and myself in a ditch.

"Hello?" Stephanie said.

"Just a sec." I pulled off the road and onto the shoulder. "Why didn't you call me right away. How much is the bail?"

"I told you I forgot about it. It got a little busy here. Harry called, Mrs. Paddy called—"

"But Stephanie, the man's in jail! Don't you think that is important?"

"Of course. But if I didn't answer the calls you'd be yelling at me. But I guess it doesn't matter because you're yelling at me anyway!"

"I'm sorry. I didn't mean to yell. Do you know the bail amount?"

"He didn't say. Just said to call."

I took a deep breath before pulling back onto the road. "Can you call and find out for me?"

I let Stephanie go and continued on, pulling into the Lott's driveway a few minutes before four. I lifted the tailgate.

"Come on boy." I encouraged Grand Ambition to jump out of the Jeep by slapping my hand against my thigh.

He didn't budge.

I grabbed his lead and tugged. He rolled over.

"Not funny. Just a few scratches and then you get your butt out of there." I scratched his tummy and he pawed at my arms.

"Ok. Out." I tugged on his lead again. He laid his head down.

I crawled into the back and pushed him toward the edge of the Jeep. Although I was tempted to roll him out onto the driveway, I couldn't guarantee he'd land on his feet. I jumped back out of the Jeep, leaned in and shoved my arms underneath him. As I lifted all sixty pounds of Grand Ambition, he began to flounder. I struggled to keep control. He sprang from my arms onto the driveway and took off running.

"Damn you!" I took off after him. He ran to the side of the house. I followed him through the open gate and into the back yard.

"No! No! No! Grand Amb—"

Splash.

I watched in horror as the professionally groomed Airedale with an upcoming show instantly transformed into a gigantic wet rat. Grand Ambition stood in the small pond, periodically thrusting his head into the waterfall as he tried to lap up water.

"Come!"

Grand Ambition, sulked his way out of the pond. Shaking vigorously, the water flew in all directions. He took off toward the sliding glass door where the twins watched, doubled over in laughter.

"You guys get a towel!" I screamed.

They both walked away. *Spoiled little brats.*

Grand Ambition sat obediently at the sliding door as Bella opened it and came outside with towels in hand.

"Mr. Lott's going to be furious," I said.

"No. Don't worry. I will not tell on you."

"Bella, you're a saint. I will see you next week."

"Wait."

I turned back. "Do you need help?"

"No. I was expecting jewelry for Mrs. Lott."

"Oh. Right. Meet you at the front door."

I headed back to the Jeep relieved Bella was going to cover for me. I couldn't afford to lose the Lott account.

I closed the back of the Jeep and went around to the passenger side to grab the bag. My heart sank. The bag was missing. If someone stole the necklace, I'd be literally working for the Lott's free of charge for the next four months just to pay them back. And that was only if they'd let me. I closed my eyes and conjured up a vision of me purchasing the necklace, tracing every step I took until I saw myself setting the bag down on my desk. I didn't remember picking it back up.

I called the office. "Stephanie, can—"

"God, Aspen. I haven't had a chance to call the jail yet. What do you think I am Superwoman?"

No. No I don't. You're more like the villainess Vertigo only with red hair.

"Stephanie. I just need you to look at my desk and tell me if you see a bag from Varriano's on top."

"Yes. I see it."

"Can you please put it in my desk drawer before you leave for the day? And please make sure you lock up. Oh, and text me with the amount right away. I need to figure out how to post his bail."

I hung up. The already postponed sexy event with Jack looked like it might be postponed again. I had to run back to the office and then back to the Lott's house to deliver the necklace, plus I still had to bail out Mr. Q. I walked to the front door ready to give Bella the bad news, but she wasn't at the door so I rang the bell.

"Hello, Miss Moore."

"Oh. Uh, hello. I didn't know you were home."

Oliver Lott leaned against the door jamb, his big gun wannabes sticking out from under his starched tee-shirt. "Bella claimed she let Grand Ambition out, but I saw him run into the yard and do a swan dive into the pond."

"Oh."

"We had to pull out of the show."

"I am so sorry. I should have had a hold of his lead. I'll make—"

"It wasn't your fault. His handler is sick and Grand only works well with his handler. We'll get him in another one. He only needs a couple of more points to attain Grand Champion."

Oliver was not so much a proud pop as a pompous one. He talked about Grand Ambition as if he were a commodity. Eventually the conversation about dog shows and breeding turned into Oliver's successful business.

"I'm sorry Mr. Lott. I left the gift for Mrs. Lott back at my office. I'm running back to get it now."

"Don't worry about the gift tonight. I don't need it until Saturday."

"I'll make sure you have it in time. Good night Mr. Lott."

The pressure eased a bit when I got back into my Jeep. I still had to run to the office, but at least I didn't need to come back to the Lott's house which meant I might be able to salvage a night with Jack. And maybe I could use Jack for something other than sex. For the first time since I'd moved to St. Louis, I decided to turn to Jack for help instead of Peter.

"Hey, Good Looking," Jack said when he answered.

I blushed. "Jack. I need some help."

"You name it."

"My client, Mr. Quetzalcoatl, is in jail."

"Mr. who?"

"You know. The guy I call Mr. Q."

"What's he in for? Drugs, DWI?"

"I think, well, I think murder."

———

The bag with the necklace was inside my desk drawer as I'd requested. Now all I needed was to get the necklace safely back to my place so I could relax and have a great night with Jack.

I tucked the bag under my arm. The USB flash drive I'd swiped back from Peter fell to the floor when I pulled my car keys out of my jacket pocket. What was I thinking? How could Jack and I have a sexy night while Mrs. Rippetoe was still missing? Nothing would be normal until I found her. I popped the drive into my laptop and pulled up the kidnapper's telephone number. I picked up my office phone. I put the phone down. After a few deep breaths, I picked it up again and dialed. I didn't hear a ringing sound when I put the handset to my ear, but there was no out of service message either.

"Is anyone there?" I asked, teetering between wanting someone to answer and wanting to end up with dead air.

"Why wouldn't there be?"

"I'm calling the number like you asked. I'm sorry I missed the first deadline."

"Who is this?" the man asked.

Maybe the cellular phone company already re-issued the kidnapper's number to someone else. I wasn't sure how long they held a number before re-assignment. I proceeded as if I'd reached the right guy. "You know who this is. Why don't you tell me who you are?"

"I'm Jack Arbon and I thought I called my girlfriend's office."

"Jack? Is that you?"

"Aspen?"

Holy cow.

"Did you just call me your girlfriend?"

"No. Don't think I did. But if it makes you happy, sure. Now what about a missed deadline?"

I fought with my finger as it moved dangerously close to the button on the phone that could end the call. *What the hell was that about? He'll call me his girlfriend if it makes me happy?* I was trying to handle this relationship with a light touch. I didn't want to push, but I wasn't about to be patronized. If I didn't need his help with Mr. Q, I'd let my finger do as it pleased.

I ignored his statement and his question. "Weird. You must have been calling in while I was calling out. I didn't even hear the phone ring. Sort of serendipitous, don't you think?"

Jack made no comment. "I was calling to talk to you about Mr. Quetzalcoatl. Why'd you think your client was in for murder?"

Crap. I hadn't even entertained the thought of Mr. Q getting arrested for something else.

"I, uh, I don't know. I know his neighbor died and they hadn't ruled out homicide," I said.

"Sure, that's the leap I'd make."

"Cut it out. What's he in for?" I asked.

"Trespassing and possible tampering of evidence, for now."

"What do you mean, for now?"

"He could be in big trouble if they end up ruling it a homicide. Might even become a suspect."

"How much do I need to post his bail?"

"I already posted it."

"Why'd you do that? He's not your client, he's mine."

"You're very welcome."

"Sorry. It's just...well...why didn't you just use a bail bondsman"

"It wasn't that much and he said he'd write a check and give it to you, to give to me. Oh, and he said he wanted you to pick him up at the jail."

"Looks like I won't be able to get to your place."

"I'm okay if it's late."

"I'm sorry we'll have to reschedule. I'll call you."

I couldn't fool myself no matter how hard I tried. I didn't want a 'no worries' kind of relationship. I wanted more. More love, more commitment, more anything but what Jack offered. I had no plans to call Jack. He'd get his check in the mail.

Important people needed me. Jack wasn't one of them, but Mrs. Rippetoe was and I was failing her. I had to find out if she'd been kidnapped. I dialed the number again. As the phone rang I closed my eyes and prayed I wouldn't get a recorded message.

"Listen and listen carefully."

The voice could belong to a man, but it was hard to tell. The person sounded like they were using one of those wacky voice changers.

"Okay, but can you use your real voice? I'm having a hard time understanding you."

"Shut up and listen. We have the old lady and she wants to come home. We need—"

"How do I know she's alive."

"Shut up and listen. Your employer Mr. Lott has—"

"He's not my employer. Hello? Hello?"

Amelia. You idiot. Referring to myself by my birth name was a warning sign. My subconscious used it whenever I needed to be brought back to reality. But I was already back because the guy hanging up on me was like having reality smack me in the face.

I redialed, ready to plead with the man.

"Are you going to shut your trap?" he asked before I could get out my first word.

"Yes," I said, listening for any background sounds.

"Oliver Lott has the diamond. I want you to get it. Don't call any police, the security guard, or anyone. You need to go alone. You'll get another thumb drive with instructions. Call the new number on Monday or the old lady becomes a dead lady."

I thought I heard a train. I needed to stall so I could hear more to be sure. "How do I know she's not already dead? Hello? Hello?"

Damn it. He'd ended the call. I started to call him back when my phone beeped. It was a text with an image of Mrs. Rippetoe chained to a table leg.

———

In my line of work, I sometimes did things I didn't want to do and this was one of those times. I opened the door to the police station and kept my head down. For some reason I couldn't shake the feeling the police would one day be responsible for Marshal Cutter shipping me off to some remote location. The less time I spent around the police the better.

"Aspen, how are you?"

I couldn't ignore him, so I lifted my head. "Hi, Officer Storey. I mean, Eli."

"Now, that's more like it young lady. You been staying out of trouble?"

Eli had arrested me a while back. A mistake, of course. He'd turned out to be more of a father figure in the end, telling me to call him whenever I needed anything. With the bag of evidence from Mr. Q's place in my Jeep, I'd probably end up taking him up on his offer.

"Squeaky clean, sir."

He laughed. "Mmmmhuh. So, what you doing here?"

"I'm picking up my client, Mr. Quetzalcoatl."

"Oh yes. I heard about him. Got himself in a little pickle I hear."

"I'm not real sure. I'm just giving him a ride home."

"Best be all you do. Not sure about that one."

"Yes, sir. Just a ride."

"None of that sir stuff." He tossed a smile my way and advanced down the corridor.

I continued to the main desk to ask where I could find Mr. Q, but I didn't need to because I could hear him calling my name.

"Aspen. Aspen. Hey, Aspen."

"I hear you. No need to yell," I said, keeping my head low.

"Thank God you're here. Get me out of this place."

I tried hard to smile. Mr. Q looked awful. I couldn't imagine him surviving if he were locked up for a long time.

"Why didn't you call for a taxi?"

"I don't usually carry much cash with me."

There must be more to it than that. Mr. Q always acted like he didn't need anyone. I never heard him talk about family and the only friend I knew about was now dead. "Let's get you home. Mr. P is waiting."

After we settled ourselves into my Jeep, I scanned the windshield for a flash drive before backing out of the parking space. "What happened?"

"I got caught at Gavri...I mean Greg's place and they hadn't unsealed the house."

"What on earth made you think it was a smart idea to go into his house?"

"I was looking for my comic book."

"Did you say comic book?" I wondered about Mr. Q.

"Yes. A very expensive comic book."

"Even if it was worth a few thousand, is that enough to take the risk you took?"

"A few thousand? The comic book's worth over three hundred thousand."

Complete craziness. How could a comic book be worth that much and why would he loan it to anyone. "If you don't mind me asking, why'd you let Greg borrow it?"

"I didn't. The comic is missing."

"Did he steal it?"

"No...I don't know. It's gone is all I know and I got caught before I could finish searching his house. And I was thinking, maybe you—"

"No. Don't even ask." I had to stop the madness that was Mr. Q. If I didn't I was going to end up in jail myself.

"You don't even know what I was going to say."

"You're right. Sorry I interrupted."

"So. I only had two rooms left to search and you—"

"Stop there. I'm not going to break into Greg's house and enter an active investigation scene to find your comic book. Can't afford to take the risk."

"You sure think you know everything, don't you? I wasn't going to say that at all."

Sheepish, that's exactly how I felt. I'd interrupted the man twice and been wrong. "I'm sorry. Go ahead. I promise I won't interrupt this time."

"What I was going to say was, you could sit outside Greg's house and text me if someone is coming."

We continued our discussion as we made our way to his house. Mr. Q aggressively listed all the reasons he needed to once again break into his dead neighbor's house. And I listed all the reasons why I couldn't help. We pulled up in front of his townhouse. I got out of the Jeep and walked with him to his front door so we could finish our conversation.

"I thought your company did anything for anybody?"

"The answer is no, Mr. Quetzalcoatl," I said boldly and perhaps a little too firmly. "And the slogan is, 'just about anything for just about anybody'."

Mr. Q opened his front door, scooped Mr. P into his arms, planted kisses on the dog's face and closed the door in mine. Normally I would have knocked and insisted he open the door so we could discuss the matter further. I would have stood firm, suggested we review our needs and work together to reach a compromise. But, I wasn't sure I wanted to compromise because I was beginning to have even more doubts about Mr. Q.

12

"EIGHT SHARP. You told me you'd be here at eight. Am I going to need to find a new concierge?" Mrs. Paddy asked when I answered the phone, my eyes barely open.

"No, ma'am, Mrs. Paddy. I'm on my way."

"How could you be on your way when you're talking to me on the phone?"

"You called my cell phone Mrs. Paddy. I'm in the car."

"Don't forget to ask Edward to call when you get here."

"Yes, Ma'am."

I yanked the covers off and hopped out of bed, putting on yesterday's clothes so I could race outside with PJ and Sassy. The lack of a pause before lying to Mrs. Paddy struck me. Aspen Moore had become a skilled liar, something Amelia would never have accepted.

"What are you guys doing staying up late and partying? I can't believe you let me oversleep again."

PJ and Sassy responded with a whine.

"Yeah, yeah. I know it's not your fault." I ran them outside and hustled back to my apartment to fill their bowls with kibble.

With no time to take a shower, I switched my old clothes for fresh ones and pulled my hair back in a ponytail. *Eight-thirty.* I could feel another lie coming. I threw the tube of tinted moisturizer and some mascara into my briefcase and took off.

My cell phone rang. I picked it up off the passenger seat. "Hello, Mrs. Paddy. I'm almost there."

"You were almost here a half hour ago. Somebody named Stephanie is downstairs. She says you sent her to clean up my home. I thought you were coming to clean up?"

"I am. Stephanie is my assistant. She can stay in the lobby until I get there."

"Somebody needs to start the work. I'll tell Edward to send her up."

"No."

"Why not?"

"I'd like to make sure she starts in the right place."

"It's my home, I think I can handle telling her where to start."

"No, Mrs. Paddy. I'd rather she wait."

"You make it sound like something is wrong with her. She's not one of those prison release workers, is she? I believe in second chances as much as anyone else, but I don't want a prisoner in my house."

"No, Ma'am, she's not a prisoner."

"That's a relief. Is she slow or something?"

"She is fine. I just prefer to be there before we start the job."

Mrs. Paddy stopped her line of questioning and said goodbye.

Last night, Mrs. Paddy had called and requested I come clean up the items that remained scattered throughout her penthouse apartment. I'd in turn called Stephanie and asked for her to be there at eight-thirty. For once she was on time and for once I wished she'd been late.

I dialed Stephanie's number, but she didn't answer. I kept dialing until she picked up.

"Hey, Aspen."

"I'll be there in a few minutes."

"Don't worry. Mrs. Paddy and I are having a cup of tea."

"Oh. Well, don't touch anything. I mean don't start picking up until I get there."

Stephanie was silent. I was sure I'd hurt her feelings. "Stephanie?"

"I understand."

"I didn't mean it that way."

"In what way, Aspen?"

Oh boy.

"Never mind. I'll be there in a few minutes."

Guilt nibbled at my brain as I ended the call. The same kind of guilt that brought PJ into my life. The kind that might end up causing me to give Stephanie a raise.

I had a few more minutes before I reached Falcon Ridge Towers, enough time to phone Peter. When he didn't answer, I called his store.

"Parker Security."

"Hi, Victor, it's Aspen. Is Peter around?"

"No, he flew out to California yesterday."

"He never mentioned going to California. Was there some sort of emergency?"

"No. He's surprising Madeline."

"Oh. That's nice." I thought I sounded convincing. I was happy for Madeline. It was swell she had such a fantastic

158

guy. A guy who would drop everything, even the case of his kidnapped landlady, in order to surprise her.

"He'll be back Monday."

"Thanks, Victor."

Monday? Monday? What was going to happen to Mrs. Rippetoe? If Peter didn't have my back, I thought he'd at least have hers. What the hell was I going to do now?

My mind was on overload. I'd been waiting for Peter's help and never suspected he wouldn't come through for me. My insides hurt. Peter was the one person I thought I could trust in this new world of mine. I had an overwhelming sense of nothingness. A disconnect. I sat at the traffic light waiting for myself to re-engage, but it didn't happen. The light changed and I stepped on the gas.

Pulling up in front of Mrs. Paddy's building, I still had no feelings. I was detached. I didn't like it, but I could use it to my advantage. I intended to elicit information from Mrs. Paddy about what the police found in their investigation of the break-in. Detachment, wasn't that an attribute of a good detective?

Edward waved me through. I didn't bother asking him to call ahead. I didn't want my arrival announced. I wanted to see what was happening while it was happening, not five minutes after.

I tried Mrs. Paddy's front door and it opened. I walked into the parlor where I found Mrs. Paddy and Stephanie almost in tears from laughter. "You shouldn't have left the door unlocked, Stephanie."

"I left the door unlocked," Mrs. Paddy said. Her words coming to Stephanie's defense.

"It's not safe." I moved my arm away from my body, my palm up, drawing attention to the items strewn across the floor to emphasize my point.

"They already broke in. Why would they bother coming back?" Mrs. Paddy asked, while Stephanie sat in silence.

"Maybe they didn't find what they were looking for the first time. Or maybe they want to steal more valuables. Or perhaps they decided they needed to eliminate the only eye witness."

My words hung in the air as a tiny gasp escaped Mrs. Paddy's mouth and Stephanie's eyes widened.

"Aspen, can I talk to you for a minute?" Stephanie asked.

"Sure."

"We'll be right back Mrs. Paddy," Stephanie said. She took my arm and dragged me into the foyer and down the hall to the library.

"What is wrong with you Aspen? Why are you acting like this? You could have given her a heart attack. She probably won't be able to sleep now because she'll be thinking someone's coming to kill her."

I didn't say anything. I wasn't used to Stephanie being the voice of reason.

"And you were late!" Stephanie used the same tone I used whenever she was late and I wasn't sure I liked it.

"Everything is okay. Let's just get cleaning. I have tons of things to get done today." I walked out of the library and back into the parlor. Stephanie followed.

"Sorry, Mrs. Paddy. I didn't mean to scare you. I was trying to make a point. I want you to be safe."

"I know you do. You're a good girl, Aspen."

The nothingness snapped and I felt a surge of tears working their way into my tear ducts. I cleared my throat praying the tears wouldn't run down my cheeks. "Stephanie and I will get started in the bedroom first."

As Stephanie and I straightened up, neither of us spoke. I convinced myself I could leave Stephanie to finish the bedroom without any of Mrs. Paddy's items making their way into her pockets and went back into the parlor.

"How are you doing Mrs. Paddy?"

"I'll feel better when this mess is cleaned up."

"Did the police figure out who broke in?"

"I don't know. They talked to me. Asked me about who was here. I told them nobody but you."

My heart skipped a beat and I bent down to retrieve a throw pillow and book off the floor. "What about the person who tied you up?"

"Of course I told them about him. Wanted to know if I recognized him, but he had one of those knit hats on his face. The police might be calling you because they asked for your number."

Great.

"Not sure what I could add." That was the truth.

"They asked me about a lot of people. Even Junior. I know I talk about Junior wanting me in a nursing home, but he would never steal from me, do you think?"

"Of course not, Mrs. Paddy. You're his grandmother and he loves you." Junior didn't need to steal from her because she gave him so much. Plus, I had a feeling this break-in was connected to the blue diamond because why else would two of my client's homes be broken into and their possessions rifled through? It seemed I wasn't the only one looking for the diamond.

"What did they steal?"

"I don't think they took anything. Isn't that strange? Why would someone break in and not take a thing?"

Because they were looking for the blue diamond? "The criminals could have been looking for drugs."

"Young lady. I do not do drugs. That is preposterous."

"Not illegal drugs, prescription drugs."

"Oh, well I don't think I'm missing any prescriptions."

"I'm sure the police will find who did this as soon as they review the buildings security video."

"No. Something was wrong with the equipment, that is what Edward told me."

"Was it broken?"

"I don't know. Edward said someone had messed with it is all he said."

"Can you describe the man who tied you up?"

"I already told you I didn't see him."

"But what do you remember about his body, his height. Did he speak while he was here?"

"He was regular height. Not short, but not too tall either. He didn't say a word. I tried to get him to talk to me. That's what all the crime shows on television say to do. Try to humanize yourself. But, I don't think he was listening."

"Were there any tattoos or other marks?"

"What do you think you are, a detective?"

"I'm sorry. I am trying to help. My questions might help you remember something and then you can tell the police."

"I already told you, my memory is fine. I told the police everything, even about some little mole I saw when the man's sleeve moved."

I continued picking up the few items that were still on the floor. A candlestick, a broken Tiffany vase, and a broken picture frame with a photograph of Mr. and Mrs. Paddy on the day of their wedding. "I'll get you a new frame for your photograph Mrs. Paddy."

"Thank you. I don't understand why someone would come into my home and tear it up." Mrs. Paddy raised her hand to her face and wiped away a tear.

"I don't either. I'm really sorry someone did this to your place and scared you."

"You don't have anything to be sorry about. It wasn't your fault."

Or was it? If I'd called the kidnapper immediately maybe Mrs. Paddy's place wouldn't be in shambles and Mrs. Rippetoe would be at her home sipping on tea and petting Sassy.

"Are you sure nothing was taken? I couldn't help but see there is a safe behind the picture in the library. Was it broken into?"

"No because it isn't locked. I stopped keeping valuables in the safe after my husband passed. Only thing in there is my shopping money and a few papers. Nothing inside was disturbed. I don't think they even tried to open it. Strange."

Stephanie walk toward Mrs. Paddy and sat in the chair next to her. "I'm through in the bedroom."

"What about the library?" I asked.

"I didn't think you wanted me to start without you."

"Oh. Why don't we do it together then. It will go faster."

Stephanie and I left Mrs. Paddy to her own thoughts and hurried through the rest of the penthouse picking up everything we found on the floor. I grabbed a duster from the hall closet and dusted off the knobs to the doors, removing any leftover fingerprint powder.

"You didn't have to wait for me, Stephanie."

"I was afraid you might think I was stealing something."

"I wouldn't think that."

"Oh come on, Aspen. We both know you don't trust me and that's okay. I wouldn't trust me either if I were you."

That wasn't very comforting to hear. "Stephanie, I understand you have an illness and it isn't that I don't trust you, I am just cautious."

"I know. I am thankful you are such a good friend and good boss," Stephanie said.

"You know you can go if you like. Do you have lunch plans with Roberto?"

"Yes. I do." The smile on her face accented the twinkle in her eyes.

It was nice to see someone in serious like. I wondered what my face looked like now when I thought of Jack. Or Peter.

"You all are seeing each other almost every day, aren't you?"

"Actually. Every day! He's so awesome. He's really in to me. He's always asking questions. Wanting to know everything about me and my family. He's interested in my friends and my job. He's so attentive. And he's always stopping by work, just to say hi. I mean, oh, I...well, he isn't always at work. I mean I'm doing my jo—"

"It's okay. Don't worry. I am sure he just stops by for a few minutes and as long as you're doing your job it should be okay."

"Of course. I always do my job. He doesn't stay too long."

Both of those statements were debatable. "Why don't you run along. I'll finish up with Mrs. Paddy and see you back at the office after lunch."

"I almost forgot." Stephanie dug in her purse.

I hated to admit it, but I couldn't stop myself from sneaking a peek inside her purse. Wondering if I might find some of Mrs. Paddy's possessions.

"I set up an appointment for you on Saturday to look at two RV's. Before you yell at me, I tried to set them up for a week day but the owners couldn't do it." Stephanie handed me a piece of paper before heading off to say goodbye to Mrs. Paddy, her new best friend.

———

I pulled into the McDonald's and rolled up to the speaker.

"A number one. Supersize it with a Coke. Please."

"Is that all?"

"Yes. Thank you."

"That will be—"

Kkkkkzzzzzzzztttkzzt. "Please pull for—" *Kkkkzzzzttkzzt.*

I assumed the guy had been trying to tell me to pull forward, so I stepped on the gas. My New Year's resolution consisted of a single goal, swearing off fast food, but I needed something to make me feel good.

"Six dollars and thirty-two cents."

I paid the guy seven dollars in exchange for my sin.

The bag was open before I pulled out of the parking lot. My hands, without my direction, pulled out a few hot fries. "Mmmmm." I followed the fries with a gigantic sip of Coke. "Aaaaaahh."

I opened the Big Mac container so I could take a bite at the next red light. But, I kept hitting green lights. When a yellow light finally appeared, I slowed down. I salivated in anticipation of my first Big Mac bite in over a month. I raised the burger to my mouth and my phone rang. Seeing Jack's number, triggered me to acknowledge the number of calories I was getting ready to shove into my mouth.

Damn him.

I reached over and hit ignore on my phone, brought the Big Mac to my mouth and bit down hard. The burger tasted delicious, salty with the tang of the special sauce. I savored the flavor. Worth every calorie.

By the time I reached my office, I'd not only finished the entire Big Mac, but all the fries, and over three-quarters of my drink. I reminded myself it was a treat, something to make me feel better. It wasn't about the calories it was about the comfort.

I gathered my purse and briefcase from the passenger seat and left the evidence of my indulgence in the Jeep to dispose of later. I walked by Peter's store. The pressure built in my head as I thought of how easily Peter tossed me aside, leaving me on my own to take care of bringing Mrs. Rippetoe back home. I'd accepted being the number two woman in Peter's life, but I never thought Peter would turn his back on an elderly woman. And not just any elderly woman, but one who cared about him and his well-being. I looked away from the storefront so I wouldn't have to face Victor.

Stephanie hadn't made it back yet from lunch, so I snooped around the reception desk to see what she'd been up to the day before. The desk was neat and her notes organized. Maybe dating Roberto was having a positive effect on her after all. The only evidence of daydreaming was a notepad full of doodles, mostly Roberto's name written in fancy cursive, surrounded by varying sizes of hearts. I smiled. At least someone was head over heels.

I walked back to my desk and pulled up my schedule for the day. I could check off taking the birthday necklace to the Lott's house because I'd dropped that off with Bella before stopping by McDonald's. I noticed Stephanie had set an appointment with a new client for three o'clock.

My eye caught the flashing dot on my phone, reminding me of Jack's call that I ignored earlier. The least I could do was listen to what he had to say, so I tapped the voicemail icon. "Aspen. This is Jack. It's important. Please call me at the office."

That was it? Why couldn't he tell me what he needed? Why did I have to call his office? I was suddenly fearful. What if Jack found out something about my previous life? It's not like the case I testified in made nationwide news, but it could have been of interest to someone whose job it was to know all about the business of white collar crime, and that was Jack's specialty.

I went to the bathroom. I made a pot of coffee. I cleaned out my briefcase and my purse. I cleaned out my email inbox. An hour remained before my meeting with the new client. Then I thought about Jack's call again. What if something had happened to Peter or Mrs. Rippetoe? I stopped stalling and dialed Jack's office.

"Granson, Pollock, and Bernstein."

I knew Jack hoped someday it would be Granson, Pollock, Bernstein, and Arbon. I'd had ambition like that once. But now my main goal in life was working hard at being a nobody. Blending in with the average people of the world.

"Jack Arbon, please. Let him know it's Aspen Moore."

I listened to the music while I waited for the receptionist to transfer the call.

"Aspen. I wanted to tell you before you heard it on the news."

"Oh, God. Is Peter okay?"

"I don't know. It's not about Peter."

"Is it Mrs. Rippetoe. Oh. I think I'm going to be sick."

"No."

I'd been outed. That's what it had to be. I knew the day would come. I braced myself. Marshal Anthony Cutter would be calling soon and whisking me away to another location. "What are they saying about me?"

"I'm never going to understand how your brain works. How did you go from the news being about Peter or Mrs. Rippetoe to it being something about you? And why would you even think someone would be saying something about you? Is there something I should know?"

"Just tell me what it is then. Stop making me guess."

"I wasn't asking you to guess. Never mind. It's about Mr. Q. He's been arrested."

"He is so stubborn. I told him not to go over to Greg's house again. What is it trespassing? Burglary? And why did he call you?"

"Murder, and I'm his lawyer."

13

I LOCKED UP MR. Q'S TOWNHOUSE, walked to my Jeep and placed Mr. P in the passenger seat. He was oblivious, unaware of how his life might change. My experience with unexpected serious life changes left me vehemently wishing they never happened to anyone else, even a dog. I owed it to Mr. P to do everything I could to keep Mr. Q out of jail even if I wasn't so sure of his innocence.

"Stephanie. Can you please reschedule the new client for some time tomorrow? I canceled on him at the last minute. I'll call you later to explain. And schedule both of us to meet with him. He deserves extra attention." I hoped Stephanie would check her voice mail soon.

Getting home seemed to take forever. The sense of sadness persisted not only for Mr. P, but for myself. Somehow I'd meandered into a pity party. When I finally made my way through my front door with Mr. P in tow, PJ pounced on both of us. A one dog revival, spreading his joy to whoever would accept it. I gladly obliged, giving back a little joy in return by scratching the base of his tail. He wiggled his butt in gratitude. If I could only live every day as happy as PJ.

Sassy lifted her head up off the couch, looked longingly through me, then laid her head back down. She looked depressed and Mrs. Rippetoe's absence was most likely the cause. I began to doubt my decision not to involve the police in Mrs. Rippetoe's disappearance and wondered if I'd made that decision for my benefit or hers.

I clipped the leads on the dogs, hustled them down the steps and out the front door. They needed no prompting to go to the bathroom. Within minutes we were back inside the fourplex. Passing by Mrs. Rippetoe's place I told myself anyone would feel depressed if they had a friend who'd been kidnapped. But how many people experienced a kidnapping? Few, really, or at least I hoped the number was small.

Like dark energy, my feelings were dragging me down. If I didn't act soon, my sadness would swallow me whole. I hesitated doing what I knew needed to be done. But, it was time, time to reach out to the only person who could take my sadness and turn it into something productive.

Once again I was going to break the honor code of the Witness Protection Program. It was risky for everyone involved. The tiniest bit of information in the wrong hands made me vulnerable to the actions of the criminals I'd once helped convict, but it was a risk I had to take. I had to talk to her. I had to talk to my mom.

I extracted my pre-paid cell phone from its hiding place and punched in her number. I began to panic when the phone continued to ring, but as always my mom came through.

"Amelia? Is everything okay? I thought you weren't supposed to call until next month?"

Hearing her say my real name, the one I'd grown up with, the one I now missed like a warm blanket on a cold night, caused a lump to form in my throat. Tears began to well.

"Amelia, honey, are you there?"

"I'm here."

"Honey, are you crying? What's the matter?"

Her words opened the gate and the sobs escaped as though held prisoner for a million years. I wasn't sure I could live like this any longer. I wasn't sure I could be as strong as I needed to be in order to take this strange life and mold it into something half as beautiful as my old one.

"Mom, I can't do this anymore."

"Oh, sweetie, I know it's tough. Every day I think about the friends we left behind and how much I miss my little girl, but this is our life now. We must make the best of it. I know it is easier on me because I have Daddy-O. I can't even imagine what it is like for you. But look at the good things. Peter always seems to be there for you and you're dating Jack, a great guy with whom you have a bright future."

When I heard Peter's name, anger rose inside me. I was so mad at him for abandoning me. But my heart soon skipped a beat, not the type of palpitation produced when overcome with anxiety, but the kind the heart welcomes, the kind that appears when you're in love. Irritation followed at the sound of Jack's name and then another explosion of tears.

"Honey, cry. Cry if you need to. I'll hang on the line as long as it takes."

I did as my mother told me. I cried. The release was incredible. I wasn't sure how much time passed, but when I finished crying it was as if I'd been baptized by my own tears. I felt free and happy to be alive. I knew if I wanted to stay that way leaving the Witness Protection Program wasn't an option.

"Mom?"

"Yes, honey. I'm here."

"Can you hold on a sec?" I liberated some tissue from the box on my nightstand and blew my nose, tossed it into the trash, grabbed another one and dabbed the remaining dampness from my face and neck.

"Ok. I'm back. I feel so much better."

"Amelia, remember that even when things are hard you are a strong woman and incredibly smarter than your blonde hair advertises."

I laughed. She was right. I was strong. I'd remained silent throughout my ex-fiancé's murder. The strength I'd demonstrated that day had saved my life and allowed me to put the man who killed Kevin, in prison.

"Thanks, Mom. I don't know what I'd do if I could never talk to you."

"Honey, you say that now, but you'd be fine. Like I said, you are strong. You can accomplish anything you set your mind to."

"Thanks for helping me through this. I love you."

"I love you too, Amelia."

My mother's reassurance refocused my attention to the most pressing problem in my life. I hung up knowing I was ready to find and rescue Mrs. Rippetoe as soon as I got back to my office.

————

The image texted to me by the kidnapper had contained no GPS data. Either the kidnapper used a phone without that capability or knew how to delete the geotags, which made them smart enough to be dangerous. The only thing I could think to do was search for Mrs. Rippetoe in the area where she'd previously been held.

East St. Louis might only be a little over fourteen square miles, but in my mind that came to fourteen square miles too many. Haphazardly running around the streets of East St. Louis expecting to hear Mrs. Rippetoe screaming for help didn't sound like an intelligent move, but if I could narrow the field, it might be worth pursuing.

I'd definitely heard the sound of trains in the background. The only problem – there were train tracks all over East St. Louis. I remembered the cab driver saying he'd come across her up by the river. I wished I'd asked him for more details, but train tracks by the river narrowed it down enough to merit a drive by the area.

I took a few tools from my office closet in case I found Mrs. Rippetoe and needed to break her out. But what I really needed was a gadget to verify her presence in the building. For the first time, I was happy Peter was out of town because he had a gadget that would do the job and would never have agreed to loan me such an expensive piece of equipment.

I put the tools in a backpack. I locked the office door and walked to Peter's shop.

"Hey, Aspen. Peter's not here. You going on some kind of cat burglar job?" Victor asked, continuing to stare.

"What?"

"You're all dressed in black."

Suddenly I was self-conscious of my black sweatpants and sweatshirt, with my black beanie hat covering my dirty hair. "Oh, funny. No, I'm thinking of going to the gym."

"Good for you. Always good to get some exercise."

Thin and geeky, Victor didn't look like the exercise type. Maybe Peter had brainwashed him or something. The gym I'd belonged to was one with spa facilities. One where I never touched a piece of exercise equipment. Even though my statement to Victor was a lie, it held an element of truth because I'd been thinking of renewing my membership.

"I wanted to leave something on Peter's desk if you don't mind."

"Sure, if it's open. He usually locks it."

Damn. I crossed my fingers and headed back to his office and got excited when I spotted a slight crack in the door. I pushed it open and shut it behind me.

The other day, in Peter's office, I saw the C-Thru 1000 in a box on the file cabinet next to his desk, but it was no longer there. I peeked behind his desk and found it sitting on the floor. I picked up the equipment and instructions and stuffed them inside my backpack. I hoped to put it back inside his office before he discovered it was missing, but just in case, I wrote a quick note. I apologized to Peter, asking him not to be mad, then apologized a second time before signing my name. Who was I kidding? I took a military grade piece of equipment for which Peter probably paid a fortune. He wasn't going to be mad, he was going to be furious.

"Have a great night," I said, waving to Victor as I left the shop. I didn't want to stop for fear Victor would see the guilt in my eyes or the change in the shape of my backpack.

I laid the backpack gently on my passenger seat, fastened my seatbelt, and turned the key that would start my journey to the wilds of East St. Louis.

Heading up I-55 toward the Poplar Street bridge, the sun was setting behind me. I crossed over the Mississippi river and then a set of railroad tracks, following the signs for 4th Street. The view of the fiery orange and pale pink sky behind the Gateway Arch and the image of Mrs. Rippetoe chained to a table leg juxtaposed in my mind. How could there be so much evil in such a beautiful world?

I made my way on to the unkempt road leading to the river. The only thing that kept me heading down the uninviting street was a railroad crossing sign. A sign that might lead me to Mrs. Rippetoe. I continued until I found myself at the Malcolm W Martin Memorial park. Had it been summertime, I'd be staring at people watching the erupting Gateway Geyser, but in the middle of February, the park was deserted.

Across the river, the St. Louis Arch framed the city lights that were beginning to twinkle. I drove north past the Casino Queen, the East St. Louis police station, and under the Martin Luther King bridge hoping to locate the kidnapper's headquarters. None of the buildings fit the description Mrs. Rippetoe had given when she'd told me about her escape. And I doubted the cab driver would have been this far north. So I backtracked and headed south.

I came across an industrial style building divided into separate units. Other than a restaurant and a strip club, all the other units appeared to contain daytime businesses or nothing at all. I drove through the parking lot and got excited when I spotted a railroad track running parallel to the building and just beyond it, the river.

Cars were parked in front of a few of the units, so I parked near the back of the building. I pulled out my flashlight and the booklet to the C-Thru 1000. The instructions seemed straight forward. Mrs. Rippetoe wouldn't appear on the screen, just a neon dot. This meant anyone could be inside. I scanned the units, deciding which ones to investigate.

Although an interesting place to hide an old woman, I scratched the strip club from my list because Mrs. Rippetoe would have mentioned the loud music. She also didn't mention the smell of food, so I scratched the restaurant off the list too. That left an insurance company, a used furniture store, a plumbing company, and what appeared to be two empty units.

My phone rang and I watched Peter's name turn into a missed call. Why was he calling me during his surprise rendezvous with Madeline? I wondered if Victor had figured out I took the C-Thru 1000.

I read the instructions one more time. The subject had to be no more than fifty feet away in order for them to be registered by the radar, which meant I was screwed if Mrs. Rippetoe had been placed in the middle.

The good thing about this building was the lack of outdoor lighting, which was also a bad thing since the area came across as a little rough. I ran my mom's words through my head, reminding myself of my inner strength before grabbing my pepper spray, flashlight, and Peter's C-Thru 1000.

The men in front of the strip club were hooting and hollering as they entered the club. In an odd way it made me feel safe. I started with the empty end unit. I turned on the radar and held it up with both hands, aiming it at the wall. Nothing appeared on the screen. To verify the equipment worked, I strolled down toward the strip club, tucked myself behind a dumpster and took aim. The screen filled with ten to fifteen neon dots moving around in various directions like a video game.

Knowing the equipment worked, I made my way back to the next unit, which housed the insurance company. I held the machine up again and waited. No neon dots. I moved on to the used furniture store. I took aim once again and two dots appeared. One dot moved back and forth across the screen and the other sort of vibrated in place. My heart began to pound. I'd bet anything Mrs. Rippetoe was inside with her captor, though she never mentioned seeing a bunch of furniture in the place. They could have brought her in through the back or something. When one of the dots appeared to be moving in my direction I took cover behind a nearby RV and tractor trailer.

If I got caught, I'd be screwed because I wouldn't be able to rescue Mrs. Rippetoe. If I couldn't rescue her or steal the diamond before Monday so they'd set her free, then who would? I watched the door to the unit open and squinted trying to get a visual of the person. The door closed, without anyone stepping outside.

"MMMMMM. MMMMMM." I struggled to scream through the hand covering my mouth. I jabbed my elbows behind me, trying to save myself and the C-Thru 1000. My damn pepper spray was lodged in my pocket. *Smart move.* I tried keeping my feet firmly planted on the ground, but I was being dragged away from the trailer and toward the railroad tracks.

My heart pounded. My head screamed. Snot ran down my nose as I struggled for air.

"Hold it right there, buddy. Don't move."

My eyes filled with tears as I recognized the voice.

"Let her go and get the hell out of here before I shoot your nuts off."

The hand left my mouth and I heard feet pounding the ground and didn't dare turn around until they had become a distant sound. "Peter!"

"Are you okay?" Peter pulled me toward him and held me tight. I let my tears flow for only a few seconds.

"I thought you were out of town. How'd you know I was here?"

"Don't worry about it. Just be glad I knew."

"No, really, how could you know I was here?"

"Did you think I wouldn't put a tracking device on such an expensive piece of equipment? Victor called me when he noticed your backpack looked a bit larger than it had when you entered the store."

"Oh."

"I have to say you were pretty impressive holding onto that thing even though you were being dragged to your possible demise."

I handed the C-Thru 1000 over to Peter. "Sorry. I know I should have asked, but you were in California. Why are you back already?"

"Flew all the way there and found out Madeline is out of town shooting a commercial. She texted me and said it was a last minute thing."

"That's a bummer. Long trip for nothing."

"Yeah. Especially because I planned to ask her to marry me."

I stood. Stunned. I mean, I knew Peter was unavailable, but something about his relationship with Madeline made me think there might someday be a small crack in the door. I'd had no idea Peter intended to slam that door shut and lock it up tight. "I, uh, that's, well, wow."

"I know. Shocking."

"Well, yes. I guess you could say that."

"It's been six years. It was time."

I didn't want to talk about Peter marrying Madeline any longer. My sweats seemed unseasonably warm. I hiked up my sleeves. "Sorry again about the equipment. I know I should have called to ask you, but I figured it might be too expensive for you to let me borrow it."

"So you decided to steal it?"

"No. I borrowed it."

"You do know that when you take something without someone's permission it's considered stealing, right?"

"But, I—"

"Right?"

"Yes." I hung my head in shame like Amelia Milhauser, the good girl, but in my mind I was Aspen Moore, a murderer's accomplice, a liar, and now, a thief.

"I'm going to forgive you, but you've got to ask me if you need something. Stop trying to do it all yourself. So why are we here?"

"I think Mrs. Rippetoe is in one of these buildings," I said. My eyes were drawn to a woman getting into a car outside the furniture store.

"I'm not even going to ask you why you think that. I'm just going to tell you that you can't tell with this machine who is in the building, only that someone is in the building. And, we can't go breaking in to every unit where we suspect someone is inside."

"But, what if she's here?"

"You said Mrs. Rippetoe got away from the place she was being held last time. Did she mention anything about strippers, or a restaurant, or a plumbing comp—"

"No. She didn't mention anything about anything. Only that there had been a bed in the office."

"A bed is a piece of furniture isn't it?" he asked.

"She didn't say there was a lot of furniture around."

"A bed is a piece of furniture, right?"

If I didn't answer his stupid question, he wouldn't stop. "Yes."

"Good. Now that we settled that, I would say the empty spaces would be your best bet."

"What about the furniture store?"

"If I were going to kidnap someone I'd hide them in a place they wouldn't be seen."

"If we scan all the empty spaces, will you promise me you'll be satisfied and leave with me?"

"You bet."

We walked by each unit and Peter held up the C-Thru 1000 with both hands. Each time nothing registered. I was disappointed when the last empty unit showed no people inside.

"Can we at least knock on the door of the furniture store?"

"Aspen you promised we'd leave if we checked out the empty units. Wouldn't she have mentioned furniture?"

Finally, a chance to whip a rhetorical question back at him. "A bed is furniture isn't it?

"Let me take a look," Peter said, shaking his head. He held the equipment up to the furniture store and one neon dot appeared.

"See. That's her. There were two people, but one started coming toward the door. That's how I ended up behind the trailer."

"You don't know if Mrs. Rippetoe is inside."

"Well whoever it is, they're sitting awfully still. Like their chained to a bed or table or something."

"What makes you think they'd chain her to a bed?"

He was going to be even more pissed if I told him the truth, but there was no reason not to tell him except to avoid conflict and I was better than that. "The kidnapper texted me a photo of her."

"You've been in contact with the kidnapper?"

"I called the number. They want me to get the diamond."

Peter was silent. From my experience it meant one of two things, either he was angry or he was thinking. The small bulging vein by his temple gave it away. I waited for him to yell at me.

A few minutes passed and it was getting harder to hold my words. "Remember, this is about Mrs. Rippetoe. Our land lady, the sweetest woman in the world. The woman who makes us awesome fresh lemonade in the summer and tasty hot chocolate in the winter. The woman who would give you the shoes off her feet if you needed them."

"Oh yeah. Those Velcro strapped, Vibram soled shoes are just what I need."

"Peter, seriously, she needs us."

"Ok. Let's go. I'm going to view the inside while you knock so I can tell if they are moving towards the door."

We both walked up to the unit. Peter aimed the device and I knocked.

"Their moving. So it can't be her," he said.

"Are they coming to the door?"

"No. Knock again. Now they're coming. And pretty damn fas—"

A loud banging sound came from the other side and the deep growling was enough to send Peter heading in the other direction.

"Come on Aspen, let's go."

I turned back toward the door. "But, I'm good with dogs. I bet we could go check out the place and the dog would calm down. I've got some tools to get the door open. Can't we try Peter? Peter?" I turned around and he was almost to the end of the building. "Hey, wait up!"

14

THE GUY BEHIND ME HONKED HIS HORN and woke me up. I glanced in my rearview mirror. I couldn't have been asleep for too long, yet the traffic light was now green. I hadn't slept well last night due to the failed attempt to find Mrs. Rippetoe, the news about Peter proposing to Madeline, and the unexpected phone call from Jack at one o'clock in the morning.

Jack's effort to convince me to let him come over had been met with my silence. Not because I was still mad at him, but because I'd fallen asleep during the call. My eye twitched as I vaguely recollected agreeing to show up at his home tonight for another attempt at a sexy rendezvous.

As soon as I got to my office I'd shut my eyes for a few minutes, for a cat nap, a small escape before I began my day. Maybe I'd made a mistake trying to work on the weekend. I had so much to do and I was running out of time, but I had to make sure my business didn't fall apart which meant I had some RVs to inspect.

"Hello," I mumbled into the phone.

"Aspen, it's Stephanie. Where are you?"

"I know I'm late. I'll be at the office in five minutes."

"No. We were supposed to be meeting at the new client's home."

"You didn't tell me that."

"Yes. I texted you last night."

"You texted me jumbled letters. I thought it was a mistake."

"No. I typed the man's name, address, and the time."

"No you didn't. You typed something like SXU and some numbers or something."

"Oh God. I wondered why I never heard from Roberto."

"What?"

"I was sexting Roberto!"

"TMI. Just text me the address!"

My phone chimed. I pulled into a parking lot and entered the address from Stephanie's text into the navigation app on my phone. I wasn't sure what the new client wanted and why they'd insisted on meeting me in person before discussing the services they needed. Stephanie had verified their information, otherwise, I would have insisted the first meeting be held at our office or a public place.

The location wasn't too far and when I pulled up in front of the home I discovered Stephanie had once again beat me to a customer's house. I imagined things would only get worse until Mrs. Rippetoe was safely tucked away in her apartment with Sassy on her lap. I gathered my purse and briefcase and walk toward Stephanie. She was aggressively knocking on the front door of the small shotgun house.

"How long have you been here?"

"Ten minutes. I've knocked and rung the bell."

"I think ten minutes is long enough. That is why we should meet them at the office for the first meeting. Here, leave them a note." I jotted down 'we missed you' on the back on my business card and handed it to Stephanie.

"Do you think I got the time wrong?"

"Don't worry about it now. We have RV's lined up to see."

"Oh, about that. You know, Saturday is my day off. I'm supposed to meet Roberto at the office."

Technically both Saturday and Sunday were Stephanie's days off. I couldn't argue with that and I hadn't specifically asked her not to take the day off. "You're right. Go ahead. I'm sure I can handle it."

And once again there it was, the twinkle in Stephanie's eyes. Ugh. I hoped Stephanie and Roberto weren't going to do it on my desk. What other reason would she be meeting him at the office on a Saturday. I shuddered, not wanting to imagine my desk being christened by anyone other than me.

———

The light on Manchester Road turned green and I drove over I-270 towards Wildwood, an exurban town outside of St. Louis. The first RV scheduled for preview was located next to Rockwoods Reservation. Beautiful trees, singing birds, and exactly what I needed to calm my soul.

I could commune with nature and reel in a ten-percent finder's fee at the same time if the RV fit my client's needs. Priced at more than seventy-five-thousand dollars, brokering the sale of the RV would give me a hefty chunk of change. Only a fraction would be needed for current operating expenses leaving my business with a little cushion.

Jack's name popped up on my phone. I hesitated. My confusion about what I wanted was driving me crazy. One minute our undefined relationship was satisfactory and the next I was mad as hell at him for acting non-committal. I wondered if the inconsistency that plagued our relationship was my fault. Had I been holding Jack at position number two in favor of Peter? It was a valid question because Peter was my unavailable friend, who would soon be mega-unavailable, with a capital M for Married.

"Hey, Jack. How are you?"

"A little perturbed if you really want to know. A slot opened up on yesterday's docket and I tried to pull some strings and get Mr. Quetzalcoatl's arraignment moved. The damn clerk wouldn't budge. She's still mad at me and unprofessional if you ask me. Now he's spending the weekend in jail."

"Oh. He's not going to like that."

"Who would? I can't believe she's still upset."

"What made her so mad?"

"A big mix up. I... let's just drop it. Are we still on?"

"Yes, we are. And I'm looking forward to it," I said even though I was feeling a bit agitated in response to Jack's side-stepping the story about the court clerk.

"It wasn't apparent during last night's call."

Breathe. Jack deserved a fresh start. Which meant tossing out the past, even the angry court clerk. "I was extremely tired. I really am excited."

"Great. And I've got a surprise for you."

"Can't wait. I'll see you later."

I thought our conversation went well. Did Jack and I need a defined relationship? Whatever we had, I wasn't helping the situation by holding him up to high standards while I let Peter shred my heart strings.

"Moore Time. How may I help you?" I asked when I accepted a call from a number I didn't recognize.

"Ms. Moore? This is Junior."

"Junior who?"

"Junior Paddy."

His name sent me directly to a bad place. "Is...is your grandmother okay?"

"Oh. Yes, except for her forgetting things all the time."

Was he talking about the same woman? For her age she was still quite alert. "What do you mean?"

"Oh. You know."

No, I didn't know. "Did you need me to assist your grandmother with something."

"No. I am not sure how to say this, so I'll just say it. Your services are no longer needed."

"Your grandmother didn't indicate any problems with our service."

"It isn't that she's unhappy. It's because I'm moving her into a nursing home since she's become so forgetful."

"And she wants to go?"

"Haven't told her yet. I don't think she'll know the difference."

What? I wasn't going to let him move her to a nursing home without talking to her first. Maybe Mrs. Paddy had been right to suspect Junior for her ransacked apartment. "Thanks for calling. I'll schedule an exit interview with her soon."

"No. She doesn't need an exit interview. Call me, I can do the exit interview."

"Ok. Goodbye Junior."

The only person I wanted to interview was Mrs. Paddy. I dialed her number.

"Hello," Junior said.

I pressed the end call button and immediately called Stephanie. Junior had never met Stephanie, so she'd be the perfect person to schedule the interview. I left a message.

Inhale.

Exhale.

The average brain held a limited amount of data and mine was about to explode. Either I had a very small brain or I was on overload. If something didn't change soon I'd need a database to keep track of all my problems.

I pulled into the driveway at the address where the first RV was located, parked my Jeep and trotted up to the door. Nobody answered after I rang the bell several times. *Awesome.* The second appointment of the day and another no show. One more crappy event in my crappy day. I didn't see the RV and wondered if I went to the wrong address. I pulled my phone out of my purse to call Stephanie when I heard a faint noise.

"Yoo hoo. Yoo de hoo. Hoo hoo hoo."

What the heck was that?

"Oh yoo hoo. Helloooo."

I looked to my left and saw a pair of eyes barely peeking over a small wooden fence. I walked toward the gate. "Hello?"

"Yes, yoo hoo. Over here."

As I approached the gate, it opened and there stood the tiniest woman I'd ever seen. She wasn't a little person, but she was definitely short and thin, and downright fragile looking.

"I'm here to look at the RV."

"Yes, come on back."

I followed her down a path to the rear of the house where a humongous carport housed an equally humongous RV.

She opened the door to the RV. "This is it."

Something about the RV seemed familiar. I stepped up into it, amazed at how beautiful it was for a vehicle. The leather seating was spectacular. The kitchen much nicer than the one in my apartment. Once back in the bedroom, the feeling of familiarity left. It has a good sized, well-appointed bedroom and I thought about how wonderful it might be to live in the RV instead of my small apartment.

The interior was immaculate and a perfect fit for the doctor, his wife, and their five-year-old twins. He'd have many happy family camping trips in this RV without having to give up his luxurious lifestyle. I followed her down the steps. When I turned to close the door the image of Mrs. Rippetoe chained to a table leg popped into my head.

"Oh my god," I said to no one.

"What? What's wrong?" she asked.

I looked at Tiny Lady. "Uh, oh nothing, it's perfect. Let me discuss it with my client and we'll give you a call back."

"I'm not sure how long it's going to last. I've had many a people call to see it."

"Yes. I can see why. Can I give you a small deposit to hold it for twenty-four hours?"

"Well. Let me see. How much?"

All I wanted to do was run back to the Jeep and call Peter. "One-hundred?"

"That won't get you a decent pair of shoes nowadays. You think that's worth the risk of passing up another deal? Five-hundred."

Five hundred? Tiny Lady wasn't acting so tiny. "Fine," I said, betting the doctor would love it.

I ran to my Jeep and wrote a business check then ran it back to her, and then ran back to my Jeep like I was in a relay race.

"I know where she is!" I screamed into the phone when Peter answered.

"Where who is?" Peter asked, as if there were multiple missing women.

"Mrs. Rippetoe. Well, I don't know exactly where she is, but—"

"You know, but you don't know? Have you been drinking?"

"No. I'm out looking at RV's and—"

"You planning a trip?"

"Stop interrupting me! I'm trying to tell you that Mrs. Rippetoe is being held in an RV."

"Why would you think that?"

"When I looked at the RV, the leg to the table, it just hit me."

"You got hit with a table leg?"

Peter was irritating, but I held steady. "No, the table leg reminded me of the thing Mrs. Rippetoe was chained up to!"

"Why didn't you just say that?"

Suddenly I wondered why I was so enamored with him. "I tried. Can you go with me tonight to check out that RV we saw in East St. Louis?"

"I guess I could. It's not like I'm busy with anything else."

Peter had that 'woe is me' tone. I had a feeling it had something to do with Madeline but I wasn't going to bring her name up. "Good. I've got some errands to run and then I'll come to your office around eight o'clock, so we can load up on spy gear."

"It's not spy ge—"

"I got another call. Bye."

I pushed the button to accept the call. "Moore Time. How may I help you?"

"Miss Moore. It's Oliver Lott."

My mind immediately ran through everything I'd done for Oliver Lott to see if I'd screwed up somewhere. "What can I do for you Mr. Lott?"

"Actually, I want to do something for you. I have two extra tickets for tonight's charity event and Bella suggested I invite you."

"Thank you, but I don't think I can make it." I hated to say no because not only did I want to cultivate a good relationship with him, but a charity event was just the type of place I could network to gain more business.

"I insist. You can't deny it's a great place to pick up more business."

Eerie. I'd already been trying to figure out how to nicely cancel my plans with Jack so Peter and I could make a trip to East St. Louis. I couldn't possibly go to a charity event, unless I ran over to East St. Louis this afternoon.

"Are you sure Bella doesn't want to go?"

"She already is. I think that's why she suggested I ask you. She says she likes you and would like to become friends because she doesn't have many here in the states. You would actually be doing us a favor."

A hard invitation to turn down. "Sure. That would be great."

"And don't forget, there are two tickets, so bring a friend. It's at the Four Seasons. I'll leave the tickets with the front desk."

My night in red sneakers had now turned into a night in red heels. The only question – who would I ask, Jack or Peter?

15

My hands couldn't stop touching my hair and I felt like a traitor. One of the best stylist in town had a cancellation and I got my hair done. I'd been conflicted, but I was desperate to look presentable for the charity event this evening. An event that might allow me to connect with rich people who could afford to buy blue diamonds.

I touched my hair again. My frizzes were banished and my curls defined. I should have felt sexy, but instead I felt guilty. Mrs. Rippetoe was somewhere trapped in an RV, which was why I was headed back to East St. Louis to check the inside of the RV I'd been next to the other night.

As I neared the strip joint, I noticed a motorcycle behind me, the same one that followed me over the bridge. I turned into the lot and the motorcycle turned too. I drove through the parking lot to the end of the building and relaxed when the motorcycle pulled in front of the strip club. I drove around back and met with disappointment. The RV was no longer there.

I continued along the train track and river's edge, making my way back to the road. I caught sight of Harry Corbitt outside the strip club, helmet in hand, standing next to the motorcycle that had been following me.

Harry mounted his bike. I pressed on the gas. My creep meter ticked upward as Harry closed in behind me. I worried he was interested in me, but not for planning his wedding. I doubted there actually was anyone willing to marry him.

Whatever he was doing, I didn't like it. He'd already popped into my life once on the premise of getting married and my world had turned into a vortex, going down the drain. Once again he wanted me to plan his wedding and again my life was swirling. I didn't get why he was in my life. If he wanted to harm me, he could have done it behind the building near the train tracks. I checked my rearview once more before getting on the interstate. Harry slowed to a leisurely pace and I breathed a guarded sigh of relief. If Harry was up to something, today wasn't the day.

I crossed the bridge into St. Louis and kept my eye on Harry. A few miles into St. Louis, he gave up the chase and exited the interstate. I felt relieved, but still anxious about not finding the RV in the building's parking lot. In another hour, it was decision time. Call Peter or call Jack and extend an invitation to the charity event. But first, I needed to seek professional help in my investigation of Greg's murder.

"Officer Storey. Eli, it's Aspen Moore"

"What can I do for you?"

"You said if I ever needed anything to call, right?"

"Yes, those were the exact words."

"Can we meet in twenty minutes? "

"Sure, I'm off duty now anyway. Want to join me for a cup of coffee?"

"I don't have a lot of time because I'm going to a charity event tonight. I'm on I-64 near the Chaifetz Arena. Are you far from the World's Fair Pavilion in Forest Park?"

"Are you driving and talking on your cell phone?"

"Ummm. It's not illegal is it?"

"Not yet. But, it isn't safe."

If I wasn't breaking the law, why did I feel guilty?

———

The parking lot of the World's Fair Pavilion was empty. I'd only been about five minutes away, which meant Eli should arrive in another five. I got the paper bag with the evidence collected from Mr. Q's house and took out the plastic baggie with the long hair. I plucked one of my hairs from the back of my head and placed it inside an empty baggie. I rummaged through my briefcase, pulled out a permanent marker and marked the bag containing my hair with an 'A' and the other baggie with a 'B'. The next thing I pulled out was the baggie with the small curly hairs. I wasn't sure if I should give them to Eli or not.

Eli pulled into the parking lot. I grabbed all the baggies of hair and got out of my Jeep. My hands were shaking. I was nervous about asking him for a favor because I was afraid he might ask a lot of questions. But, if I hoped to get anywhere with my investigation of Greg's death, I needed professional help.

"What's so urgent?" Eli asked after stepping out of his car.

"First, you promise to keep this between you and me?

"That depends."

"I don't want you telling Marshal Cutter."

"Are you in some kind of trouble?"

"It's personal." I lowered my eyes.

"Man trouble?"

He'd gone in the exact direction I'd hoped he would, but now I felt bad about outright lying to him. But, Greg was a man and I considered being dead trouble. "Maybe."

"I promise not to call Marshal Cutter."

"Thank you. Here." I handed him the baggies.

"What's this?"

"I'd like to see if you can find someone to compare the two long hairs. See if they are from the same person. Uh, and well, I'm not sure what you can find out by looking at the other, uh, hairs. Maybe if they are male or female?"

"Ah. You sure you want to do this? Maybe it's better not knowing."

"I'm sure. How long will it take?"

"I've got a few people who owe me favors, but in this situation I need to select someone I can trust who won't ask questions. So, I'll get back to you."

"Can you get DNA too?"

"DNA? Are you sure everything is okay?"

I knew I'd just made an error in judgment. I should have kept my mouth shut. "Yeah. I was just curious."

Eli raised one eyebrow and pursed his lips. The look said he knew everything wasn't okay, but he'd respect my request to not tell Cutter.

"Thanks so much for coming through for me."

"I haven't come through for you yet, but I am sure going to try. Is this anything you'd like to talk about? Remember I'm a father to a daughter, so I'm pretty good at this stuff."

"No, but thanks for offering. Can I get the hairs back when you're done in case I need them?"

"I'll make sure to tell them you need them back."

"I better go. I need to get ready for the Charity event tonight."

"You enjoy yourself and I'll let you know if I find someone to take a look at this." He held the baggies up as if I didn't know what he was talking about.

"Thanks." I turned to get into my Jeep.

"Aspen?"

When I turned back toward Eli, the smile lines that usually ticked upward around his eyes were flatlined. "You know you can come to me for anything, right?"

I smiled hoping to bring those tiny wrinkles back to life, but they didn't move. "Thanks." I turned and hopped back into my Jeep, feeling wistful. There wasn't a single soul I could express myself to within the totality of my life, not Eli, not Peter, not Jack, not Cutter, not even my mother.

By the time I ended my pity party, I was almost home. I couldn't delay the call any longer. "Hey, it's Aspen."

"I know your voice and I know your tones. You're calling to cancel, aren't you?"

"Not exactly."

Jack didn't respond.

"I have a charity event I need to go to."

"So, you're cancelling."

"No, I'm redirecting. Would you like to go with me?"

Again, Jack didn't respond.

"Jack, are you still there?"

"Yes. I'm thinking."

"If you need to think then it must mean you're not interested." My stomach felt dense, it ached and a heaviness let me know I was worrying about the relationship status again. Jack and I had been out to dinner several times and to both our homes, but we'd never done anything as grand as a well-known and well-attended charity event.

"I'm interested. I'm not sure if you sound like you really want me to go. The excitement you had earlier today seems to have dimmed."

"It was either Peter or you and I chose you because you're the one I wanted to spend the evening with, no one else. If this event hadn't come up short notice like it did, I'd be over your house like we planned."

"You were considering taking Peter?"

I shouldn't have mentioned that. "Didn't you hear what I just said? I want to spend the evening with you."

"Are we coming back to my place afterward?"

"I wouldn't have it any other way."

———

Five dress changes and three pair of shoes later, I pulled into the valet parking lane at the Four Seasons hotel. I'd finally settled on a low-back red dress with matching red heels. I was meeting Jack at the front desk.

The valet opened my door. I picked up my small clutch, but left my coat behind. The cold air smacked me. I ran toward the lobby doors, easily entering with the assistance of the doorman.

The lobby was striking and so was Jack. I approached the front desk. Jack's eyes gave off a reflective glow from the gold in his paisley tie. It was like I'd found a secret stash of Egyptian treasure. My body slightly quivered.

"You look beautiful," Jack said, his eyes focused on my chest.

I couldn't help but glance down. My nipples were ready to party. I folded my arms across my breasts. "Uh, thank you?"

"Sorry, my bad. But, you look so sexy. Why don't we just skip the event and head up to my hotel room?"

"You got a hotel room?" Jack and I had never stayed the night together in a hotel room. I took a breath, trying to stop the quivering from turning into a full blast earthquake.

"Do you not approve?"

"I definitely approve."

Jack leaned in and his lips touched my ear. "You sure you don't want to skip the event? We're in room nine-ten with a beautiful view of the Arch?"

The moisture from his whisper, tingled. "You aren't making this easy, you know?"

Jack's lips were pressed together in a devious smile and I was tempted, but Oliver Lott had been gracious enough and I knew better than to disappoint a client. I turned my attention away from Jack to the woman behind the front desk.

A little groan escaped Jack's mouth.

"Oliver Lott should have left two tickets for the charity event tonight," I said, nudging Jack just a little.

She opened a drawer and pulled out a group of envelopes. "Your name?"

"Aspen Moore." I wondered how many others Oliver Lott had invited.

"Here you are. Have a nice evening." She turned her attention to Jack. "Don't hesitate to find me if you need anything."

"Definitely." Jack's smile was awkward, not quite a full-sized pleasant smile and not quite a full on sexy smile either. I could tell he was struggling.

"Okay, then. You ready?" I waited for Jack's response.

Jack broke eye contact with the desk clerk, but didn't immediately make contact with me, instead, he lowered his head slightly.

"You ready?" I asked again.

"Oh, sorry. Yes. I 'm ready."

I took Jack's hand and we strolled toward the ballroom in silence. A person at the door took our tickets and we entered a huge and lavish room. I wondered how much of the money raised for the function actually made it to those the charity was supposed to be helping.

"You ever been to this? I heard it's an annual event," I said, finally releasing Jack's hand.

"Yes."

His answer was short, which meant there was more to the story, but I wasn't going to ask. I saw wine, food and a band who had yet to begin playing. It looked like a fantastic place to have fun and I intended to do just that.

We walked side by side to the open bar, a place I promised myself I wouldn't frequent this evening. The bartender slid Jack's bourbon on the rocks to him, and to me, my Cuba Libre. My face stiffened and I kept my eyes directed at the small mole on the bartender's left arm. The exact same place Mrs. Paddy had described when asked about her assailant. Moles weren't unique like fingerprints. If the mole had been unusually shaped, like Mary with the baby Jesus or something, I could have turned him in, but small and round, wasn't enough to lock the guy up. I shook loose my stare long enough to notice the Lott's across the room.

"Thank you so much for the tickets," I said, as we approached Oliver Lott and his ensemble, most of who dispersed when I'd addressed Oliver. Mrs. Lott stayed by his side, wearing the necklace I'd chosen for her, but noticeably the diamond initial no longer dangled from the chain. Carmine had sworn she'd love it, but I guess he didn't know her as well as he thought.

"You're welcome. And you brought a date!" Oliver extended his hand toward Jack.

"Yes, Mr. Lott, this is Jack Arbon. Jack, Oliver Lott."

Jack and Oliver shook hands and started up a conversation, so I excused myself and walked over to one of the hors d'oeuvre tables where Bella munched on a piece of shrimp.

"Don't you like cocktail sauce?" I asked.

"Yes. Love it. But dress is white."

She didn't need to explain any further as I understood exactly what she was talking about. My chest became a food magnet whenever I ate. I took her advice and took a piece of shrimp sans the cocktail sauce. "Thanks for asking Mr. Lott to invite me. Are you here with anyone?"

"No, but my boyfriend is working here. There," she said, pointing to the bartender with the mole on his arm.

I couldn't imagine Bella getting involved with someone capable of ransacking an old lady's apartment, which was a relief. Her boyfriend was just one of the thousands with arm moles. "I didn't know you had a boyfriend. He's handsome"

"Thank you. I met him on the airplane when I came to America. He was born here."

"That's interesting." I glanced over toward Jack. "I better go rescue my date from Mr. Lott."

Bella's eyebrows raised. "Why rescue?"

"It's only a figure of speech. It means Jack might be bored."

"Mr. Lott is never boring."

It seemed pointless to explain. "I'll catch up with you later."

"You should try some of the shrimp," I said when I walked up to Jack. I grasped his hand.

"The woman is always right. Nice to meet you, Oliver." Jack shook Oliver's hand, removed his other hand from mine and placed it around my shoulders.

"Perfect timing."

"Really, how so?"

"You ready to go up to the hotel room?"

"Jack! You're like a boy with a brand new twenty-dollar bill burning a hole in his pocket."

"It's not a twenty-dollar bill burning a hole in my pocket."

I laughed. "Sorry, it'll just have to keep burning for a while. I still need to schmooze for an appropriate amount of time."

"Fine, but take this in case we get separated." Jack slid a hotel keycard into my hand. I tucked it into my small clutch.

"Thank you, but I'm sure we won't get separated again."

"You know I was serious when I said you have perfect timing."

I'm sure there would be plenty of people, including me, who'd argue that statement. "What was so perfect about it?"

"You rescued me. Oliver Lott was just about to go into more detail on how technology played a big part in his success. I'm all for technology, but he's sort of like Peter. There are only so many times you can get excited about hardware and software."

Inside, I snickered. "Oh, yeah, that technology stuff can be boring." What would Jack think if he knew I was a geek?

"Right." Jack put a few shrimp on a plate with a small scoop of cocktail sauce and handed it to me. Then he picked up his own plate and loaded it with shrimp, tiny puff pastries, olives, small blocks of expensive cheeses, and some bacon wrapped steak and mushroom bits.

"There is a regular dinner later, you know," I said.

"Yes, but it usually isn't as good as the appetizers. I suggest you load up. He dropped a couple of the bacon wrapped steak thingies onto my plate.

We walked around for a while, people watching, only stopping when Bella approached. "Hello again, Bella."

"Hello." She looked up at Jack and smiled.

I wanted to see Jack's reaction to the woman I'd dreamed of looking like when I was a child. I scooted closer to Bella so I could face him. "Jack, this is Bella. She's the Lott's nanny."

"Pleasure to meet you." Jack reached out and took Bella's hand.

He looked like some sort of prince charming, ready to kiss her hand, but then he stopped midway. His eyes flashed to a place somewhere behind me and I wished I hadn't changed my position.

"Pardon me, I need to run to the men's room. I'll be right back." Jack turned and walked away, heading in the opposite direction of whoever had been standing behind me.

When he was gone, I turned around to see who scared him off and I locked eyes with the brunette who'd been with Jack at the pet parade. She smiled and headed toward me.

"So, Bella. How long have you been dating the bartender?" I asked, desperate to keep Bella close to me so I wouldn't have to face the brunette by myself.

"We only go out fo—"

"Hi, I'm Jennifer Tanner." She extended her hand toward me.

"Aspen Moore. And this is Bella."

"I saw you were talking to Jack Arbon. He's a great guy."

"Do you work with him?"

"Oh no," she said and then let out an adorable laugh. "I'm his ex."

16

MY THOUGHTS were on Jennifer Whatever-Her-Name-Was the entire time I drove to the Lott's home. I swear I didn't run away. Bella had begged me to go and let Grand Ambition outside. It was a win-win. Bella got to spend more time with her boyfriend during his break and I got a chance to inspect the safe in the Lott's house.

Bella had promised to let Jack know I'd be back soon. It bothered me that he took off when he saw his ex. And ex what? Ex-girlfriend? Ex-wife? It had to be girlfriend because otherwise Jack or Peter would have mentioned her to me.

I pulled into the Lott's driveway and strolled to the door with pen, paper, and magnifying glass in hand. I planned to take down every bit of information I could find on the safe, so I'd be able to research the best way of getting inside it.

Grand Ambition was excited to see me and I tried the best I could to fend him off and save my dress, but I was no match for his crazy tongue and wet muzzle. "Down, Grand!"

He finally obeyed and I surveyed the wet spots on my dress. If they didn't dry without stains, I'd have to change.

"Come on boy." I walked to the back and opened the sliding door, releasing him to the freedom of the fenced yard. While he rummaged around the back yard, I'd spend my time trying to get into the safe.

I found my way upstairs to the three display alcoves in the hall and pushed the button behind the statue. The alcove opened exposing the safe. Without Bella obstructing my view as she had when she originally showed me the safe, I could see it sported a digital lock. I wrote down the specifics of the safe and eyeballed the measurements before pushing the button, sending the safe back into hiding. I started down the stairs until I heard the front door open and the Lott boys arguing.

Crap.

Bella told me the boys were out of town. If she knew they'd be home, why wouldn't she just phone them and have them let Grand Ambition outside?

"It's all your fault! If you weren't such a butthead they wouldn't have kicked us out of the resort!" one of them screamed.

That explains it.

"Screw you. Douche bag. I'm going downstairs to watch a movie."

"No. I'm going to watch a movie."

I heard Grand Ambition barking. The door to the basement slammed, the boys having ignored Grand Ambition's plea to come back inside. They were oblivious to the fact another human being was in their home.

Grand Ambition brushed by me when I opened the sliding door. He bee-lined it to the basement door and began scratching.

"Come on down, G. A.," one of the boys said, opening the basement door and shutting it after Grand Ambition headed down the stairs.

Unbelievable. The Lott's could be robbed blind and the twins would never know. I didn't bother saying hello to the boys. I simply slipped out the front door and into my car.

I drove to my apartment to pick up a change of clothes. I looked forward to spending an evening in the hotel with Jack. I knew I'd be restless thinking about Mrs. Rippetoe, but I hoped Jack would help keep my mind and other parts of my body occupied.

I took a detour to the hardware store and made a copy of the key Bella gave me. At some point I was going to have to go back and find out what was inside the safe.

I'd been gone quite a long time and hoped Jack wasn't upset that I'd missed the dinner. The band should be playing by now and the party in full swing. I pulled in front of the hotel and let the valet take my car. I entered the hotel lobby and ran to catch the elevator, my overnight bag banged against my side.

The elevator bell dinged and the doors opened when I reached the ninth floor. I stepped out and took a right toward the room. I planned to drop my overnight bag off, freshen up a bit, and then head downstairs to the party and Jack. Maybe we could skip the rest of the event and come back to the room.

The light turned green when I slid the key card into the slot. For a second, I thought I heard Jack talking to someone. I entered the room and set my bag down by the closet. When a woman giggled, I froze. I wanted to see who was there, but then again, I didn't. The thought of walking out into the open and looking at the bed petrified me. The memories of my ex-fiancé in bed with my intended maid of honor flared up. My heart gasped.

If I didn't see who was in the hotel room with Jack, I'd always wonder. I held my breath and approached the corner easing out just enough to catch site of Jack lying back on the bed with his ex and her dog. *Her dog?*

I stepped back, relieved they hadn't been naked. But still, it didn't matter. Dog or no dog, Jack was in a hotel room, lying in the bed with his ex.

"Woof."

"Quiet Beasley!" Jack commanded.

I held my breath. *Please don't get up. Please.* I backed up to the hotel door, turned the handle and let myself out.

———

Damn it. Stupid. Stupid. Stupid. I ignored Jack's phone call. I still couldn't believe I'd left my overnight bag sitting on the hotel room floor last night. My plan was to never speak to Jack again, but if I wanted my bag back that plan needed to change.

"Get out of my way!" I screamed at the car in front of me.

I was angry at Jack for his thoughtlessness, but even more angry at myself. I didn't get inside the Lott's safe, didn't connect with any rich person that might lead me to the diamond if it turned out not to be in the Lott's safe, and I didn't spend any time searching for Mrs. Rippetoe.

Time was running out. Monday was the kidnapper's deadline. Either I snatched the blue diamond so they'd set her free or I rescued her. Both seemed impossible, but I had no choice. If I went to the police it almost guaranteed she wouldn't be making lemonade for me this summer or ever again. Besides wasting an entire evening, I had come close to allowing myself to spend an entire Sunday morning wrapped in Jack's arms. In reality, finding Jack with his ex had been a good thing. My priorities were now straight.

I parked in front of my office and went inside to wait for Stephanie. She was coming in on her day off so I could prepare her to run my business for the next couple of days without me. I was going to put everything into saving Mrs. Rippetoe and there'd be no time to spare.

"Peter?" I positioned the phone so it covered my ear.

"By the tone of your voice I can tell you know you did something wrong."

"I'm sorry. It's...well, I screwed up. I was supposed to go out with Jack last night and then I asked you to help me and I was going to cancel with Jack, then Oliver Lott called—"

"Skip it all."

"What?" I asked, not understanding why he sounded so angry.

"Just skip all the excuses. The fact is you left me hanging."

After all these months, I finally discovered a little bit of jerk inside Peter. "Oh, like you kept me hanging when you ran off to fawn all over Madeline and propose to her?"

I waited for his reply. "Hello?"

Nothing.

"Hello? Peter, are you there?" I looked at my cell phone and saw the call had ended. I called him back.

"Did you just hang up on me?" I asked before he said anything.

"Yes, because you were out of line. I know you're upset that I'm with Madeline. I feel it every time her name is mentioned."

"I'm sorry."

"No, Aspen. I'm sorry. I am. I'm sorry I couldn't fall for you the night you kissed me. Things might have turned out differently had Madeline not been in my life. Maybe that's why I find myself flirting with you and getting upset when you're with Jack. I'm not sure what our friendship is about, but I do know it's not fair to you."

Peter's words permeated the air, surrounding me, making it difficult to breathe. He finally spoke the truth. The constant anticipation of our flirtatious friendship transforming into a passionate long term relationship kept me bound to Peter in an unhealthy way. I wiped the tears from my cheeks, keeping silent so Peter wouldn't know I was crying. "What now?"

"What do you mean?"

"It sounds like you're breaking up our friendship."

The length of silence made me check my phone to see if he'd hung up on me again. "You are, aren't you?"

"I care about you and I don't want to end our friendship. This is hard for me too. I find myself attracted to you when I shouldn't be. I'm a faithful man and have always been one."

Silence again, but this time from me. I couldn't talk. All I could do was think about Peter saying he was attracted to me. My heart jumped up and down, high fiving itself. Peter was attracted to me and he cared for me. "I don't know what to say."

"There is nothing to say," Peter said.

"So, are we ending our friendship?"

"Why do you keep asking me that?"

"Because you said you are attracted to me, but you are faithful. You are upset I'm with Jack, but you don't want to be with me. What are we supposed to do?"

"Do you want to remain friends?"

The warning light in my brain flashed. I wasn't one to always make the healthiest choices. Regular soda or diet? Regular. Watch TV or exercise? TV. Alone and strong or caught in a dysfunctional relationship where the passion would never be realized? "Of course I do."

"Then, let's not do anything. Let's just promise one another we won't leave each other hanging. I'll work on easing up on the Jack front, if you'll ease up on the Madeline front. Does that work for you?"

"Yes, but what about the flirting?"

"We'll both need to work on it. If either of us gets too uncomfortable we let the other one know. Sound like a deal?"

"Sure." My answer lacked enthusiasm.

"You sure, you're sure?"

"You're my friend, Peter. In fact, you're my best friend." The words I spoke were the truth. And I just didn't have it in me to let that go.

"So, let's do what best friends do and find our kidnapped landlady."

"Or steal a blue diamond," I said.

"There is a limit you know."

"But what else are we going to do? We have no idea where she...Can I call you right back?" I looked out the office window as a car pulled to the curb.

"Sure."

I hung up, dabbed my eyes with a tissue and went to the front of the store. I watched as Stephanie made out with a guy in the front seat of the car. I assumed it was Roberto. She got out, walked toward the office, paused and turned back. When she did, Roberto turned to look at her. That's when I felt my knees buckle. I realized I'd never seen

Roberto's face before and unless he had a twin, Roberto had been the one tending bar at the Four Seasons last night.

At first, I ached for Stephanie because Bella claimed the bartender was her boyfriend. If Roberto really was a two-timer, Stephanie would be devastated. But then I stopped thinking about Stephanie and listened to what my brain was saying. *Who is Roberto?*

"I'm in looooooove," Stephanie sang as she entered the door.

I almost burst into tears. Partly for Stephanie and partly for me and my situation with Peter and Jack. In a way I guess I'd finally found something in common with Stephanie. We both had feelings for men who possessed feelings for someone else.

There was no reason to tell Stephanie about Roberto and Bella. I needed to to be sure about the situation before I risked taking a sledge hammer to Stephanie's heart. "I noticed he brought you to work today. Did you stay over his place last night?"

"No. He had to work."

"Work at night? I thought he did computer stuff or something, oh, right, you said he gambled for a living."

"Yeah. He played poker at the casino downtown."

"It's too bad you couldn't go with him."

"I would've but he says he gets nervous when he's being watched."

I bet he did. "Thanks for coming in today. You know, Roberto could have waited. We shouldn't be too long."

"That's okay. He's going to help a friend clean up a motorhome their getting ready to sell. I asked him about it in case you were interested for the doctor."

I raised my eyebrows and my lips parted. Stephanie had taken initiative. Maybe there was hope. "I think the doctor is interested in the one I looked at yesterday. But it never hurts to have a plan B. What kind is it and how big?"

"I think he said it was a FreeRoader and thirty-two or thirty-four feet. He said it's really nice, but needed a little cleaning. There's a place near the storage lot in Fenton where they can wash it. It's a little cold, that's why I was glad to come in today. I didn't want to be freezing my hiney off watching him wash an RV. As soon as you think we're close to being finished here, I need to call him so he can come get me. I'm making him dinner tonight."

"So are you guys getting serious?"

"We're in love! Of course we're serious. Can you keep a secret?"

If I hadn't known she was serious, I would have burst out laughing. Stephanie was the worst at keeping secrets. "Yes."

"I overheard him talking about diamonds. I think he's going to propose!"

17

I ACTED EXCITED for Stephanie and when she wasn't looking I texted Peter that our hunt was on. A few minutes later Peter was in front of the store in his Citation.

"Sorry, Steph. Peter and I have an errand to run for our landlady," I said, heading out the door before she could say anything.

I climbed into Peter's car.

"This sounds like another one of your wild moose chases," Peter said, stepping on the gas.

"It's wild goose chase and no, it isn't."

"In your case, things always seem bigger, more complicated. So I'd say wild moose chase is spot on."

Peter was more right than wrong. I never intended for things to get so out of control. I should have gone to the police when Mrs. Rippetoe first disappeared, but I didn't and now it seemed too late. I'd made some poor decisions and now it was my responsibility to make sure things turned out right. I needed to investigate every lead I had.

"Am I crazy for thinking Roberto's mention of diamonds and having access to the RV are related?" I realized what I asked the minute I finished talking.

Peter briefly took his eyes off the road and looked at me. "Yes. You are definitely crazy."

"I'm serious."

"Me too. Maybe Roberto really is going to ask Stephanie to marry him."

"Really?"

"Yeah, you're right. It'll take someone special to commit to a lifetime with wild Stephanie."

"So? Do you think all of this is a coincidence?"

"Maybe. Maybe not."

"And you call yourself a PI?"

"It's a Security and surveillance company, not a private investigation company. Remember?"

"But you've done investigations, right? What is it, five? Ten?"

"It's irrelevant. Any smart investigator would make sure they keep all lanes of investigation open until there's enough evidence to close one or proceed down another path full speed ahead. We have neither of those situations here."

"Are you saying I'm not a good investigator? I'm a really good investigator!"

"You're a personal concierge."

"There, turn left," I said, pointing to the street sign scaled for one of Thomas Brackford's model trains.

Peter made a quick left. "You sure this is right?"

"What? Now I'm not even good at giving directions? Of course I'm sure. It's mapped on my phone." I turned up the volume.

"Your destination is ahead two miles," the sexy navigation lady said.

Peter's hands tightened around the steering wheel. "Who would take their RV down this crappy road?"

"Roberto's friend."

The road was peppered with dips and bumps, dirt and gravel. The dust kicked up as if it hadn't rained in years.

"Glad I brought the Dumpster," Peter said referring to his Chevrolet Citation.

The car had probably been decent back in the eighties. Now he used it for surveillance, when he wasn't in a ritzy neighborhood. For some unknown reason, his neatness in all other aspects of his life hadn't trickled down to the Citation. The car was full of trash. The last time I'd ridden in it, I'd complained about the filth the entire time and called it a dumpster. Instead of cleaning it up, he named it.

"Slow down!" I shouted.

Peter slammed on the brakes. "What is it? Is there something in the road?"

"No."

"Why'd the hell you yell?"

"You were going too fast. What if Roberto hasn't left to go get Stephanie? How are we supposed to arrive incognito when your sending out smoke signals?"

"Jesus, Aspen. You scared the hell out of me. I thought I was going to hit something." Peter clenched his hand to his chest, like he was going to keel over.

"Sorry."

"Your destination is ahead on the right," the phone lady said.

I turned off the navigation. "There isn't much around here. How are we going to do this?"

Peter pointed off to the right. "I think I should let you off here. You can hide out in those trees."

There'd been no reason to point to a specific place because there was nothing but trees, and a little too thick and brushy for my taste. "I don't think so. What happens if someone carjacks you and then I'm left out here in the woods. I'm going with you."

"Oh, I see you're only worried about yourself." Peter winked.

I stiffened up.

"I'm sorry," Peter said, "I shouldn't have winked."

"No, that's okay. It's habit. I know."

"You can't go with me. Someone needs to stay with the car. I have one more idea, but I don't think you're going to like it."

"I know and I don't like it, but I'll do it. Pull over and I'll climb into the back seat floor board."

"Actually, I was going to suggest you get in the trunk."

I sat back waiting for him to laugh.

"You're serious. Unbelievable!"

"You can't blame me for wanting to hide you. Your shirt's bright red and highlighting the girls. Not exactly what I would call camouflage."

"The girls? Did you just call my breasts, the girls?"

"Sorry. All I'm trying to say is, in that shirt, you are hard not to notice."

My large breasts had always felt like an asset, except where my back was concerned. But, at the moment Peter had labeled them a hindrance. I expertly maneuvered a button into the buttonhole to hide more of my cleavage. "Apology accepted. But, I'm still not getting into the trunk."

"Fine. You can hang out in the back seat in case Roberto is still here. If he isn't, I'll come get you."

While Peter walked toward the storage grounds, I undid my seatbelt and began my climb over the seat and into the back. "This is disgusting!" A pile of garbage comprised of dirty socks, empty chip bags, one of his wigs he used when he was undercover, and a collection of crumbs, covered the seat. I grit my teeth, wiped it off, and plopped onto the back seat.

"Hey, it's not that bad."

"Then you get back here."

"No can do." Peter pulled onto the storage grounds and got out of the car.

I laid in the back praying a bug didn't crawl up my pants. Time ticked away. I wanted to ease up from the back seat and check out the scene, but I didn't want to endanger Peter. I was sort of fond of the guy.

My fondness for Peter gave way to thoughts about Jack. Why would he have his ex-girlfriend up to his hotel room? If Bella specifically told him I'd left the charity event with no plans to return, then it was obvious why What's-Her-Name had been in the room. But, if Bella had told him the truth, why would he be so stupid to invite her up to his room?

I heard Peter open the driver's door and I sat up. "Can I come out and help you look now?"

"No. RV's not here. Hasn't been here for a few weeks."

"Hmm. Wonder why Roberto told Stephanie he was coming here?"

"Did she say he was coming here?"

I thought for a second. "No. No, she didn't. I assumed because she said this was where it was stored."

"The guy says he thinks they're at a park somewhere in Illinois, not too far. Somewhere south of Cahokia."

"Now that makes sense. That wouldn't be too far from East St. louis. Are we heading that way?"

"Sure. See if you can find the location with your phone."

I brought up Google, searched and found two parks in the Cahokia area. I entered one of the addresses into Waze.

We turned off the gravel road onto the paved road and the car suddenly seemed quiet.

"So, what are we going to do when we get there? You aren't going to make me get in that dirty ass back seat again, are you?"

Peter laughed.

"Not funny. It's disgusting! How can you leave it like that?"

"Oh. Let's not talk about that. Let's talk about Jack."

I knew I was sporting the deer in the headlights look. "Why?"

"I wasn't going to say anything, but since we had our, uh, conversation earlier, seems we ought to talk about the elephant in the hotel room."

"Oh God! What did he say happened? It wasn't a damn elephant it was an ex-girlfriend! And I saw him with her at the pet parade too. So she seems more current than ex."

Peter had a little smirk on his face.

"What's so amusing about that?" I asked, fighting the urge to grab the dirty socks from the back and wipe the grin off his face.

"What else did you see at the pet parade and in the hotel room?"

I thought for a few minutes. "A dog?"

"Ding, ding. ding. Correct. That's their dog. They got the animal when they were together and when they split they agreed on joint custody. Personally, I'd have given up my parental rights."

"One day I'll make a dog lover out of you."

"Pass."

"Why didn't he tell me about the dog?"

"I'm guessing because it would have required him to tell you about Jennifer."

"So what. It's not like I thought I was the first person he ever dated."

"Right. But they weren't just dating, they were engaged."

All sorts of questions popped into my head. Why had they broken up? Was it him? Her? But then one niggling question demanded to be asked. "Why didn't you tell me he had been engaged before?"

I knew it wasn't Peter's responsibility, but I viewed him as my best friend. And a best friend would have passed along that kind of news.

"I thought about telling you, but I figured Jack would tell you when the time was right. I guess the right time hadn't arrived."

"I wish you would have told me. Not that it matters, but the dynamics definitely change. A broken engagement comes with a lot more baggage than a simple ex-girlfriend."

Jack was in the same situation. I hadn't told him about my broken engagement and I never would. My baggage was covered by an invisibility cloak and Jack would have to battle my baggage without even knowing exactly what he was fighting.

Peter looked me in the eyes, his own eyes relaxed and soft. "Sorry," Peter said. The single word was layered with emotion. The easiest type of apology to accept.

"Not your fault. I do appreciate you telling me now. I didn't know why he was attentive one minute and scarce the next. Makes a little more sense now. Oh. Sorry. Are you okay talking about Jack?"

"Actually, I think it would be good for us to talk not only about Jack, but Madeline too. If we keep them in the forefront of our own relationship, then we are less likely to cross the line."

What kind of incentive was that? I never wanted to talk about either of them if it would get Peter to cross the line. *Not true.* My brain was right. I didn't want Peter to become a cheater and neither did I.

"You're right. So, let's talk about Madeline," I said, forcing a lighthearted chirpy sound to accompany my words.

"Boy, words can't get any more forced than those."

Damn. "You know, fake it till you make it. The more we talk about her the easier things will be for me in the long run. So have you talked to her since you returned?"

"No. I guess she's still filming."

"What are you going to do? I mean, if she says yes? Where are you going to live?"

"You have doubts she'll say yes?" Peter asked.

"Do you?"

"No. Not really. Getting married was all she ever wanted. I'm not worried about that, but I am worried about our living arrangements. I don't want to be away from her so much, but relocating my business is going to be tough. Like starting over."

"Why don't you open a second location?"

"That might work. I could fly back and forth at the beginning and then after the second location becomes more profitable I could just fly out here a few times a year or whenever Victor needed me. Thanks for the idea."

I wished I could take the idea back. The thought of seeing Peter only a few times a year made me incredibly sad. I tried to keep a smile on my face. "You're welcome, but you need to promise to come back at least four times a year. You're my best friend."

"Don't you worry. We'll keep in touch. And besides, by that time Jack and you will be so involved you won't even notice I'm gone."

"Not sure what makes you think that."

"Despite what I've said about Jack. You need to give him a chance. I know he seems all playa like, but his insides are sort of gooey, like chocolate chip cookie dough."

"Hmm. I've only ever had the frozen kind and it's always hard as a rock."

"Very funny. You know what I'm trying to say. Even though I warned you against getting too involved, he's a decent guy at heart. I'm afraid some of my warnings were coming from a selfish place and that isn't fair to you. Let him in. I think you'll be surprised."

"Who are you? Dr. Phil?"

"I'm just saying."

———

It was Sunday and for many that was a day of rest, but there was no time to waste. I had only today to find Mrs. Rippetoe or the diamond.

PJ whined.

"I know buddy. I promise things are going to be a lot better in a few days and we're going to spend a lot more time together." The words flowed from my mouth, but my brain didn't believe a single one.

PJ whined again.

"Look PJ, if you're a good boy, I'll take you to the P. A. R. K. in a few days." If I spoke the word, the spaz inside PJ would be unleashed and he would not be ignored.

When Mr. P barked, I realized I'd forgotten to take them out. I grabbed the leads off the table. PJ twirled, Mr. P bounced up and down, and Sassy sat like a lady barking her muzzle off. I was exhausted by the time I got the leads clipped on to their respective collars. I hustled all of us outside and breathed in the cool air.

While I walked the dogs, I decided to heed Peter's advice and listen to Jack's messages. Even though he'd called me five times, my voicemail only showed two messages.

"Aspen, it's Jack. I know you're upset and I know it seems like I'm always asking you to let me explain. But seriously, you need to let me explain. Call me. Please."

I deleted it and listened to the next one. "It's Jack again. It's important you call me. It's about Mr. Quetzalcoatl."

The one message I couldn't ignore. If he was using it as an excuse to get me to call or not, it didn't matter. Jack was the only one getting inside the jail and if Mr. Q. needed something I had to help. The question was whether or not it had to be right away.

"Let's go people," I said, gently yanking the leads to get the attention of the three musketeers.

I tossed a snack on the floor for each of them and sat down on my couch. I was tired and I was afraid. I scooched down and rested my head on the throw pillow.

Ringing. Phone. "Hello?" I said. The man asked for Mrs. Rippetoe. I glanced at PJ sitting in the corner like an angel. "Who's calling?" The man said he was her son. He was worried. He hadn't heard from her. I looked at PJ again. Something was wrong. He was behaving. "Did you say you were going to call the police?" I said to the man, trying to hide the panic in my voice. I didn't hear his answer because PJ was floating in the air, tiny angel wings behind him. He floated toward me...

"Arrrumph. Pffft." I brushed PJ's fur off my face as I shot up off the couch. "PJ!"

I tried shaking off my dream, but there was truth in it and it wasn't the part about PJ being an angel. At some point Mrs. Rippetoe's son would call I didn't know what I would tell him. I had to get her back. I'd really made a mess of things. I wasn't sure what else I could do which meant it was time to reach out to Marshal Cutter.

I walked over to the counter to get Cutter's card out of my purse. It wasn't in the main section of my bag, so I unzipped the small pocket. It contained Cutter's card and the copy of the Lott's key. I tossed Cutter's card back into my purse, put the key in my pocket and walked out door.

18

IT WAS DARK as I sat in my Jeep outside the Stanley apartment complex located less than a mile from the Lott's house. I turned Cutter's card over and over with my fingers. Contemplating. Considering. One last attempt, that's all. If I failed I'd call Cutter.

I pulled my hood over my head, loaded my screwdriver, mallet, cell phone and the key to the Lott's house into the front pocket of my sweatshirt. I'd forgotten my pepper spray so I tucked the car key between my fingers like a weapon, ready to key somebody's eye out if they tried to attack me.

I walked with my back to the traffic, staying as far away from the edge of the road as possible. The darkness was my shining star. It kept me hidden. It was beautiful and scary at the same time. A slight chill hit me and the hairs on my neck jumped to attention. I turned around. No one was following me. A pizza delivery person drove by, followed by a couple of motorcycles and then it was dark again.

My heart beat in double time. Doubt crept in. What kind of idiot does something like this alone? I took slow deep breaths and reminded myself that I was alone because I was about to commit a felony. I couldn't ask anyone to come with me because I wouldn't risk taking down anyone but myself.

I kept my head down, the lights in the Lott's neighborhood were a little too bright. As I approached the Lott's driveway, a motorcycle passed by the house. Instinctively, I turned my head and caught sight of a motorcycle like the one Harry Corbitt rode. I ran up the driveway, my heart hammering with every breath causing me to gasp. I had hoped to case the place first to make sure that Bella and the family were actually gone. Too late for that. I jammed the key into the lock and wrestled with the handle. The door finally opened and I locked it behind me. Maybe I was wrong. Maybe my imagination was getting the best of me. Harry wasn't the only person in the world who rode a black Harley Davidson. I was being paranoid.

I pulled the front window curtain aside to see if the motorcycle was still around and spotted Harry, barely visible, tucked behind some bushes down the street. *Oh god. Oh no. This is it.* I knew Harry was up to something from the very first time he contacted me. What if tonight was the night?

What the hell was I going to do? I pulled my hood off. Grand Ambition barked from his space down in the basement. *Crap.* That meant Bella didn't go with the family. The place was dark so she must be out, but that meant I had a limited amount of time to see what was inside the safe.

There wasn't time to worry about Grand Ambition or Harry Corbitt or Bella coming home. The diamond was my only focus. Mrs. Rippetoe's life depended on it. I ran up the stairs. I pushed the button behind the statue and opened the alcove. My eyes focused on something I hadn't paid attention to before – drywall. A sense of doom fell over me. The instructions I'd found on the Internet covered breaking into a digital safe with a few tools. But, I'd have to remove the surrounding drywall. It seemed silly, but the thought of damaging the Lott's property bothered me.

I positioned the flathead screwdriver against the wall and brought the mallet back in order to get as much forward motion as Newton would allow. Cocked and ready to swing, I heard a car pull into the driveway. *Bella.* I put the tools back in the pocket of my sweatshirt and ran into one of the twins' rooms to look out the window. One of the twin's Range Rover's was in the driveway and it hadn't been there when I broke in. I ran back into the hallway, pushed the button to hide the safe, and hustled myself into the Master bedroom. It's the one place I knew the twins would avoid.

My eyes took their time adjusting to the dark. Someone was talking, though it was more a mumble. The voice kept getting louder until I realized they were heading in my direction.

I dove underneath the bed, crawling to the far side and thanking God it was king size. I wriggled a tiny bit trying to get comfortable, but stopped all movement when I recognized Oliver Lott's voice. I could hear his voice, a one-sided conversation, so I assumed he was on the phone.

"I'm sorry I couldn't stay too, but my meeting tomorrow morning is important. No. Bella's not back. I told you she was planning on coming back in the morning. Yes. I'll remember to take Grand Ambition out. Yes. Me too."

Oliver stopped talking and I assumed he'd finished his call. *Terrible.* I was stuck unless I figured out how to distract him or until he fell asleep. On the up side, the entire Lott family could have walked through the door. Then I would have died of dehydration waiting for them all to leave the house at the same time.

I heard Oliver talking again. "Hi Babe, yes, I'm home. They all stayed. She thinks I have a meeting tomorrow so we'll have the house to ourselves this evening. I'll see you soon."

No. I needed Oliver to go to bed. I needed to hear him snoring so I could make my escape. But his phone call made it clear I'd be hearing a totally different sound.

I checked the service bars on my phone. The glow from the phone lit up the area beneath the bed. I tucked it under my shirt while I considered who I was going to text to help me escape. Cutter was out, for the obvious reason. Not Jack because although I planned to patch things up with him, doing so by asking him to rescue me from a botched B & E was probably not a good idea. Peter would do it, but I'd have to pay by responding to all his questions. Plus, I wasn't going to risk getting him in trouble. Stephanie could do it. She'd be loud enough to distract Oliver and men seemed to love her. I pulled the phone out, sent a quick text and put it on vibrate before tucking it back under my sweatshirt.

Oliver hadn't said a word since the last call and it worried me. Without his voice I couldn't keep track of his location. I imagined him downstairs in the kitchen pouring himself some wine, dimming the lights, and queuing the mood music. My mind wandered. Ten minutes had passed since I texted Stephanie. I checked my phone. She hadn't replied yet and Oliver's guest would be arriving soon.

My mind trekked down the gloomy side. If I didn't get someone to help get me out of here, I'd have to attempt to escape all by myself. I saw the dominoes falling, Oliver would catch me, then he'd fire me, and after that he'd have me arrested. I'd no longer be able to save Mrs. Rippetoe, and I'd have to call Cutter. Then, the final domino, the one that would mean it's over, would fall. I'd be relocated and left to start all over again.

I didn't hear Oliver and figured it was safe to look on my phone again to find another rescuer. And there it was, the one person who could get here quickly. I'd officially lost whatever was left of my mind, the minute I selected Harry Corbitt's name and sent the text: CAN YOU CREATE A DIVERSION?

A few minutes passed with no response. *Crap.* I never thought I'd be upset that Harry wasn't around. Then, the doorbell rang.

Grand Ambition barked. I heard the mumbling of two loud voices and then the sound of the front door slamming. *Was Oliver gone?* I didn't know what to do. My phone vibrated. The text message from Harry was like a message from heaven: GET OUT NOW. I didn't hesitate. I was sure I only had minutes. I made sure all my tools were in my pocket, scooted out from under the bed and made my way down the stairs.

Stepping outside into the back yard, the cold air shocked me. I closed the sliding glass door and froze at the sound of a motorcycle throttling. Despite the cold, I was sweating, sweating fear. What if Harry had attacked Oliver and was waiting for me? I ran behind the garage and crossed into the neighbor's yard. I took cover behind a bush, my eyes focused on the back of the Lott's house.

My body shivered. The silence left me feeling exposed. With no noises, I couldn't figure out where Oliver or Harry were located. I wouldn't leave until I knew it was safe to make the trip back to my car.

———

Mulch filaments lay scattered across my pillow. Somehow, even with all the adrenaline, I'd fallen asleep behind the bush last night as I waited for the right time to flee. I didn't get home until almost four o'clock in the morning. I'd walked the dogs, torn off my clothes and jumped into bed.

I brushed the filaments onto the floor and went into the bathroom. Indentations made by the mulch covered my cheeks and I smelled outdoorsy, but not the pleasant pine tree sort of smell. It was more like roadkill.

I scooped last night's smelly clothes up off the floor and put them on because the dogs were circling my feet and whining. The four of us made our way down the stairs and out the back of the building so I wouldn't run in to anyone. On our way back inside, I knocked on Mrs. Rippetoe's door to see if a miracle had happened.

"She's not there."

I swung around to face Peter standing in his doorway. "I know."

"You look tired. No, actually you look worn out. Were you up late or something?"

"Not too late."

"Hah. I heard you come in around four o'clock."

"Then why'd you ask me?"

"Because you appeared to be up to something. If you lied, then it would verify my assumption."

"Maybe I was at Jack's place."

"Not looking like that and definitely not smelling like that. Tell me the truth. I'm not kidding when I say you look worn out. Tell me the truth and I can help you."

229

"The truth is, it's Monday. We haven't found Mrs. Rippetoe and I don't have a blue diamond to give to the kidnappers."

"Where were you last night?"

"If I tell you, I don't want you to jump on me. Okay?"

"I promise."

"Hold up your hand boy scout style while you say it and maybe I'll believe you."

Peter held up his hand and I was relieved to see more than one finger.

"I went to steal the diamond, but I got trapped. Took me a while to get out."

"Where's the diamond?"

"At one of my clients' homes. I really don't want to talk about the failure any more. Look, as much as I don't want to, I have to go get ready. Can we talk later?"

"You know you can't go around avoiding things much longer. You're going to have to call the police. If you don't, I'm going to do it."

"Can you wait until the kidnappers contact me again?"

"No. By then it will be too late. I should have called them from the start."

"Oh, and risk getting her killed before we had a chance to save her?"

"I've got a few things to take care first, but then I'm making the call. You've got two hours."

"Two hours? It's not enough time to do anything." I freaked out. This was crazy.

"That's enough time for me to figure out how to best approach telling the police about our obvious lack of judgment in this situation. We should have called them from the start..." Peter held up his phone, "Take it or leave it."

Damn him. I walked out the door and stomped up the stairs. Mad. I stomped when I went into the kitchen to fill up the dog bowls. And I stomped even harder making my way to the bedroom. I wanted Peter to hear my defiance, but mostly I wanted to release the anger that boiled inside. The anger at myself for letting things get out of control.

I took a short, hot shower. My body relaxed and then my mind. My thoughts were mixed up and I needed to pluck them out one by one, address them in some sort of order so I could figure out what was happening and where they belonged.

Roberto. He was definitely up to something. I needed to talk to Mrs. Paddy and Mr. Q to see if they were eventually able to discover whether something was missing from their homes. Then I'd talk to Stephanie and Bella. If I could rule out Roberto's involvement in the kidnapping, then I could focus on other possible suspects.

I continued to process my thoughts while I got ready to go to Mrs. Paddy's house. Monday was Junior's golf day and the only time I could guarantee he wouldn't be at her house so I could talk with Mrs. Paddy alone. I'd use the drive time to decide if there was anything I could do in less than two hours to find Mrs. Rippetoe.

———

I stopped at the front desk in Mrs. Paddy's building. "Hi Edward. Can you let Mrs. Paddy know I'm here and on my way up?"

"Sure thing, but I think she has a real estate agent up there."

"Thanks." I walked toward the elevators, hopped on when the door opened, and pushed the 'P' button for the penthouse.

"Oh, and Junior's up there too." Edward said as the doors were closing. I hit the open-door button but it was too late. I headed for the top floor on what felt like an express elevator.

I couldn't run away anyhow because Mrs. Paddy knew I was on my way up. Maybe it was a good thing. I no longer believed Junior was incapable of causing harm to his grandmother. It was time he and I had a talk.

"This isn't a good time," Junior said when he pulled the door open.

"Your grandmother wanted me to come up. I'll only be a few minutes."

"I never heard the phone ring."

"Edward called up. If you don't believe me call the front desk."

"Fine, come in, but don't stay too long. She's old and needs her rest."

"I won't, but first, did they ever find out who broke in to your grandmother's place?"

"Uh. No."

"Isn't that weird how the security camera wasn't working? You think Edward was involved?"

"I don't know."

"You don't think somebody you know did this, do you? Maybe somebody in a bind needing money or something?"

"No. And besides, nothing was taken."

I walked into the parlor. "Where is she?"

"I'm telling you, she's old. She's in her bedroom."

I marched down the hall, with Junior on my tail. "Do you happen to know a guy named Roberto who tends bar?"

Junior stopped. "What's with all the questions?"

"Oh nothing. Just making conversation." I peeked into the library and saw an attractive young woman fiddling with some folders, appearing to be busy.

"I'm not in the mood, really."

"But, do you know Roberto?"

"I said I don't want to have a conversation with you."

I wasn't sure if he didn't want to admit to knowing Roberto or if he truly didn't want to have a conversation with me. "Sorry."

"Remember. Only a few minutes."

I ignored his words and took a right into Mrs. Paddy's room. "How are you Mrs. Paddy?"

"I'm okay. I guess." She glanced past my shoulder.

I turned around. Junior had planted himself in the doorway. I walked over and began to close the door. "Excuse me."

Junior put his arm out. "You don't need to close it."

"I'm sorry, but your Grandmother and I need privacy to discuss some woman stuff. Isn't that right, Mrs. Paddy."

"Yes. Junior, please give us some privacy."

"Five minutes." Junior removed his arm and walked back down the hall.

I closed the door and locked it. "So, Mrs. Paddy, I was surprised that you wanted to move into an assisted care place."

"What? I didn't raise my children here, but I've lived here a long time. It's my home and I'm going to die here."

"Oh. I thought the young woman in your library was a real estate agent."

"No. That's Junior's girlfriend."

She was way too attractive for Junior. That young woman was a ten and Junior, well, he was closer to a three.

Ah, perhaps that's why he's wanting to discard his grandmother. If Junior got his hands on Mrs. Paddy's money, he'd skyrocket to at least an eight, maybe even a nine.

I didn't want to alarm Mrs. Paddy by telling her about Junior's plan, but I had to at least drop a hint about looking into her affairs after I finished asking her a few questions.

"Mrs. Paddy. I was wondering about the break-in here the other day. Did you ever get a chance to go back and look through everything to see if something was missing?"

"Yes, and I found something. My husband's Rolex watch. I stored the watch in a box in my dresser drawer. It was old, don't know why anyone would take that when I had a perfectly beautiful Chinese vase on the dresser worth almost a quarter of a million dollars."

I gasped. I couldn't help it. "Two hundred and fifty thousand?"

"Yes. But don't tell anyone. Only a collector would be aware of its value, to anyone else it looks like something I won on eBay."

"You buy items on eBay?"

"Of course I do. Edward's helped me buy a few things on there. Auctions are very exciting."

Hmmm. Edward. I hadn't considered him a suspect in the break-in, but maybe he'd been looking for a few things to sell on his own.

"I should go. Junior didn't want me to wear you out. But I...I...here's the thing...I, uh—"

"Just say it!"

I jumped. "Mrs. Paddy, you scared the crap out of me."

"Crap's not a nice word for a lady to be saying."

Crap.

"I'm sorry, but I wasn't expecting you to yell out like that."

"If you have something to say to me then you need to stop skittering in and out of your mind trying to find the words. You just need to say it."

"Okay. I think you should make sure you have a trust or something."

"My affairs are my affairs. But, if you think you are so smart, I already have a trust and a power of attorney. So if I turn senile like you always think I am, Junior will be able to take care of things."

Double Crap.

"Mrs. Paddy. I think you need to watch Junior. That young lady in your library is a real estate agent."

"Well, a real estate agent is a fine career."

"Mrs. Paddy, Junior's going to put your place up for sale and stick you in a home!"

"What's going on in there?" Junior banged on the door.

Mrs. Paddy looked me in the eyes, "What's wrong with you today?"

"Open up." Junior banged even harder on the door.

"We're almost finished," I said.

I leaned in close to Mrs. Paddy. "I'm begging you Mrs. Paddy. Ask Edward about the real estate agent. Then call your attorney."

"I think you worry too much."

"Humor me Mrs. Paddy, please? If you aren't able to use your regular phone, call me on this and don't tell Junior you have it." I gave her one of my older pay-as-you-go phones that still had some time left on it.

"I'll humor you if you agree to go see a doctor about your paranoia."

"If it turns out to be nothing, I'll take you with me to my appointment."

Junior banged on the door again. Mrs. Paddy shoved the phone inside the pillowcase on her bed.

I mouthed "Thank You," as I unlocked and opened the door.

"You need to leave now. Look how exhausted my grandmother is," Junior mumbled as he grasped my arm.

"Let me go."

I looked back at Mrs. Paddy and saw her place her hand on the pillow next to her where she had stashed the phone.

"Goodbye, Mrs. Paddy."

I pulled my arm from Junior's grasp. "I can find my own way out."

The front door seemed far away. Junior followed me. I reached for the handle and opened the door. Junior pushed it shut with his hand.

"I told you before. Your services are no longer needed."

I pushed Junior. "You don't want to mess with me."

"Bitch."

"Your grandmother would be appalled at that kind of language." I yanked the door open and shut it firmly behind me.

Having escaped Junior, I rode the elevator down and stopped by the front desk to talk with Edward.

"Hi, Edward."

"Hey. Did you find out how much they're going to list her penthouse for?"

"No, why? You thinking about moving up?"

"Ha. I wish. I can barely make my car payments."

"Is that why you help Mrs. Paddy with the eBay stuff?"

"Sort of. Mostly I help her buy things and I don't get anything for that. When she sells something, I get a percentage."

"She's been selling things on eBay too?"

"Yeah. Junior always handles the sales."

That was all I needed to hear. Mrs. Paddy never said a thing about selling her items on eBay. It had to be all Junior's doing. It appeared Edward was an innocent bystander.

"Hey. What's your seller id? I wouldn't mind bidding on some of that stuff."

"Sure. It's MrEdSellsStuff"

I entered the information into my phone.

"How much money have you been making?"

"I'm not sure I should be discussing this with you."

Maybe Edward's toe was dipped in the dark side of the pond after all. "What's it matter? Everything's above board, isn't it?"

"Wh-wh-why of course!"

Edwards stuttering was the crack in the door I'd been looking for. "You know, if you're selling Mrs. Paddy's stuff and she doesn't know about it, you could get in a lot of trouble."

"I'm only s-s-s-selling what Junior asks me to sell."

I wagged my finger at Edward. "I'd watch out for that Junior if I were you. That's all I have to say."

I left Edward with his thoughts and made my way to the revolving doors. My phone rang. I waited until I'd been scooted outside by the glass partitions before answering. "Moore Time how—"

"Come pick me up!"

"Mr. Q? Where are you?"

"I'm at the jail. This place sucks. Please come get me."

Mr. Q sounded like a frightened teenager. "I believe Jack is still working on getting you released."

"It's done and I'm waiting on you."

I wasn't expecting to provide transportation for Mr. Q. I wanted to work on finding Mrs. Rippetoe. "Ok. I'll be right there."

I pressed the end call button and Eli's name popped up. "Hi Eli."

"Can you meet me at the pavilion again?" he asked.

"Do you have information for me already?

"Yes."

"Wow. That was super quick!"

"I thought you'd like to know."

"Sure, but I have to give Mr. Quetzalcoatl a ride."

"That's fine. Twenty minutes at the pavilion okay?"

"Sure. What were the results?"

"I need to give them to you face to face."

19

"I DON'T UNDERSTAND how they could arrest you for Greg's murder. Did someone see you moving his body?" I asked Mr. Q once he buckled his seatbelt and got settled into the passenger side of my Jeep.

"Fingerprints."

"What do you mean?"

"They found my fingerprints on the wine glasses. Rumblings are that it was poison that killed him and I think it was in one of those glasses."

"How are you doing?"

"Your vehicle is nasty." Mr. Q brushed dog hair off the dashboard.

"Really? You've been charged with Greg's death and you want to talk about the cleanliness of my Jeep?"

"No. What I really want to talk about is the Blue Monkey diamond."

"What about it?"

"I haven't been completely honest with you."

"You know something about the blue diamond?"

"I own the Blue Monkey diamond."

I said nothing. Mr. Q said nothing. It was like a bullhorn had been used to amplify the silence. How could he own the diamond if the kidnappers said Oliver Lott had the diamond? We drove for a few minutes with only the road noise lingering in the background. I cleared my throat.

"Did you just say you own the Blue Monkey diamond?"

"Yes."

"Where is it?"

"I don't know. That's why I was going through Greg's house."

"I knew there was no such thing as a comic book costing three-hundred thousand dollars."

"No, there is such a thing, but it's tucked away in my safety deposit box."

Lying. Not completely honest. Bad luck didn't just appear like a pop-up ad. This had to be the curse. The legend was pretty clear – if the owner of the Blue Monkey diamond was dishonest, their luck would turn bad. What could be unluckier than having your friend killed in your home and then being arrested for the murder? And why would the bad luck be limited to the owner when in reality we are all connected. Mr. Q was my bad luck charm.

"Why didn't you tell me about the diamond when I asked?"

"Because you didn't need to know. The things worth a lot of money and the less people who knew the better. Look, very few people knew and now the diamond's gone!"

He lied to me before, what if he was lying now? What if the safety deposit box also contained the diamond? But, what if he was telling the truth?

"You're right. So, who knew?" I asked.

"I did, of course. And Greg. That's all."

"What about the auction house?"

"Yes, well, the auction house had to know. But, that was in Denmark."

"And the insurance company?"

Mr. Q didn't respond.

"Please tell me you insured the diamond," I said.

Mr. Q sat silent.

"Oh my God. You didn't insure the diamond? Why wouldn't you insure the diamond?"

"I did. I bought a short-term policy to cover the diamond while in transit. Once I had the diamond I hid...I put it in a safe place. I was planning on getting insurance the following week, but somehow it slipped my mind."

Was he that rich that a three-million-dollar diamond would slip his mind? I'd have to consider renegotiating my contract, that is if Mr. Q didn't get sent to prison for life. I dropped the subject of insurance because his hands started to shake.

"Do you want to swing by my place first, to get Mr. P?"

"Yes. I miss him."

Now that I had PJ in my life, I totally got what Mr. Q was saying. It was like having a four-legged child.

"Did you kill Greg?"

I'm not sure why I decided to ask Mr. Q that question at that particular time since the thought of no insurance had made him tremble, but I did and it was too late to take it back. I waited for him to answer, but instead he clutched his chest with his right arm. Sweat formed on his forehead.

"Mr. Q, are you alright?"

"Just indigestion." He continued clutching his chest. His left arm appeared heavy and limp.

"We're going to the ER. Or should I pull into that fire station up ahead." I pressed my foot on the gas pedal.

"No really. It's indigestion. Bwaaaaaauuuuurrrrrp. That's better."

"Are you sure?"

"You're like some mother hen."

I didn't dare ask him the question again, though I'd have to later. I needed to hear his response while I looked into his eyes. I didn't want to think that Mr. Q, with all his idiosyncrasies, could be capable of taking another person's life for no reason.

"What do you think happened to the diamond?" I asked, curious of how it might have gotten into the hands of Oliver Lott if in fact it did.

"I don't know. I thought Greg had ripped me off, but he was my friend. I'm wondering now if he tried to stop someone else from taking the diamond and that's what got him killed."

"Are you saying you didn't kill Greg?" I knew I was asking the same question, but it sounded different.

Mr. Q burped again. "That's what I'm saying."

I didn't exactly get to look him in the eyes, but the way he answered reminded me of the night he told me about Greg being in witness protection. He was timid, vulnerable, and the tone in his voice wreaked of honesty.

"Then we need to figure out who killed Greg so we can keep you from going to prison," I said, looking over at Mr. Q.

Crap.

His face was the color of salt. I wanted to spend more time with Mr. Q, but based on his reaction I thought it was time to stop before I killed him. Besides, Eli was expecting me at the pavilion.

No police cars were in sight when I pulled into the parking lot of the World's Fair Pavilion. I parked in the same space I'd parked in the last time we rendezvoused figuring I'd be easy to find.

I left the car running with the heat on and closed my eyes. Maybe, just maybe it might spawn some incredible idea of how to find and rescue Mrs. Rippetoe, but the only thing I thought about was Eli's insisting we meet face to face. The paranoia started. What if this was a set up? What if he knew I cleaned up the primary crime scene? It scared me that the conclusion of our meeting might end with handcuffs. I reached into the small pocket in my purse and fondled Marshal Cutter's card.

Tap. Rap. Tap.

"Oh. You scared me!" I said, rolling down the window.

Eli smiled. "Sorry. Didn't know it was nap time."

"Just closed my eyes to think."

"Sorry I'm late. I was dealing with a two-one-five."

"A what?"

"A little carjacking problem. Everything's fine, but I've got to get back and finish some paperwork, so don't have much time."

"To be honest, I'm surprised you called so soon. It hasn't even been a full business day."

"I figured this was important to you."

"What did you find out?"

"The short dark hairs were from a domestic animal. The—"

"Really? Were they from a dog or cat?"

"Couldn't say definitively because there were no roots, but it's either a dog or a curly-coated cat if there is such a thing."

"And what about the other hairs, did they match?"

"Both human and no, no, they didn't match. You okay?"

I knew Eli thought I'd be upset, figuring the positive human hair identification meant my man had been with someone else. "I'm okay. I sort of expected it. I guess I better let you go."

"You sure you're okay?"

"I'm sure. I can't thank you enough. If you ever need a personal concierge let me know."

"I think I'm okay doing things on my own, but thank you for the offer. You take care."

Being dishonest with Eli bothered me, but I had a feeling he already knew I wasn't telling him the truth and somehow he was okay with it. He was a sweet man. *Like maple syrup.* My stomach growled at the thought. I'd barely been eating because of all the drama. I swung through a McDonald's drive through, ordered a sausage biscuit with egg and a coffee, then pulled into a parking space to think.

The missing item from Mrs. Paddy's house made it more plausible that the break-in had nothing to do with the blue diamond and the disappearance of Mrs. Rippetoe. Roberto had to be scamming Stephanie and Bella too. Although it was alarming, I'd wait to address that situation. I focused on what I knew about Mrs. Rippetoe's disappearance. I knew she was chained to a table probably in an RV. I knew the blue diamond was supposed to be in the hands of Oliver Lott. That was it.

"Hello Mr. Brackford." I welcomed his call to take my mind off the fact that I had no idea what I was doing in regards to Mrs. Rippetoe.

"I need to see you. Can you come over now?"

"What's this about?"

"I'll tell you when you get here."

"Sorry. I won't be able to get by there for several hours." The truth was I didn't know when I could meet him because I had lost control of my life.

"Ok. But you got to be here before seven o'clock because Belinda's coming and I don't want you to be here." Thomas Brackford hung up.

Technically, I could have gone to see him immediately, but I wasn't up to the task. All I wanted to do was find Mrs. Rippetoe without endangering her life.

I pulled out of the parking lot not knowing where I was going. After driving around, I found myself parked in front of my apartment. I trudged up the stairs, settled the dogs down then retrieved my box from its hiding place. I curled up on my couch with my secret memory box. My two hours were quickly ticking away but I didn't have a clue what to do. I felt like a failure. I was ready to give up, ready to call Peter and tell him to place the call, but first I dialed my lifeline.

"Mom?"

"Is everything okay honey?"

"I'm having a little bit of a hard time. I'm trying to solve a business problem and my mind seems to have shut down."

"Amelia, your mind never shuts down. Stop trying so hard."

Hearing my real name created a warmth around my heart, quickly followed by an ache. I couldn't tell her how bad things had gotten.

"You're right. That's why I thought I would call you and we could just chat."

"Well then, let's chat. Tell me how my grandson is doing."

I laughed. "PJ is, well – PJ. He's misbehaving and having a good time. He's the one bright thing in my life."

"You have so many bright things in your life."

"It doesn't feel like it at the moment. I'm overwhelmed. I wish you were here to help me. You'd be so good at this business."

"I wish I were there too honey. I miss you."

I started to cry.

"I'm sorry sweetie. Look, you are good at what you do. I'm so proud of you. You're building a successful business. It has to bring you some happiness."

My business. She was talking about the same business that seemed to continually hurl me into dangerous situations. "It does and business is good."

"What are you working on now? Any interesting clients?'

No matter what, I would never tell my mother the truth about my situation. It would tear her apart. She'd had such a difficult time when I'd made the decision to enter the Witness Protection Program. Although I reached out to her for support, I had to limit what I told her.

I laughed. "Believe it or not I have a guy who wants me to plan his wedding."

"That sounds like it might be fun. A good change of pace."

"Yeah, but well, he's a little creepy." What I wanted to say was he was super creepy and I had no idea why he was following me around, but that would just make my mother worry.

"Creepy how? Did you tell Peter or Jack about him? You should decline. You need to be careful."

"He's just persistent. I'm not sure what is wrong with this guy. Harry Corbitt's, well, sort of—"

"Harry Corbitt?"

"Yeah. That's the guy's name. Something is off about him."

"Is he Australian?"

"Wha...Yeah. Do you know him?"

"Oh, Amelia."

"Who is he?"

"Sweetie, he's, well, let me have you talk to Daddy-O."

I listened as my mom called out to Daddy-O, my step-dad and the only true father figure I'd known. I heard the two of them exchanging words. She wasn't happy and Daddy-O answered her questions like he was guilty of something. My mother told him to take the phone.

"Amelia?"

"Daddy-O. Who is this guy?"

"I'm sorry. I made a mistake. I'm so proud of you and your business and I let the name of it slip out the last time I talked to Harry. He's an old friend. I caught myself before I said anything else. The conversation was short. I figured it was in his one ear and out the other and didn't give it another thought."

I could hear my mother talking in the background and Daddy-O said, "Okay. Okay."

"What's she saying?"

"She wants me to tell you about Harry's background. He's harmless really, but well, he used to be a member of Sons of Retribution."

"What's that?"

"It's a motorcycle club. But he doesn't belong to the club any longer. He didn't like being involved with a one-percenter club. And he isn—"

"One percent of what?"

"One-percenter clubs. They're usually involved in illegal activities. You know, clubs like the Hells Angels, the Banditos, the Outla—"

"You mean he belongs to a motorcycle gang? A GANG?"

"They call it a club. And he isn't a member any longer. He's actually a nice person. I can't believe he remembered the name of your business after all this time."

"This isn't the first time he's been here! He's scary and really odd. Not only does he frighten me, but every time he's here the problems in my life grow exponentially. I can't believe you told someone about me. Are you trying to get me killed? What am I going to do now? I might as well—"

"Amelia! Amelia! Calm down. It's going to be okay."

"How? How is it going to be okay when someone in St. Louis, other than Marshal Cutter, knows my true identity? And not just anybody, but a member of a motorcycle gang."

Daddy-O didn't respond. The silence signaled I'd gone too far. "I'm sorry Daddy-O. I didn't mean it. I'm just afraid of what he might do or who he might tell."

"I'll take care of it. He may be a little odd, but he really is good to the core. I'm going to call him and find out what he's doing. What did he say to you?"

"First time he showed was a ruse. Obviously he planned it. He'd said he wanted me to plan his wedding, and then ta-da, like magic his fiancée ran off with someone. Now he's back wanting me to plan a wedding again. He must think I'm stupid."

"Harry's getting married? Did you hear that honey? Harry's getting married."

Daddy-O's exchange with my mother was the small break I needed. The happiness in her voice when she received the news of Harry's upcoming nuptials meant I should be happy for Harry too.

"Daddy-O." I tried to bring his attention back to me.

"I'll take care of it, Amelia. I'll call him right after we get off the phone."

"No. Don't do that. If you think he's okay, then I'll call him and set up a time to talk to him myself. Just one last question. You don't think he's rejoined the gang do you?"

"There's no way."

"But how can you be sure?"

"I just know."

Daddy-O sounded confident.

"But how?"

"Amelia. Believe me when I say I know. I would tell you if I could, but it's not my story to tell, it's Harry's."

"Ok. Remember, don't contact him. I will take care of it. We've already been talking too much lately. It doesn't seem like it at times, but it's still dangerous for us to be communicating."

"I know sweetie. You want to talk to your mom again?"

"No. I better go. Tell her I love her. And Daddy-O?"

"Yes."

"I'm sorry for jumping on you and I love you too."

When we hung up I felt better. My call to my mother had become my call to action. I looked up at the pendulum clock. My time was running out.

20

I MICROWAVED AN INSTANT MAC AND CHEESE and sat on my couch thinking of what my next move should be when Peter called.

"Times up," Peter said.

"Please? One last look." I held my phone in one hand and poured some kibble into the dog's bowls with the other.

"You have no respect for rules and deadlines do you?"

"Please? Just one last look at this other RV park before you go to the police?"

"You don't, do you?"

Inside my head I ranted and raved at Peter for his obsession with questions. They were maddening. But I wanted his help, so I gave him what he wanted.

"No. I guess I don't. It's what makes me a ferocious concierge, working hard to get the job done. And I know this is the right thing to do. Think. It makes sense. The two RV parks are in such close proximity that they're easy to travel between."

"Ok. One last look."

Some sort of crazy squeal came out of my mouth and I blurted out, "I could kiss you!"

There were a few seconds of silence before Peter spoke. "You already tried and it didn't work out so good."

"Sorry. Didn't mean it. Just a figure of speech." The truth was I meant every word of it. Then it hit me that he'd caved quickly. "That was a little too easy. What's going on?"

"I think we waited too long to call the police. We should have done it right away so they could have tried to control the situation. Now we've basically put Mrs. Rippetoe's life in jeopardy and we've left ourselves open to possible legal problems. I'm so angry with you right now."

"I'm sorry. I know. You're right. We both screwed up. But I feel really good about this direction. I'm positive we'll find her in the RV park."

"Let's get going then. Where are you?" Peter asked.

"We can't go now. We need to wait until it's getting dark." I got up and dropped the empty mac and cheese container in the trash.

"Seven o'clock?"

"Great. I'll go to my office and do some more research on the RV parks. I've got to go to Thomas Brackford's place too. So I'll see you back at our apartment building when I'm done. We can pack up a few necessities and head out. Oh and bring some spy stuff from your store with you."

I ended the call, walked back over to the sofa and scratched PJ's and Sassy's ears. "See you two in a little while. Be good." I aimed the last statement at PJ. He looked at me and cocked his head like he was responding, "Who me?"

After I got my jacket on, I took a mozzarella string cheese out of the fridge and prayed it wasn't more than a few weeks past the expiration date. One more glance at the dogs and I was out the door.

It was freezer-cold inside my Jeep. I couldn't get the engine and heater warmed up fast enough. My teeth chattered as I waited for a smooth idle before pulling onto the road.

I mapped out my plan for this evening's hunt as I drove to Brackford's house. First stop, the RV park we went to the other day. This time, we weren't contacting the park manager in case he'd given these outlaws a heads up. We'd do a quick drive through, peep into a few windows. If we didn't find the RV I'd have to give in to Peter. We'd have to figure out what to tell the police and I'd have to come up with a creative excuse to stay out of the middle of the investigation. If we found them that would require an entirely different plan. One that included all of us coming out alive.

By the time I pulled into Brackford's driveway I felt a little more in control of the kidnapping situation. The keyword – little. I hopped out of the Jeep and made my way to the door.

Brackford answered after only one knock. "Come in. Come in," he said, scanning the road outside in both directions.

"What's going on? Are you in some sort of trouble?"

"Yes. Sort of."

"What do you mean sort of? Either you are or you aren't."

"Let's go in the kitchen. Do you want a coffee or some hot chocolate?"

He must not be in real trouble if he was offering me a drink. "Hot chocolate, please. It's cold outside."

"I know. Our city was on The Weather Channel. They're predicting up to six inches of snow tonight."

Crap.

He wheeled himself into the kitchen and I followed. He filled a cup with water, then tore open a package of Swiss Miss Hot Chocolate and dumped it in. A few seconds after the microwave beeped, I sipped a cup of steaming hot chocolate with tiny marshmallows.

"So what kind of trouble are you in, Mr. Brackford."

"Didn't I tell you to call me Thomas?"

"Yes. So what is the trouble?"

"The other day I asked Belinda to move in with me."

"That's great."

"No, it's not."

"Are you having second thoughts?"

"No. I want her to move in with me, but she said no."

"Mr. Br—Thomas, I'm so sorry."

"It's not that she doesn't want to live with me, but she wants to be married first."

"Oh."

"Right? She said something about free cows and milk or something. It was all so confusing. I wasn't expecting her to say no. After she said the word married, I didn't hear anything else she said."

"What did you say to her?"

"I didn't say anything. I was in shock. She got upset and left."

"But everything is okay, right? You said she was coming over tonight?"

"She is, but I had to beg her to come over."

"So, what do you want me to do? Do you need me to cook something for you? Clean up?"

"No. After thinking about how much I love her and now even more because she wants to marry me, there should be no reason to be scared. So I'm going to ask her to marry me tonight and I want you to plan the wedding."

Why did people think I was good at planning weddings? Actually not people, just men. Maybe they didn't know the importance of wedding planning and figured any woman should know how to do it. "I'm flattered Mr. Brackford, but I'm not really a wedding planner. There are real wedding planners out there."

"But you were the one responsible for turning our first dinner into a real date. If you hadn't done that, we might not be getting married. That's why I want you to do it."

What could I say to that? "Well then, I'd be honored."

"Oh, and I'm pretty sure that Belinda will want you to be her maid or whatever that is. Maid of honor, right?"

"Yes. But, that is usually the bride's sister or best friend."

"She doesn't have a sister and come to think of it, I don't think I've ever met any of her friends."

"Before we jump ahead, why don't we wait for your proposal and see what Belinda says about who she wants as maid of honor?"

"We can do that, but I know she'll want you. So I'd like to get married next weekend."

"Mr. Brackford, that is such short notice. Why don't we wait to see what Belinda says?"

"Are you saying you don't think she's going to say yes to my proposal?"

I took another sip of my hot chocolate, slurping in a few marshmallows. What if she didn't accept his proposal? What if her refusal to move in without being married was a ruse, thinking he would never ask her to marry him? I couldn't spring those thoughts on Brackford.

"Not at all. I'm saying that women have their ideas of what they want their wedding to be like and perhaps Belinda might want more time to plan."

"We'll see. I'm sure she'll want something small. You as the maid of honor and I think Christopher as best man. And if for some reason he can't do it, you could ask that friend of yours, Peter, to consider being the best man. I liked him from the first time I met him."

"Who's Christopher?"

"Mr. Quetzalcoatl! We've gotten to be fairly good friends. He even treated me to dinner once. And he took me to buy Belinda's ring."

Oh lord. Mr. Brackford and Mr. Q had bonded behind my back. I was unaware that their trip to the transportation museum, hadn't been the end of their contact. Mr. Q helping Brackford with the engagement ring meant a full fledge friendship had developed. It wasn't a bad thing. Peculiar personalities naturally found one another. But, why would he think Mr. Q would be available? Perhaps he had only been watching The Weather Channel and not the local news.

I had to tell him about Mr. Q's arrest. But first I wanted to hear more about the shiny object. "Where is Belinda's ring?"

"Is that what all you girls are focused on?"

"We do like our diamonds. Where'd you get it?"

"Christopher took me to this little family-owned jewelry store by your office called Varriano's. He must buy a lot of jewelry there because they seemed to know him well and treated him like royalty. I got a beautiful ring for a great price, but you'll have to wait until Belinda shows it to you. I don't want to ruin her excitement."

Very interesting. I'd have to nose around the jewelry store again, determine if they played a role in the purchase of the blue diamond or worse, in its disappearance.

"You know, Thomas, Mr. Quetzalcoatl was arrested for murder the other day."

"Yes. What do you think I am a hermit?"

Well, yes, I do. "No, of course not. I didn't know if you watched the news."

"I watch the news every day. He didn't do it. He just isn't that kind of man."

At one point in my relationship with Mr. Q, I'd have agreed, but now I wasn't so sure. He'd been keeping secrets, moved a body, and broke into an active crime scene. Then again, I'd done some of those things too and I would never murder anyone.

"You have a point." I glanced up at Brackford's kitchen clock. "I better get going, Belinda will be here soon and I'm assuming you didn't want me to be here when you popped the question."

"You're right. You better go."

"Call me tomorrow and let me know what Belinda says. And if you're serious about getting married this weekend you better get your marriage license."

I took my cup to the sink and rinsed it, then I put it inside the dishwasher. "Wouldn't want Belinda to think you had company, especially one who wears lip gloss."

Brackford laughed. "Yes, good thinking."

———

Peter and I sat outside the RV park in his dirty Citation.

"Would you please clean this nasty car?"

"Dumpsters are supposed to be dirty."

I ignored his response. "I came up with a plan. We should drive through once and identify any suspicious RVs. Then we leave the park and drop the car down the road. We walk back to do a more detailed review of each RV that we think might hold Mrs. Rippetoe—"

"You'll freeze to death."

He had a point. The predicted snow had started to fall. Even though I'd known it was supposed to snow, I still forgot to change into my heavier coat. "Do you want me to drive and you peek inside the RVs?"

"Not particularly."

"You got any other ideas?"

Peter looked at me. "Call the police?"

"You promised me, Peter."

"I know, but at this point Mrs. Rippetoe is running out of time."

"Please, Peter? I promise if we don't find her at either of the parks you can call the police. But you know, once we call the police it's a guaranteed death sentence for her."

"That's not necessarily true. I'll tell you what I'll do. I'll drive first and you scan the RV's, I'll even let you hop out if you need a closer look. Then if we think there's a need to do a more detailed search, you can sit in the car and I'll walk back."

"No way. We should both walk back."

"I need you to be in the car so you can rush in if I get into a bind."

"Fine."

Peter pulled into the RV park and turned the opposite direction of the manager's office. I don't think it would have mattered anyway because the office was closed.

As we drove along, I checked out the RV's using the DarkSight night vision monocular Peter brought along. It was even better than the night vision lens he had for his camera. "Why didn't you bring that C-Thru 1000?"

"Too many people. And besides if someone caught us with that in the RV park we'd probably get arrested. With the night vision monocular we can just say we were looking for nocturnal animals or something."

I guess he made sense. As I watched through the monocular, I wished I had the C-Thru 1000. I didn't like not being able to see if there were people inside the RVs. "Wait. Slow down."

"What do you see?"

"I'm not sure, that's why I said slow down. I think there's one guy inside that RV over there." I pointed up the street to the left.

"So?"

"So, the guy keeps walking back and forth. Pacing. I want to take a closer look. Pull up past the RV and I'll go back and check it out."

Peter sped up and pulled past the RV in question. He parked in a barely lit section of the road. I hopped out. *Brrrrr.* I ran back to the RV and positioned myself behind some bushes that had been planted to separate the RV lots, luckily I was hiding in an empty lot. In fact, there were several empty lots in the park. I understood. Who wanted to camp in the winter?

The man continued to pace. I didn't recognize him. My phone rang. I dropped down to the ground and took the phone out of my jacket pocket.

"Do you have the diamond?"

What was I going to say? I needed to stall until I got back to Peter. "Can you hold for one second please?"

"What the...."

The kidnapper babbled as I held the phone down. I popped back up and peered in the window. The man continued to pace. He wasn't on the phone, but that didn't mean he couldn't be the one tasked with keeping an eye on Mrs. Rippetoe. I ran back to Peter's car and heard the person yelling on the phone.

"I'm sorry. One more second please," I said to whoever was on the other end of the phone.

I pressed my thumb over the cell phone's microphone. "It's the kidnapper. He wants to know if I have the diamond. What do I say?"

"Say yes. Ask him where he wants you to meet him."

I trembled. "I'm sorry. Someone walked by and I didn't want them to overhear. Yes, I have the diamond. Where do you want to meet?"

"Not now." The kidnapper hung up.

"Can you believe it? They hung up."

"We need to call the police now."

"No please. Something is up in that RV back there and I think you should check it out."

"You are helplessly crazy. You know that don't you?"

This time I answered his question without hesitation. "I know I am, but isn't that what you like about me?"

Peter smiled. Without a word, he got out of the car.

"Text me when you want me to come back to get you," I said, before he closed the door.

I scooted over the console and into the driver's seat. Once I adjusted the seat and mirrors, I exited the park and pulled over a few hundred feet down the road.

"God, please let this be the right RV. And please let Peter rescue Mrs. Rippetoe unharmed." I knew my request was a long shot since God and I hadn't been corresponding lately.

I sat, waiting for Peter's text. It drove me nuts. Was he still spying on the guy? Was he breaking into the RV and rescuing Mrs. Rippetoe? I felt like texting Peter and asking him what was happening.

My phone rang. I was excited but confused when I saw Peter's name pop up. "What's happening, do you need me to come get you?"

He didn't respond. I listened close, thinking Peter had butt dialed me. When I overheard the conversation going on between Peter and someone else I knew Peter dialed me on purpose so I'd know he was in trouble.

"What are you doing poking around my motorhome? You a peeper?" asked a man.

"Put away your gun buddy, I mean no harm," Peter answered.

My heart ramped up. I was sure the guy had the gun pointed at Peter.

"Sorr-eee, bud-eee, but you need to step on inside."

I pushed the speaker button and kept the line open. I shifted the Citation into drive and drove back into the park. I approached the RV where Peter was now being held hostage and pulled into the unused RV lot next to it.

I sat for a few minutes listening to their conversation.

"What do you want from me?" the man asked.

If he had to ask what Peter wanted from him then he probably didn't have Mrs. Rippetoe. But that made it even worse. By the way he paced, he could be some frantic lunatic. I had to think of a way to get Peter out of his clutches.

"Honest, buddy, I've had a little bit to drink and I was trying to find my RV. If you don't believe me...I think you should call nine-one-one."

Call nine-one-one? He's talking to me! Inside my head, the left side screamed, "Call nine-one-one!", while my right side was busy thinking of a way to rescue Peter.

"Act like your drunk," declared the right side. The left side piped up, "That might work, but..."

There wasn't time for the left side to run through all the reasons why it would be too risky to attempt Peter's rescue. I pressed the end call button and dropped the phone in my jacket pocket. I searched Peter's filthy car for props that might help give me a believable cover. I was surprised to find an open pint of whiskey, three-quarters empty. It wasn't illegal to have the container in his car, but it did fill my head with tons of questions.

Peter pretended to be drunk one time during his first side job as a private investigator and it had served him well. I hoped I could be just as convincing as he had been. I opened the bottle and wiped a small amount of whiskey near my mouth. The smell caused my eyes to water. I tossed the bottle back on the rear floorboard and jumped out of the car.

I walked over to the RV and flung myself up against it. "Ouch!" I screamed, then went with a softer more slurred accent. "Where you Bubby Boo? I seen you go in one of these R-fees! Bubeeee Booooze. Ha. Ha. Boooooze."

When I heard the RV door open I knew the man had taken the bait. "What the hell. Are you drunk?"

"Noffff. I'm lookin for my Booby Boo." I walked toward the man as he stood in the door.

"You smell like you've been drinking. Look lady, you need to shut the hell up and get out of here."

"There's my Bubby Boof!" I pointed through the door at Peter.

"I'm soooorryy. I luffff you." I pushed past the man and ran into Peter's arms.

"Did you call nine-one-one?" Peter whispered.

All I had to do was look at him and he knew the answer. He seemed unhappy.

"Stop!" The man yelled.

He got my attention and I turned around. His gun was pointed in our direction.

"She's drunk. Don't get all hopped up. Why don't you just let us leave and go back to our RV?"

"Sorry, no can do."

This wasn't turning out as I'd expected. Maybe if I caused a scene Peter could figure out how to use it to our advantage.

"I don't...urrrgggh...feel good."

"Oh buddy. You need to let her get to the bathroom. She's gonna urp all over the place. I've seen her do it before and believe me you don't want to witness the disaster." Peter pretended to help me up.

"Sit down!"

Peter and I obeyed.

"Oh no. Oh no. Oh no. I really don't feel good." I pretended to collapse and fall to the floor. I laid on the floor transfixed by a shiny object at the edge of the sofa.

"Get up off the floor." The man nudged his foot into my ribs.

"Okay. Okay. Stopffff." I extended my arm as I pushed my body up, grabbing the object and dropping it in my front pocket as I stood up. "I told you I didn't feel good! I really gotta go to the bathroom."

"She's not kidding, buddy."

I gagged. "Please?"

"Go, but don't try anything. I got my gun pointed at your lover boy."

I walked back to the rear of the RV. "Where is it?" I asked, opening the door to the bedroom. It was empty and I was disappointed.

The man was pissed. "It's not in the back stupid idiot! It's the small door on the right side."

I threw myself on the bed. I plucked a couple of lashes from my eyelids to help me form some tears. "I luuufff him, my bubbey boo. Please don't hurt him. I want him to take me home."

"Holy shit! How do you put up with that?" the man asked.

I assumed he was directing that toward Peter who was probably now bonding with the man.

"Go get her. Get her now!" the man shouted.

I sat up and watched Peter as he came down the hall. The man kept his gun pointed at Peter's back. I jumped off the bed and thrust myself toward Peter and wrapped my arms around him. "She's not here, but I want to look in the bathroom." I whispered.

Peter put his arm around me and even in our current situation, staring at the barrel of a gun, his arms were warm and made me tingle.

"Let's go in here my sweet little drunk." Peter opened the door to the bathroom.

"It's too small. I'm gonna throw up all over myself."

Peter turned to address the guy. "Even all drunk she's still concerned about her looks."

We started walking back toward the front of the RV.

"She's a real peach. You two lovebirds get the hell out of here and don't come back else I'll shoot you and stuff you both in the RV storage compartments outside."

"Sorry, we won't be bothering you again," Peter said, then opened the door and almost pushed me down the stairs.

"What do you mean we won't be bothering him again?" I asked Peter when we were out of earshot and almost back to the car.

"No reason. I assume you proved that Mrs. Rippetoe wasn't in the RV, right? "

"She wasn't in the bedroom or bathroom. But..." The words were too terrible for me to speak, but I had to express my thoughts to Peter, "...what...what if she's stuffed inside one of the storage compartments on the outside?"

Peter's eyes widened and his brows crimped. A look that conveyed a very specific message. I knew he was horrified by the words that had departed my mouth, wondering how I could think such a thing.

"I'm just saying, the guy practically projected the situation. We need to go back and check the compartments but we need the C-Thru 1000."

"If what you say is true, then she'd probably be dead, and the C-Thru only picks up warmth, like that within the body of a live human."

"I'm not even going to acknowledge that idea. She can't be dead. We just need to figure this out. Look." I pulled the object from my pocket, hoping the clue would point us in some direction.

"Whoa."

"What?" Peter asked.

"I'm pretty sure it's part of a necklace Oliver Lott had me purchase for his wife. Ingrid Lott had to have been in that RV or this is one heck of a coincidence."

"You think she's behind the kidnapping? If they already have the diamond, then why steal it?"

The truth was, I didn't really know who had the diamond. Mr. Q could be lying. What if he never had the diamond? What if the Lott's had it all along? I had to think motive.

"They could be trying to commit insurance fraud. Have me steal it and then get it back from me using Mrs. Rippetoe as the leverage?"

"I think you're just pulling stuff out of the air. It's time to call the police."

"I'm not. When I saw Mrs. Lott at the charity event Saturday night the diamond initial wasn't hanging on her necklace."

"You promised we'd call the police."

"Only if we went to both RV parks."

"But if you think that's the RV, there's no reason to go to the other RV park."

"I know, but I could use the time to talk to their nanny, Bella, and see if I can find out anything."

Peter shook his head. His lips contracted, and his nose scrunched in disgust I couldn't blame him. I was being stubborn, because I feared involving the police would make our mission go from rescue to recovery.

"Please Peter. Just a little more time?"

"No. The kidnappers hung up on you. It means Mrs. Rippetoe is already on borrowed time."

"Could be they weren't prepared and they're trying to decide what the best way was to do the exchange. Why would they kill her? I told them I have the diamond and isn't that what they want?"

"If you're right about the Lott's, maybe their checking to see if the diamond is no longer in the spot where they kept it."

"I didn't even think about that. Why'd you tell me to tell them I had the diamond? Damn it. No wonder they hung up."

"We need to bring the police in on this." Peter reached for his phone.

"Wait! I wasn't completely open with you. I need to tell you something."

Peter leaned his head back and closed his eyes. "I can't do this. How do you expect me to help you when you don't tell me the truth or you tell me half-truths? Why do you insist on secrets? Did something happen to you in your past?"

My body involuntarily jerked. I wanted to answer his questions. I wanted to tell him everything about my past, but I focused on the immediate past. "I'm not sure who has the diamond. The kidnapper said the Lott's had it, but... please don't repeat what I'm about to tell you, okay?"

"I'm not guaranteeing anything."

"Then I can't tell you."

"Then I'm calling the police." Peter punched some numbers on his phone.

"Wait! Fine. But, if you say anything it could damage my company's reputation. I'm known for keeping things confidential."

"I think that's the least of your worries, don't you?"

"Yes." I answered his rhetorical question without complaint.

"So, tell me."

"Mr. Q told me he had the diamond."

"What?"

"I know. I'm not sure if I believe him. He said it's missing. Anyone could have it."

"That's just fantastic." Peter leaned his head back again, but this time he didn't close his eyes.

"What are you thinking?"

"If anyone could have it then we know even less about the kidnappers than we did before. They could be amateurs. Maybe there is no plan. And if that's the case, they won't be playing by the normal kidnapping rules, which puts Mrs. Rippetoe at greater risk."

"Or maybe they're so nervous that they changed their minds? Maybe they'll just let her go."

"Or maybe they'll just kill her and act like nothing happened."

"Peter!"

21

As soon as the clock hit seven, I threw on some clothes and ran down to Peter's apartment. Last night he said we could sleep on it instead of going to the police.

Peter greeted me with a cup of coffee like he'd been listening to me scamper about in my apartment. "You didn't sleep did you?"

"Thanks for the coffee and no, I didn't sleep at all. I tossed everything around in my head, analyzing the data and hoped I could pinpoint who kidnapped Mrs. Rippetoe and who killed Greg."

"What does it matter who killed Mr. Q's neighbor? The important thing is to make sure Mrs. Rippetoe comes home safe."

I stared out the window, relieved that the heavy snow had landed south of the St. Louis area. We ended up with just a dusting. I took a sip of my coffee. "It matters because I think the two are connected."

"Why?"

Peter knew nothing about me helping to clean up the crime scene after Mr. Q moved Greg's body, so I couldn't tell him about the evidence I'd found in the room. I tried to come up with a quick response.

"Aspen? Did you hear me ask why?"

"No. I think I dozed off. Why, what?"

"Why do you think the kidnapping and murder are connected?"

Last night I'd looked over the initial 'I' pendant. The diamonds found at Mr. Q's house were the same size and shape as the diamonds in the pendant. There were no missing diamonds but it had to be related. "I just have a hunch."

"What have I told you about hunches?"

"I know. A hunch is like lunch. It's never free."

"Right. Either way this is going to cost you something and I'm going to make sure it isn't your life." Peter reached for his phone.

"Wait! Please! If you call the police, Mrs. Rippetoe doesn't have any chance."

"Why are you so sure the kidnapping and murder are connected?"

"I told you. It's a hunch."

"Not good enough."

He wasn't going to let this go. I needed to get to a point where he thought my logic was, well, logical. Even though I thought the break-in at Mrs. Paddy's house was only Roberto pulling off a burglary, I was going to use it to bring the logic to Peter.

"Then here's the truth. If you call the police, it's probably going to be bad for me, like, Aspen goes to jail bad."

"What did you do?"

"I can't go into detail, but a couple of my wealthier clients had their homes broken into last week. I figure the kidnappers might be setting me up, making it look like I'd been burglarizing my own clients!"

"What does that have to do with Greg?"

"Put two and two together and I'm sure you'll solve it."

"Obviously there are some missing pieces to the puzzle. And that means you don't know either or you're holding something back."

"Just like your job, I can't disclose everything."

"Aspen, this isn't a game. It's serious. I told you last night, if you don't share everything with me, I can't help you."

"Peter, please stop asking so many questions. I've told you almost everything. I need to talk to Mrs. Lott. I'm pretty sure the encrusted initial I found in the RV last night is hers and I can tell you that the Lott's weren't one of the clients who had their house broken into."

"Then go, but meet her in a public place. If she's involved in the kidnapping, I don't want you to disappear too. And if the kidnapper calls, stop whatever you're doing and call me. I swear, I don't know why I let you talk me in to things."

"Because I'm so smart?"

"Yeah. That's it. Has nothing to do with how adorable you are. Now get going and keep your phone next to you at all times and if I call, answer it."

———

After leaving Peter's place I stopped by my office to snoop on Stephanie. Incredibly everything seemed to be in order. I completed a few phone calls related to weddings since I had a few coming up in my future.

It was easing into lunch time so I rang Mrs. Lott.

"Hi Mrs. Lott. I wondered if we could get together. I have something important I'd like to speak to you about."

"Of course Aspen. You can come over right now," Mrs. Lott said.

"Actually, I'm a little hungry."

"Perfect, I'll make us something to eat and drink. Pick your poison and I'll have it ready and waiting for our little get together. I insist."

Poison? No way. I wasn't going to meet her at the Lott's house and I definitely wasn't eating anything she prepared. "It would be better for me if it were somewhere in between."

"Then I'll meet you in twenty minutes at Tequila Tom's."

Mrs. Lott didn't even say goodbye and she never asked what I wanted to talk to her about, which bothered me.

Tequila Tom's won the Riverfront Times 'Best of' award multiple times, but for their margaritas, not their food. Her choice surprised me. I'd never wish a drinking problem on anyone, but if Mrs. Lott was fond of the booze then it might make my investigation that much easier.

If I left the office right away, I'd be able to make it to the restaurant in fifteen minutes. I wanted to get there first to make sure she didn't drop anything into the salsa.

"I have to run Stephanie. I'll call you later."

I trotted out to my Jeep. The drive would give me time to plan my interrogation. It had to be well disguised. Any inkling I was on to her might jeopardize Mrs. Rippetoe's life and my own. I knew exactly how I was going to handle it. I flew through the green lights and pulled into the parking lot in under thirteen minutes.

As I entered the restaurant, I forgot everything I'd planned to say because I spied Mrs. Lott. My brain scrambled for the right words as I walked toward the table by the window where she sat with a large pitcher of frozen margaritas and two glasses.

"Thanks so much for meeting me, Mrs. Lott."

"Oh, it's my pleasure and call me Ingrid." She began filling the margarita glass on my side of the table. "I hope you don't mind I went ahead and ordered a variety of small plates for us to share."

"None for me." I said pointing at the pitcher in her hand.

"Please. It's so much better to not drink alone."

So true. "Just one then," I said.

She finished pouring mine and sat the pitcher down.

"Aren't you having any more?" I asked.

"I'm fine right now."

I snatched the pitcher and topped off her glass. "I insist we start our conversation with full glasses!"

If she stopped drinking I wouldn't start. The margaritas looked delicious. I hoped she hadn't put anything in to the pitcher.

"I called you because I wanted to discuss your satisfaction level with our services."

"Your service is great. Of course, dealing with Grand Ambition could use a little tweaking, but other than that everything has been up to our standards. How have you liked working for us?" She reached for her glass and took a large sip.

I wanted to do a happy dance, she liked our service and she drank her margarita. I licked the fine line of salt on the rim of my glass and took a sip.

"It's been a pleasure. I'm happy you're satisfied because I pride myself on knowing my clients well. Normally I wouldn't say anything, but Bella mentioned you seemed upset after you found out Mr. Lott wanted me to purchase your birthday gift."

Mrs. Lott didn't respond. She took a rather long sip of her margarita. The lingering silence made me uncomfortable and I worried that I'd overstepped or worse, that I'd gotten Bella fired for breaching some sort of confidentiality agreement.

"Yes, it upset me. I didn't realize Bella noticed me standing in the hall outside the kitchen. She never said anything—"

The waiter dropped a bowl of guacamole and basket of chips onto the table along with two plates of mini tacos and a plate of mini chalupas. I went directly for the chips.

"You were saying you were upset—"

"Right. He's changed. He doesn't seem to dote on me like he used to. I know the business is weighing on him and he doesn't have much free time." Mrs. Lott paused, tucked a tendril of her highlighted hair behind her ear and took another sip of her margarita.

The hair reminded me of the strand in the evidence bag I gave Eli. My anger percolated. It was hard to feel sorry for her when she could have been the one who murdered Greg. I took a bite of a mini taco trying to redirect my anger. While I chewed, I observed Mrs. Lott. Her face was plagued by a weightiness that shouldn't be there after drinking margaritas. Her mouth once animated now drooped, void of movement.

I was confused, she didn't come across like a person capable of kidnapping an old lady or killing another human being, but wasn't illusion part of what made criminals scary? I decide to play to the sadness emanating from her.

"I'm sorry. I hope my selection was enough to ease your disappointment."

"Yes. It was beautiful. I should be happy you were the one to pick something out. Who knows what I might have ended up with!" She let out a small chuckle.

"Right, like a toaster or some sort of lingerie he actually bought for himself!"

Mrs. Lott stiffened and her eyelids lowered slightly.

Darn. I'd definitely overstepped this time. "I'm sorry. I was trying to be humorous. I. Maybe I sho—"

"The truth is funny. You were funny. It's not your fault. It's just that Oliver's time is always focused on the business."

"Oh." I struggled with my words. Did I honor the client code or the girl code? I was expected to keep my client's private matters private and in this case Oliver had hired me, not Mrs. Lott. But from one woman to another, shouldn't I tell her that her husband appeared to be cheating? Of course she'd want to know what evidence I had. And it wasn't going to look favorably on me if my only evidence was a phone conversation overheard while hiding under their bed.

If I didn't change the conversation I might end up blurting out everything I knew about her husband. "I'm glad you liked the necklace. I was worried because I couldn't help notice the other night at the charity event that the diamond encrusted initial pendant was no longer on the necklace."

"What initial?"

So, that was how she was going to play it. I guess it was easier to say you never saw the initial than to try to explain how it ended up on the floor of an RV which at some point probably held a little old lady against her will.

"The necklace was purchased with the initial I."

"When I opened the box Oliver gave me, there was no initial."

"Maybe Oliver didn't like the way it looked," I offered.

"I guess. I'll ask him and I'll ask Bella too. I'm pretty sure she wrapped the gift. Lately Oliver doesn't seem to be doing much for me, but I'll ask him."

It was bad enough everyone but Mr. Lott was involved with her birthday gift, so it didn't seem necessary to mention the old man at Varriano's had been the one to tie the bow. I tried to remember if I'd actually seen the pendant on the necklace when it was placed in the box.

I glanced out the window. My mind entered acrobat mode, jumping and bending in directions it hadn't gone before. Maybe Mrs. Lott was innocent and it was only Mr. Lott who was guilty. I knew he'd been cheating on her. What if he took the initial and planted it in the RV in case his plans to commit insurance fraud went south or his effort to get the Blue Monkey diamond failed? I didn't know which scenario was the truth if any, but planting the pendant was a perfect way to frame his wife for the crime. She'd go to prison and he'd be free of her.

———

The kidnapper called just after I left the restaurant and set up a drop off time and place. It reminded me there was very little time left. I turned my car around. I was only a few miles away from the Lott's house. Mrs. Lott had mentioned she was going shopping and I needed to talk to Bella about the diamond pendant, alone. I drove to the house and parked in the driveway.

"Is Bella here?" I asked the twin who opened the door.

"Yep. I'm not getting her. She's in her room." The twin turned and walked away, so I headed up the stairs.

"Bella?" I knocked on the only closed door on the second floor.

She opened it looking startled. "What are you doing here?"

"I thought we could talk. I wanted to ask you about a couple of things."

"Sorry. No time right now."

"What are you doing? Anything I can help you with?"

"No. I'm to go out in a little while. You should go." Bella's eyes kept moving to the right and then back toward me.

"Are you okay?" I asked, wondering if someone was holding her hostage.

"Yes."

Her answer sounded genuine, so I assumed she had Roberto in her room or perhaps another man. "Oh. I'm sorry, uh, I've interrupted your company."

Bella looked confused, which in turn confused me. If she wasn't hiding someone then why was she so nervous?

"I need to go," Bella said.

I glanced into her room as she closed the door. My anxiety level rose when the item I saw on Bella's dresser finally registered. It was a wig stand with a brunette wig.

"Bye," I said and hurried down the steps and out the door to my car.

I phoned Peter. "I need you to come here right away and bring the Citation."

"Whoa, slow down. I think your time is up, Aspen."

"Please don't, Peter. It's Bella. I think she's the one who kidnapped Mrs. Rippetoe. Drive to the Stanley apartments off Clayton and hurry. Call when you get there."

I pulled up the road away from the Lott's house to wait for Peter's call. It would probably take twenty minutes to get to the apartments. If Bella left the house, I'd duck down until she passed then follow her and hope I could direct Peter to my whereabouts.

Peter's name popped up on my cell phone. "Hello."

"I'm at the apartments."

"There's no way you could have gotten there this soon."

"I was in the neighborhood."

"On business or spying on me?"

"Not important. I'm here."

"I'll be there in a couple of minutes. Park in the back. We have to do this quick."

"Do what quick?"

I ended the call without answering his question. I drove the half mile to the apartments and pulled around back, parking my Jeep in the visitor space next to Peter's Citation. He stood on the other side by the driver's door.

I jumped out. "You were following me weren't you?"

"And it's a good thing isn't it?"

I couldn't argue with that, but it still irked me a little. "Hurry. Let's go. We need to follow Bella."

Peter didn't ask any questions as we drove to the Lott's neighborhood and parked a few houses down from the Lott's home.

"The kidnapper called and se—"

"Don't you think you should have lead with that? What'd they say?" Peter asked.

"They set up the drop off. That's when I knew I had to follow my hunch. I know I'm on to something."

"I hope so because this is your last chance. I mean it this time. You're lucky the kidnapper contacted you again because I'm this close to calling the police." Peter held up his hand with his thumb and index finger almost touching.

We watched as Bella, sporting a brunette wig, got into one of the twin's Range Rovers.

"Nice car for a nanny."

"It's not hers, it belongs to one of the Lott twins."

"Oh, that makes me feel better."

The Citation inched away from the curb after Bella pulled out of the driveway. Peter followed her, giving her much more distance than I felt comfortable with. "Don't lose her."

"I'm not. I know how to tail someone, so stop backseat driving."

"Sorry, I just want to get Mrs. Rippetoe back and I know Bella's going to lead us straight to her."

22

"WHERE THE HELL IS SHE HEADING? Toledo?" I was getting impatient with Bella and a little bit worried to be honest. What if they'd already gotten rid of Mrs. Rippetoe and Bella was making a break for it?

"I have no idea, but this is nowhere close to Cahokia and those RV parks."

"Hey, her blinkers on!"

"You're not the only one who sees the signal."

I pushed the button on my phone to display the time. "We've been on the road for over an hour."

"She's heading into Mark Twain National Forest."

"Are you sure she didn't make us? What if she did and called someone and now she's setting up a trap?"

"She didn't even notice us. I'm sure."

"Damn. This is a whole lot of trees."

We drove behind Bella as the Range Rover kicked up dust from the gravel roads. "She's gonna know we're behind her now with all the dust."

"We aren't the only ones. There's a vehicle behind us."

"I knew it. We're being set up. What's our exit plan?"

"Calm down. This is a campground. Look, the car behind us is turning." Peter did a quick tilt and whip of his head.

"I don't see any RV's, only a few tents. Are these people crazy? It's February!"

We followed until Bella's car turned right onto another gravel road. Peter slowed to the speed of a tortoise. The dust rose from behind Bella's car. We watched until the point where no more dust signaled her advancement.

Peter parked, got out of the car and opened the trunk. I hopped out too. "Where are you going? And what's that?"

"A Taser. Here you take this one."

"Why do you get the Godzilla Taser and I get the Barbie doll-sized one?"

"Because mine is a two shot Taser and I'm not sure what I'm going to face when I infiltrate the campsite Bella pulled into. And you, Tonto, you are going to stay here in the car."

"But—"

"Don't even try."

"But—"

"I mean it. Stop trying to take control. Stay here and keep your Taser within reach."

"It's sexist, you know."

"What are you talking about?"

"This Taser. You just assumed since I'm female I'd want a pink Taser."

"For your information, I chose a pink one because I thought it would look less like a Taser in case you needed to keep it a secret."

I scanned Peter's eyes trying to decide if he was telling me the truth. The vibe I picked up was more protector than prevaricator. "Thank you. That was very thoughtful."

"You're welcome. Now, let me tell you how this works. The first thing you need to do is move the safety switch up. You need to be at least two feet away from the target before you fire."

"Don't think I'll be firing it, unless you get out of hand."

"The thing puts out fifty thousand volts so don't be playing around." Peter had his serious face on.

"Anything else I need to know?"

"You can't be more than fifteen feet away from your target. If something happens and you miss, you can use it as a stun gun by placing this end up against the person."

"If I do have to use it, what do I do after I shoot?"

"Run. You'll have maybe thirty seconds before they start to recover."

"It'll take me thirty seconds to figure out which way to run!"

"Believe me, it's more time than you think."

"And what if something happens to you?"

"Stay in the driver's seat. Keep your phone on. I know it's getting cold, but keep the window down and your ears open." Peter turned and began his trek to the campsite.

"Peter?"

Peter turned around. "What now, Aspen?"

"Be careful."

He winked and walked away.

I stuck the Taser in my left jacket pocket and got back in the car. I didn't like sitting around. What if Peter needed me? I put the window up, then down. I turned the radio on, then off, worried the sound would travel. It was quiet out in the woods and I didn't know what to do with myself when I had nothing to keep me occupied.

A cool breeze shot through the window as I stared in the direction where Peter had gone. There was nothing to see but trees and scrub. My imagination created noises and I was suddenly nervous being alone in the car. I kneeled on the seat, turned around and searched the backseat floorboard for a distraction.

Jackpot.

I picked up an old issue of Security Management magazine. It wasn't People, but it would do. I dropped back down into my seat with the magazine in hand and opened it to an article on workplace violence, which for some reason reminded me of Stephanie. I wasn't even through the first paragraph when I felt something hard press against my cheek.

"Get out of the car."

I dropped the magazine. "I was just getting ready to leave."

"Get out." The man yanked the car door open.

My mind reprocessed the instructions Peter had given me, but I couldn't find anything about what to do if my target had a gun pointed at my head.

———

"I'll put a bullet in her if you try anything," the man said as we approached Peter crouching by a bush near the campsite.

The man tightened his grip. "Get up. Get over there."

Peter rose and walked from behind the bush and toward the tent.

"Stop there."

Peter froze.

The tent flap opened and Bella came out with Roberto on her tail. I caught a glimpse of what I thought was Mrs. Rippetoe. Anger rose inside me. I was pissed at Bella,

Roberto, and the stranger with the gun who stood behind me.

"It's about time you got here." Bella walked toward us. I wasn't sure if she was talking to me or the man with the gun.

"I had a situation." The man didn't expand on his excuse.

Roberto walked toward us too.

"Stop there!" The man briefly pointed the gun at Roberto.

"Hey. I'm just going to my car so I can leave." Roberto advanced.

"Stop!"

This time Roberto obeyed.

Whatever was happening wasn't good. Peter and I needed to gain control or all of us but Bella and the mystery man were probably going to die. Bella continued to advance.

My brain negotiated with itself. *Die now or die later?* I shivered, slipping both my hands into the pockets on my jacket. *Even if I die Mrs. Rippetoe and Peter could be saved.* I felt around for the safety. *It's the right thing.* I pushed the safety up, whipped the Taser from my pocket, turned and pulled the trigger.

He went over like a falling tree. Bella ran back toward Roberto and I lunged for the gun that had dropped to the ground when I'd zapped the gunman like a super heroine. My adrenalin pumped and my eyes jiggled as they focused on the shaking gun in my hand. "Don't anybody move!"

"I'm going to move Aspen," Peter said.

"I didn't mean you. Can you tie Bella and Roberto up?"

The man moved, so I bent down to pick the Taser up off the ground. Peter yelled, "Stop." I heard two screams and two thumps. I turned and saw Bella and Roberto on the ground and Peter still with his hand on the trigger of his double Taser.

"Watch out, Aspen!" Peter yelled.

I turned back to look, but the man already had his hand around my hair and I dropped the gun. I pressed the trigger on the Taser and watched him fall to the ground once again. I kept my hand on the trigger as I bent over and picked up the gun. I barely had control of either weapon.

Peter found some rope by the tent and tied up Bella and Roberto. They both grimaced as he removed the Taser prongs from their bodies.

"Hurry Peter, I'm not sure how much battery is left."

"Peter ran to help me. I released the trigger on the Taser and Peter tied the guy up.

I looked at the guy and then at Peter. "Is he secure?"

"Yes."

"Are you sure he can't get out?"

"Of course I'm sure."

"Good." I yanked the mask off the man's face. "Mr. Lott?"

"What the hell is he doing here?" Roberto screamed at Bella.

"You didn't think I was doing all this for us, did you?" Suddenly Bella's English was more perfect than it had ever been.

"Yes. Yes, I did. Why else would I have done everything I did?" Roberto said.

What was Roberto confessing to? Breaking into my client's homes? Kidnapping Mrs. Rippetoe? Killing Greg? Everything? I walked toward Roberto. "What did you do? Did you kill for her?"

"What? What are you talking about? I didn't kill anyone. I broke into a few houses and put together some USB flash drives for her."

"And you kidnapped my landlady."

"No. I didn't kidnap anyone. Bella asked me to meet her out here. I thought we were going camping. Then I get here and find the old lady tied up."

"Did you ever love Stephanie?"

"What?" Roberto and Peter asked at the same time.

"Never mind, let's get Mrs. Rippetoe and get the hell out here."

Peter entered the tent and came right back out. "She's not here."

"But, I saw her in there. I know I did." I marched into the tent and marched right back out.

"What did you do with her?" I pointed the gun at Roberto and Bella

"Woah. Slow down now." Peter reached for the gun.

"Don't Peter. They need to tell us what they did with her."

"She was in there I swear," Roberto blurted out, his legs rattling.

"How could she get out if she was tied up or chained?" I asked.

"She wasn't. I untied her. I told you I didn't know she was going to be here."

"You idiot!" Bella shot him a glance.

Her outburst drew my attention. My sight dropped below her chin and I wanted so bad to pull the trigger and shoot that damn diamond initial off her neck. I walked toward her keeping the gun aimed at her head. I bent down and lifted the necklace with the barrel of the gun. She stiffened.

"Why did you steal Mrs. Lott's diamond pendant?"

"No. No. Oliver gave this to me before Mrs. Lott even had one!"

"But...oh, Bella. Isabella?"

She nodded. I looked more closely. Bella's initial pendant looked as though it was minus two diamonds. I knew I had to step back before I pulled the trigger, but before I took the first step, I yanked out a chunk of her hair.

"Ow. What the hell'd you do that for?"

I ignored her. "We need to go look for Mrs. Rippetoe. I'm sure she took off scared. Did anyone see where she went?"

"I didn't," Roberto said.

Bella just shook her head.

I walked back toward Mr. Lott. "What about you? You see her?" I waved the gun in his face and then withdrew it.

He reached up and grabbed my arm flinging the gun out of my hands and onto the dirt. "What the hell? He's loose Peter, he's loose!"

Peter ran toward me as I struggled to release my arm from Mr. Lott's grip. I broke away and scrambled for the gun. "Don't move or I'll blow your freaking head off. I mean it. I can't take it any longer. I want Mrs. Rippetoe back!"

Peter retied the binding around Mr. Lott's wrists, but this time behind his body instead of in the front.

"You said he was secure! How do I trust you now?"

"I'm only human. Are you faultless?"

No. I wasn't. "Listen. Is that a car?"

Peter stood up. "That's not just any car, that's my car."

"I found this car with the keys in it. Hurry up and get in!" Mrs. Rippetoe demanded.

"Why don't you scoot over and I'll drive." Peter had his hand on the driver side door handle.

"Nope. I can drive just fine."

Peter and I both hesitated.

"Suit yourself, I'll just leave you here."

"Wait. I'll get in the passenger side and Aspen you get in the back."

"No way. It's too nasty."

Peter threw up his arms. "Fine. I'll get in the back just to prove to you it's not the cesspool you claim it is."

"Where's the blue diamond?" Mr. Lott shouted as Peter and I jumped into the car.

Mrs. Rippetoe drove like an Indy race car driver. I double checked my seatbelt and did the sign of the cross. I wondered how she was able to see the road the way she was scrunched forward with a death grip on the steering wheel.

When we hit the highway she pulled over. "I'm really tired. I think I'd like to lay down."

Peter hopped in the driver's seat. With a wince, I helped Mrs. Rippetoe into the backseat. I was horrified that we were letting our little old landlady sleep in the back of Peter's dumpster.

I was tired too and nodded off until we turned onto Interstate 270.

Peter looked over at me when I woke up. "Finally. I was wondering when you were going to wake up. Check on Mrs. Rippetoe. Is she still breathing?"

I undid my seatbelt so I could turn around and look. "Oh no."

"What?" Peter asked.

I raised myself onto the seat, turned around and leaned over the seat back. "I don't see her breathing. Oh God."

I pulled myself further over the back seat so I could get a better look at Mrs. Rippetoe's chest.

Her eyes flew open. I jumped banging my head against the roof.

"Where am I?" she screamed.

"It's okay. You're okay," I said, trying to reassure her.

"What am I doing in this nasty car?"

I held back a laugh. "It's Peter's car. Don't you remember you were in a tent in the forest?"

"I'm too old to camp. I never liked camping anyway. Where are you taking me?"

"Maybe we should take her to the hospital," I whispered to Peter.

"You're not taking me any place but home. I didn't say you could take me anywhere. I should call the police and have them arrest you for kidnapping." Mrs. Rippetoe sat up.

I felt terrible for her. She didn't remember a thing, but perhaps it was a blessing. What she went through couldn't have been easy.

"You know, calling the police isn't a bad idea," Peter said.

"Can we wait just a little while longer? I have a few things to take care of first," I said.

"How long?"

"Tomorrow?"

Peter glanced at his rearview mirror, then leaned over toward me. "And leave those people out there to freeze to death overnight," he whispered.

"It's not supposed to get that cold tonight."

Peter didn't say anything. Mrs. Rippetoe didn't say anything. I hated silence, but I wasn't going to speak either. The less we talked about what happened in the forest the better.

23

I SAT IN MY JEEP OUTSIDE MY OFFICE and watched Stephanie filing papers. She had no idea what happened last night and I wasn't about to tell her. At least not until I made sure Bella and her group of evil minions were under investigation by the police. I called Jack.

"To what do I owe this pleasure?" Jack asked.

"I thought I'd give you a chance to explain and, I sort of need a favor. Can you meet me for lunch?"

"It's been three days since I left you messages. Do you really want to hear my explanation or do you just want me to do you a favor?"

"Both. And I think the least you could do is grant me the favor, after all I wasn't the one in a hotel room with an ex." I felt my cheeks heating up.

"I told you I could explain and you're right—"

"What's that?"

"Don't torture me. I said you're right. A favor isn't even enough to pay you back for what happened the other night. I should have told you about Jennifer earlier."

"Can I stop by your place?"

"Aah, so dessert too?"

I knew where he was trying to go. "Not so quick. I haven't heard your explanation. And actually, I wanted to do this at your place to make sure our conversation wouldn't be overheard."

"One o'clock? I'll be coming from the courthouse. Could you pick something up for us?"

"St. Louis Bread Company okay?" I asked.

"Sure. Surprise me."

I ended the call and took a deep breath before getting out of my Jeep. Poor Stephanie. I watched as she picked up the phone and started talking. I wished I could warn her about Roberto, but I had a plan and it needed to be set in motion before I could say a word.

"Good Morning, Steph!" I tried to be upbeat.

"Morning? It's almost noon. Why are you late?"

Her questions caught me off guard. "Who's the boss here?"

"Sorry, but I tried to call you. I've been waiting for you. I'm worried about Roberto. He was supposed to come over to my place last night and he never showed. He hasn't returned any of my calls or text messages."

"I'm sure—"

"And he was supposed to come by the office today. He always shows when he is supposed to meet me here."

Roberto no longer needs you. His days of accessing our company files to pull off burglaries are over. I couldn't tell her the truth, but it didn't feel right to lie to her either. "I'm sure he just got tied up."

"Maybe, but I think I better go check on him. I'll be back in about an hour."

"I need you here. I've got a one o'clock meeting with Jack."

"So your love life is more important than my boyfriend vanishing?"

"Stephanie. Your boyfriend hasn't vanished. I hate to say this, but maybe he needed a break."

"But he loves me!"

Exposing everything I knew about Roberto, which wasn't all that much once I thought about it, wouldn't be prudent. But I needed to tell her something to prepare her for the truth when it was finally revealed. "Steph? I didn't want to say anything to you. I know how much you like him, but—"

"I love him."

"Which is why it's important that I tell you I saw Roberto with another woman. I'm sorry."

"Who?"

"That's not important. What's important is for you to forget about Roberto right now. Worry about yourself. Get yourself focused and when he contacts you again, ask him if he's been faithful."

"Who was it?"

"Does it matter?"

"It could be his sister or a friend or—"

"Trust me it wasn't a platonic relationship. Ask him next time you see him!"

It wasn't simply a few tears that fell from Stephanie's eyes, it was damn near a downpour. I walked over and put my arms around her. "I'm sorry Stephanie. I really am. You deserve better."

The minutes ticked away and the phone went unanswered as Stephanie cried. I held her until her sobs subsided. "I'm sorry Stephanie. Look, go home. I'm going to close the office for the day. Can you forward the phones to my cell phone before you go?"

I walked back to my desk, put my purse in the drawer and retrieved the stack of phone messages.

"Thanks, Aspen. I'll see you tomorrow. Maybe."

"You have to come in tomorrow Stephanie. Promise me you won't go trying to hunt him down. Go home. Take care of yourself. I'll see you here at the office in the morning."

Stephanie didn't acknowledge me as she walked out the door and I didn't care because I was transfixed on Carmine who paced up and down the sidewalk.

I hadn't yet determined what his role was in the kidnapping and extortion. He'd been the one to suggest purchasing the diamond initial, but had it been his idea or had Mr. Lott requested him to do it?

When I saw Carmine heading for the front door I darted to lock it and flip my office sign to closed. But, he had the door open before I'd made it half way. "Sorry we're closed."

"I don't need your services. I need to talk to you."

"I'm sort of in a hurry. Can we talk later?" I kept facing him as I moved backward toward my desk, to retrieve the gun I'd confiscated from Mr. Lott. I'd lied to Peter about dropping it at the campsite because otherwise he'd take it away. As bad as it sounded, being in the Witness Protection Program made me want to carry a gun nobody knew I had.

"I'm not a bad person."

"I didn't think you were," I said.

"Then why are you backing away from me?"

"Like I said, I'm in a hurry. I need to get my stuff and I didn't want to be rude and turn my back on you."

"Right."

"You don't believe me? I'll prove it to you." I turned my back on him and headed to my desk to retrieve my purse.

"I'm not like my cousin. I actually came here to help you. I've been praying about it all week."

Praying? He didn't strike me as deeply religious, but then again, he was Italian and most likely Catholic. "About what?"

"Mr. Quetzalcoatl. I know something that might help him, but I've been worried the police might see me as an accessory or something to the murder of that guy."

Grand Canyon wide, that's how big I expected my eyes were. What did he know that I didn't? He said he wasn't a bad person, but I wasn't sure I could trust him. "Tell me what you know. I'm sure I can use it to help without getting you involved."

"This." Carmine removed his cell phone from his pocket, tapped on the screen a couple of times, and then handed me the phone.

Wow. It was a picture of Bella. This would make it easier to execute my plan. "When was this taken?"

"The night that guy got whacked."

Carmine sounded like a mobster.

"I think I can help. Actually, I know I can help. Just a sec. I need to make a call."

I dialed Jack's number and got his voicemail. I left a message that I'd be a few minutes late.

"I'm going to need to hook your phone up to my computer. Is that okay?"

"Why?"

"I'm going to print the picture. That way I can use it and it won't track back to you."

"Damn. I shoulda just done that."

I hooked up the phone and navigated to where the pictures were stored. The man had a lot of images. Lots of different women and some were a little risqué. "Um, could you get on here and find the picture. Just double click on it."

Carmine sat down. A couple of seconds later the image came up in the photo viewer program.

"I'll take it from here." I reached over and took the mouse from him and sent the image to my printer, then unplugged his phone from the USB port. "Thanks."

"No problem. Thank you for letting me help Mr. Quetzalcoatl."

"By the way. How'd you happen to get the photo of her at Greg's house?"

"I was on my way to see Mr. Quetzalcoatl about a watch he'd been looking to purchase. She caught my eye because she'd been in my store before. And you have to admit she's beautiful."

"Can I ask you a question about Mrs. Lott?"

"Sure."

"I'm pretty sure Mrs. Lott isn't a frequent customer. I mean your store is pretty great, but she lives all the way over in West County. Why did you say you knew her well?"

"I met Mr. Lott a while back at a diamond and gem show. So, I guess I knew him somewhat well, not her. He said he needed another diamond initial like the one he'd purchased from me at the show."

"But why didn't you just say that instead of pretending like you were suggesting the purchase?"

"He didn't want anyone knowing he wanted the initial. I'm not sure why. I figured he had to replace the other one. But, I didn't ask because I didn't want to lose the sale."

"Thanks, Carmine."

"Sure thing. Hey, you seeing anyone?"

"Yes. I'm heading to his place right now."

"You're empty handed?" Jack questioned when he opened the door.

"I'm sorry. I didn't think I had time to grab something."

"Good thing I snacked on some crackers before you came."

My stomach growled. I was starving.

"Follow me. I'll get you a few crackers and some cheese."

I obeyed, sitting down on a stool when we reached the kitchen.

"So. I'm sorry I didn't mention Jennifer to you. There just never seemed to be a right time."

Mentally I could feel my eyes rolling, but they weren't because they were transfixed on the plate of cheese and crackers Jack assembled. "You know. I'm not sure I want to talk about that right now."

"Exactly what I thought. You just want the favor."

"I didn't say that. I thought we'd be better off discussing it over dinner."

"Now that I like. How about tonight. Here?"

I wasn't so sure he'd want to have dinner with me after I asked him for the favor. He'd probably distance himself from me altogether, which was sad in a way. "Sounds like a fantastic plan."

"Good then its settled. Seven tonight. Now, what kind of favor do you need?"

"It's truly a big favor, but remember you said it was the least I deserved after the hotel room fiasco."

"Stop reminding me about the hotel. I feel bad enough already."

"Sorry. Okay. My favor has to do with getting Mr. Q set free."

"I'm working on that already. He's my client and that is kind of what I've been hired to do."

"I know that. But this favor is, well, it sort of sits on the unstable side of the teeter-totter."

My eyes were focused on Jack and I could tell he was seriously thinking about taking back his offer to do the favor.

"How high?"

"What"

"How high up is the unstable side of the teeter totter?"

"Pretty high."

"Max? Half max?"

"Max and you can't ask any questions."

Jack rubbed his face with his hands. It was the first time I'd seen him portray any sign of stress. "One problem—"

"I knew you wouldn't want to do it."

"I need to get back to the office, so can we talk about this tonight?"

"It really isn't going to take that long. It's simple. I need you to convince the police to go back to Greg's house to recover more evidence."

"But—"

"Remember. No questions." I slid the photo of Bella over to Jack. "This was taken the night of Greg's death and I am pretty sure there is more evidence that will point to her."

I wasn't pretty sure, I was positive. Last night I'd broken into Greg's place and strategically placed the two little diamonds and pieces of Bella's hair inside the house. And not just hair, but hair with follicles still attached.

Jack picked up the photo. "Aspen. I—"

"Please, Jack. It's Mr. Q. I know he's innocent. I can't tell you how I know, but I know she's involved. Maybe even the murderer."

Jack walked out of the kitchen. Before I'd even made it into the family room area, he was standing at the front door holding it open. "You need to go."

"But—"

"I said you need to go."

Stephanie's number popped up on my phone. I worried she might be at Roberto's, so I didn't' bother arguing with Jack. I swiped my finger on the phone and walked out the front door without looking back. "Hi Stephanie. Is everything okay?"

"Yes. Roberto finally texted me and you were right. He said he had been tied up."

Of course he had because Peter and I had left all three of them tied up in the forest. "He did?"

"Yeah. He said he'd call me later. Then I remembered I set up an appointment for three this afternoon."

"With who?"

"That new client that didn't answer the door the other day."

"The appointment better be at the office?"

"No it's at their home. I'll text you the address again so you can meet me there."

"You should call and ask them to come in to the office. They stood us up last time."

"No, actually I got the time wrong and we actually stood them up."

"Great."

24

I ARRIVED AT THE ADDRESS Stephanie had texted earlier. Her car was parked on the street.

"Hi," Stephanie said, as she opened the door.

Her face was perfectly still, only her eyes shifting.

"What's the matter?"

She didn't respond. She stood staring at me. I tried to communicate non-verbally hoping she could convey to me whether I should walk through the door or grab her arm and haul both our asses out to the Jeep.

"Don't be upset," she said.

"So that expression on your face isn't because you're in danger, but because you've done something wrong?"

Stephanie motioned for me to come inside. "I didn't know. I swear. I had no idea."

"Spit it out," I said, as I followed her into the second room of the house.

"He never told me what he wanted when I set up the appointment and never mentioned, uh, he never mentioned—"

"Never mentioned what?"

"Me," Harry Corbitt said as I entered the kitchen at the back of the house.

"Mr. Corbitt?"

"Would you have come if Bart had mentioned my name?"

"Who's Bart?"

"That would be me." A slight-framed man with dark hair and dark glasses stood up from the kitchen table and extended his hand.

I shook it briefly, trying to remember where I'd seen him before, then turned toward Harry. "Can I talk to you for a second in private?"

"Out here." Harry walked out to the four-season room at the back of the house.

"I know who you are."

"Of course you do. I'm Harry Corbitt."

"A member of the Sons of Retribution. I talked to my stepdad."

"A former member. I'm sorry. I should have left you alone or watched you from a distance, but I promised your mother I'd look out for you."

My Mom? My mind swirled. Why would she do that and worse, why would she lie to me about it?

"You're lying. That is all you do is lie. You lied about getting married before and you're lying about getting married now. My mother wouldn't ask you to do something that would put me in danger."

"She didn't ask. I saw how she worried about you when I visited them, so I made a silent promise to check on you."

That part I believed. I knew my mom worried every day.

"Well, now you've seen me. No reason for you to stay. You can leave St. Louis now. In fact, leave the whole state of Missouri."

"I'm not leaving. I'm marrying Bart."

The surprise on my face probably was no surprise to Harry Corbitt. He didn't look gay, if there was a gay look. Covered in tattoos, he was rustic, and his voice with its Australian accent was so deep, it all didn't connect for me. He was a biker and had been part of a criminal motorcycle gang. He had to be lying. "Good one. Very funny. I'm sure whenever you told your buddies in the motorcycle gang they busted a gut. For all I know you're still a gang member."

"No. I'm not. Someone else outed me to the members and then they beat the shit out of me. You think I was born with this ugly face?"

He had a point, it was hard to believe anyone could be born with a face like his. "I'm sorry."

"Don't be. I feel lucky to be alive. They could have killed me for lying to them for so long." He sat down in the rocking chair, looking frail for such a macho man.

"So you were going to marry Bart last time and you just made the fiancée story up?"

"No. My last wedding plans were entirely made up. Sorry. I needed an excuse, to make sure you were okay. And I figured what woman wouldn't want to plan a wedding? When I realized you were fine I made up the story about being ditched."

"You could have just told me the truth about who you were."

"Wasn't going to take the chance of spooking you."

"Well, you failed on that. I was spooked then and I'm spooked now. How do I know you aren't working for someone...you know...getting paid to find me?"

"And marrying a man as part of the ruse?"

"It could be possible. I mean he seems a little nerdy, like an accountant or computer guy. Like somebody who could've hacked his way to my location and could cover up all the loose ends when I mysteriously disappear."

"I just want to get married to Bart and I want you to help since you were the reason we met and fell in love."

"I had nothing to do with it."

"Sure you did. He's the guy you give your cell phone to before you enter the locker rooms at the gym you belong to."

"The phone cubby guy?"

"Don't you see him at the gym?"

"I let my membership lapse." I wondered if I could convince Bart to have the gym renew my membership at a discount.

Harry got up from the chair. "We should go back inside and talk about our wedding plans."

"Didn't the state vote against legalizing same sex marriage?"

"Yes, but it was overturned. Don't you pay attention to what's going on in the world?"

"My life's sort of messy at times. I don't always look at the news."

"Supreme court struck it down. It wouldn't have been a problem anyway because we're getting married in New York."

"I can't plan a wedding in New York."

"But you have to. Bart wants you to and so do I. I want you to be there and I'm inviting your parents too."

My parents. Could I? Should I? The thought of getting to see my mother made me want to start planning their wedding right away. But it wasn't safe for any of us. "Harry. Harry, I can't risk it. I'm sorry."

"Think about it please. We aren't planning on getting married until next year."

"I might be able to plan it but I can't attend. There will be too many people and you shouldn't ask my parents either."

"No. It's going to be small because we are paying for everyone's way. It will be Bart's family. And you and your parents."

"Why me and my parents?"

"You are the reason we found each other. And your parents have always supported me."

"You said my mom knew you were gay?"

"They both did."

"They said you weren't part of Sons of Retribution, not that you were kicked out."

"I asked them not to tell anyone about being kicked out. I'm a closet gay. But, Bart, he's proud of being gay and said I shouldn't hide it. I've never known anyone like Bart. He is so sweet and accepts me."

It was as if I'd entered the Twilight Zone. The vision of Harry with his rustic, uncomfortable to look at face, spouting words of love and acceptance was eerie. "I'm sure you are very much in love, but having someone else plan your wedding, someone from New York is best."

"You don't understand. I want you."

Creepy Harry was back. It didn't seem like I was going to be given a choice. "Harry. You can't tell Bart about me."

"I'd never do that. Besides, Bart says everyone's past is in their past. All he knows is that you were a part of our story because of the phones."

"Don't you want a beautiful wedding. A wedding planned by someone who knows the New York area?"

"No. I want a wedding planned by someone who has meaning for Bart and I. Someday you'll understand. I hope one day you find your Bart."

I did too.

———

Seven on the dot. That's when I first knocked on Jack's door. It was now five after. I should have realized dinner was going to be canceled when he'd abruptly asked me to leave his house this afternoon, but I secretly hoped we still had a date.

I headed back to my Jeep, my paranoia setting in. What if Jack planned on turning me in to the police? After all Mr. Q was his client. His loyalty to his client would be more important than his loyalty to his girlfriend or whatever I was to him. But, I was trying to help Mr. Q.

"Aspen?"

I turned around. "I didn't realize you had cancelled dinner."

"I didn't. Sorry. I fell asleep."

"It's okay. We can make it for another night."

"Absolutely not. I've got you here and I'm going to take full advantage of it." He rubbed his eyes and smoothed his hair back.

I walked back towards the front door. "But, I thought you were mad today."

"It's not that. I didn't want to talk about the favor any longer. It was heard and understood. And I don't want to talk about it tonight. Come on in." Jack held the door open.

"I'm really sorry—"

"Shhhh." Jack closed the door with one hand, using his other to grab my arm and pull me close to him.

The kiss felt unlike any other I'd had with Jack. It was gentle, loving, and ten times as sexy as the hard, passionate one's he usually gave. I felt my knees give way.

"Woah, hold on," he said.

"What was that?"

"A kiss."

"I know, but it was spectacular."

Spectacular? What kind of word was that to use for a gentle, loving kiss? I sounded like a sports commentator.

"As opposed to?"

"No. I mean all your kisses are great. But, this felt different."

Jack's face tinged with pink. He walked past me and into the kitchen. "I thought we'd just do leftovers if you don't mind."

I guessed my attempt to talk about feelings was a no go. I sat down at the counter. "Fine. I'm not all that hungry anyway."

"Did you still want to talk about Jennifer?" Jack, stuck a dish in the microwave.

I didn't really care about her. What I cared about was that he held back an important part of his past. Sure, I held back an important part of mine too, but I had a bona fide excuse. "No. It's not really about her. It's about you not feeling like you could tell me you were once engaged."

"Oh." Jack poured us each a glass of red wine. "It's lasagna, is that okay?"

The microwave beeped. Jack divvied up the lasagna and placed a plate in front of me. He stood on the other side of the counter.

"So, why didn't you tell me about her?"

"Because she's a curse."

"That's not very nice." Secretly my mind did a happy dance.

"I know. But whenever I tell a girlfriend about Jennifer it usually breaks apart the relationship. Wouldn't you call that a curse?"

Did he just infer I was his girlfriend?

"Wait. You mean Jennifer isn't the girlfriend you were breaking up with when we first met?"

"No. If you want the truth, she was four girlfriends ago."

"Four?"

"Yes and that doesn't include you."

I went all in. "Doesn't include me in the girlfriend count or doesn't include me because I'm not your girlfriend?"

"Here. Have some more wine."

I took a bite of my lasagna waiting for his response. After two more bites and no answer, I couldn't take the silence any longer. "So?"

"Oh. Yes. Four girlfriends after Jennifer and they all broke it off because of her. So see?"

No. I didn't see anything except him avoiding my question. "How long ago did you break up with Jennifer? And as for the other girlfriends, did you tell them about Jennifer in the beginning?"

"An ex-fiancée is not something you tell someone about on a first date."

"Third date?" I asked.

"I'm pretty sure I told all of them by the sixth."

"No wonder." I took the last bite of my lasagna.

"What?"

"You don't wait that long to tell someone about an ex-fiancée that continues to be an active part of your life!"

Jack collected our empty plates and put them in the dishwasher.

"You didn't say how long ago you and Jennifer split up."

"Two years ago. Guess what I picked up?"

An STD? Geez, four girlfriends in two years. "What?"

"Chocolate covered strawberries and two cans of whip cream."

I knew he meant it to be sexy, but frankly, it felt like liquid nitrogen had been poured over my hormones. "I should get going."

"Aspen. I like you. All day I thought about you. Holding you, kissing you, touching you." Jack walked around the peninsula, pressed his body against my back and put his arms around my waist. "The only thing I can think about is lying in my bed with you," he whispered.

Sigh. I felt my hormones melting. My mind not lagging far behind. The thought of lying next to Jack, naked, in his bed became my perfect escape plan. I needed to let go. Mrs. Rippetoe was safe, Mr. Q wasn't in any immediate danger, and I was a lonely woman with needs.

25

"WHA...? WHAT TIME IS IT?" I asked when Jack woke me.

"Sorry, Aspen. I need to leave."

I squinted my eyes trying to focus on the clock sitting on the end table next to Jack's side of the bed. "But, it's two a.m."

"I know. It's an emergency."

"I didn't even hear the phone ring." I pulled the cover up snugly around my neck. "I'll see you when you get back."

"Uh...I'm...uh—"

"Oh. Right." I yanked the covers back and grabbed my clothes off the floor.

"Sorry."

"No need to apologize. I should get back to PJ anyway. Is this anything related to Mr. Q?"

"No."

And there it was again. Another unexpanded answer. I worked to balance my emotions. On the outside, I was practical, logical, unaffected by being kicked out of my lover's house at two in the morning, on the inside I was seething.

Jack walked with me down the stairs to the front door.

"Brrrr." I pulled my jacket tight.

"I'll see you later," he said.

"Oh. Okay."

There was only one way to describe my exit from Jack's house. I felt as though I was being escorted from the premise of a place I was no longer welcomed. He didn't even kiss me goodbye.

By the time I made it back to my place, I was pissed. I was done. Jack didn't deserve someone like me. In fact, he didn't deserve anyone. I was tempted to keep the engine running and sleep in the Jeep since I was finally warm, especially because I'd had to park more than a block away from my place. But I braved the cold, running all the way back to the fourplex.

Peter's lights were on. My heart hurt and I wanted to knock on his door and file my complaints about his friend Jack. I knew he'd listen, but not without judgment, so I quietly opened the door to our building. I crept up the steps so he wouldn't notice I was coming home in the middle of the night. But, once inside my apartment it was a lost cause. PJ jumped and whined, twirled and jumped, twirled and whined, and every combination in between. I couldn't help but smile. Finally, someone who was excited to see me and wasn't shy about expressing it.

———

My hand scrambled across the top of the nightstand trying to find the phone. I propped one eye open to view the clock. It was seven thirty, but it still seemed dark outside. I didn't recognize the number.

"Aspen Moore. How can I help you?"

"It's Mrs. Paddy. I'm calling on the secret phone."

I sat up alert. "Are you okay?"

"He's got people here packing boxes. I don't know what to do."

"Who?"

"Junior. I told them to stop, but he grabbed my arm and took me back to my room. I can't get the door open. I never noticed before, but it looks like my doorknob was changed. I think he's got me locked in my room."

"I'll be right over!"

"I don't think you'll be able to stop him. Junior, well, the boy is pretty big."

She wasn't exaggerating. Junior was probably six-foot tall and not a pound under two-fifty.

"Don't worry I'll handle it. What's your lawyer's number?"

"I don't know."

"What's his name?"

"It's a she. Angie Oxford."

"Ok. Just stay in your bed and tell Junior your too sick to go anywhere. I'll be there as soon as I can."

I dialed Officer Storey's number.

"Eli I need your help!"

"Who...who is this?"

"Sorry, it's Aspen. I know it's early, but I wasn't sure who—"

"Are you okay?

"Yes, I'm okay, but I have an elderly client whose grandson is basically holding her hostage."

"I'm not on duty right now. Did you call the precinct?"

"No. I well, this is really a family matter. Her grandson has power of attorney, but only if she doesn't have the capacity to take care of things. She's fine, but he's taken over and he's packing up all her things as we speak."

"Shouldn't she just call her lawyer?"

"He's got her locked in her room. I'm going to contact her lawyer, but I could use some help getting her grandson to leave. I'd go over by myself, but the grandson is a big man."

"What's the address?"

"Can you come without calling it in?"

"I'm off duty. I'm doing this as your friend."

"Thank you."

I hung up the phone after giving Eli the address and immediately called Mrs. Paddy's lawyer.

"Oxford Law."

"Angie Oxford, please. It's an emergency."

"I'm sorry she's not in the office at the moment."

"You don't understand. It's regarding Penelope Paddy."

"Just one moment. I'll connect you."

I was currently experiencing the power of money.

"This is Angie."

"Ms. Oxford. I'm Aspen Moore, Mrs. Paddy's personal concierge. She needs to see you immediately. She needs—"

"I'm sorry. You're her what?"

"Mrs. Paddy employs the services of my company, Moore Time. We are a personal concierge company."

"Why isn't she calling me?"

"She's having a problem with Junior—"

"I knew this day would come. I'm not yet in the office and my schedule is full, so can you please let her know I'll stop by around six tonight on my way home?"

"No. She needs you right now. Junior is packing up her belongings as we speak. I think he may have already sold her property. Can you be there in a half hour?"

"Someone from my office will be there," she said, before the call was cut off.

I turned toward PJ. "Brrr, little man. You think you can open the door and go outside yourself?"

PJ tilted his head, his eyes expressing the fact that I was talking nonsense. His tail wagged a few times and then he pounced on me, licking my face.

"Okay." I jumped out of bed, pulled on some sweats and a coat. "Let's go."

We trotted down the steps and to the back door.

"It snowed PJ!"

He hustled out into the yard, nose down in the snow. A few minutes later, he lifted his leg on the fence.

"Brrr. Let's go back inside."

He looked up at me, his muzzle covered in snow burrs. I yanked his lead slightly. He responded by running back and forth like he was on a downhill ski slope. Left. Right. Left. "Yarrf."

I couldn't help but laugh. Who knew a tiny ball of fur covered in snow could make my life feel like it had purpose. I truly loved him.

PJ stopped running and walked up toward the door. He too was ready to leave the cold air behind.

The two of us ate a quick breakfast in the living room. I turned on the morning news. No updates on Mr. Q's case and no breaking news about three people being tied up in Mark Twain forest. I had a sudden urge to check on Mrs. Rippetoe.

I gave PJ a big kiss and set him on the couch.

"Be good," I said as I closed the door, knowing PJ didn't know the definition of those words.

Even though it was early, I knocked on Mrs. Rippetoe's door.

Peter's door opened. "She's not home."

"But it's so early."

"If you had been around last night you would know that her son flew in. He was worried about her so he took her and Sassy back to California for a few weeks."

I ignored Peter's comment. "Well that's a relief."

"Yep." Peter's face lacked emotion.

"Is there a problem?"

"No. Just haven't felt like going anywhere since yesterday. Guess I'm feeling guilty about leaving three human beings tied up in freezing weather in the middle of the forest. I should have called the police, but instead I keep listening to you and I don't know why. Now it's almost too late to call the police because they could have died of exposure. We'll probably be charged with triple homicide."

"First they aren't dead because Roberto called Stephanie yesterday. And most importantly, those guys were going to kill us!"

"Doesn't matter, still natural to feel some guilt. Plus, I was thinking about how this all got started. It was you and that blue diamond. Where is that diamond anyway?"

I looked at the time on my phone. "I'm not sure, but right now I gotta run. Problems with Mrs. Paddy. Want to have dinner tonight and talk about it?"

"Okay," Peter said, sounding a little like Eeyore.

"Are you sure it's just this situation that's got you down?"

"It's Madeline too. I've called her several times and she hasn't gotten back to me."

"You think something happened to her?"

"No. She's posted on her Facebook page so I know she's fine."

"She's probably just busy. She loves her job right?

"Yes, but, I love mine too and I have time to call her."

I didn't know what else to say. He was crazy about Madeline. I hated seeing him down like this, but I'd be lying if I said I was sorry and hoped she called him soon. I wondered if his dark and gloomy attitude might just be my small flicker of light.

———

Eli and I were standing on the sidewalk outside Mrs. Paddy's building. Our attempt to stop Junior from railroading his grandmother had ended with Junior calling the police.

"That went well," Eli said.

Sarcasm was a side of Eli I'd never seen before. "I thought you'd flash your badge and Junior would stop what he was doing. Who calls the police on the police?"

"I don't know why I agreed to do this." Eli shook his head.

"I'm sorry Eli. I hope I didn't get you in trouble."

"Not going to be an issue because I'm leaving. Remember, I wasn't here in an official capacity."

"But, what about Mrs. Paddy?"

"Aspen. I want to help you, I do, but you're gonna need to call the police and make an official complaint."

"But—" My eyes flashed over to a woman who was a little bit Stephanie and a little bit Jack's ex. Her black tailored suit screamed lawyer. "Miss Oxford?"

"Are you Mrs. Paddy's errand runner?"

"Personal Concierge."

"Right. Are you coming up?"

I looked at Eli and his eyes reiterated what he'd said moments ago. He was leaving. And to be honest, there wasn't much I could do. I had no power and I had several other clients to see today. "I really need to get going. Please call if I can help you with anything." I held out my card.

"Damn Junior." She yanked it from my hand and walked toward the revolving doors.

I turned to Eli. "Well seems like she's dealt with Junior before. Maybe he'll listen to her."

"Maybe," Eli said. "Speaking of dealing with things. I heard the lawyer handling the murder case for your client has the police investigators going back to the property. Says he's sure they missed something. Don't know what he thinks they're going to find."

I tried hard not to look guilty, but I was sure he saw the trepidation in my eyes. I'd used him to help me advance my case and I had a feeling he knew it. "Really?"

"So. You didn't know about it?"

Damn. I hated lying to Eli, but preservation mode kicked in. "No."

"You think your client's guilty?"

"I'm positive he's not."

"To be honest, Aspen, I'm worried about you. Worried you're mixed up in something you shouldn't be. I promised Marshal Cutter I'd keep an eye on you and well, I'm thinking I need to have a talk with him."

"No! I mean, I'm okay. You know I wouldn't do anything unless it was for a good reason. The right reason—"

"Stop there. I can tell I don't want to know anything else. I just hope you know what you're doing because I'd hate to see you end up behind bars. I think it's best if you don't contact me for a while."

"I'm sorry Eli."

"Take care of yourself." Eli leaned over and kissed me on my cheek.

I watched him drive away. I felt a sense of loss. I hoped sometime soon I could repair whatever damage I had done.

———

Carmine stood on the sidewalk near my store.

"What's going on?" I asked when I walked up.

"I'm not sure. I saw the cops pull up and thought you'd called them on me because of that picture. Boy, was I relieved when they walked into your store."

I stood next to Carmine peering inside the window of my own store, watching like an outsider. A policeman was talking to Stephanie and Roberto was standing next to her handcuffed. He exchanged some words with the officer, then leaned over and kissed Stephanie. When he was finished, the officer escorted Roberto out of the store and into a police car.

"Aren't you going to go inside and find out what's going on?" Carmine asked, turning his head to look behind him where I'd taken up hiding when the police began exiting my store.

"Nope. Don't really want to get involved."

"Woman after my own heart. You sure you're dating someone?"

"I'm sure. Sorry, but I need to make a call." I took out my cell phone and walked in the opposite direction of my office.

"Uh. Excuse me officer. Moore Time. How may I help you?" Stephanie said when she answered the phone.

"I heard you talking to an officer. You could scare away customers."

"But you're not a customer. And what makes you think it is something bad? Where are you?"

"I'm outside."

"Well get in here. It's awful. The police took Roberto away. I need you!"

I watched the last police car drive away. "I'm coming."

Before the shop door had shut behind me, Stephanie blurted out, "It was terrible. I didn't know what to do. I tried to call you lots of times. Why didn't you answer?"

I looked at my phone. "I'm sorry. I guess I had it on vibrate. What happened?"

"Roberto came in and asked me to run away with him. Said he'd done some bad things."

"What kind of things?" I asked innocently.

"He said he broke into some of our customer's homes. I couldn't believe it. Then he said the person he was working with killed someone. He wanted me to run away with him because he thought they were going to try to blame him for the murder."

"Who killed who?"

"That nanny girl at the Lott's place. She killed Mr. Q's neighbor! Oh. That's the girl. The girl you saw Roberto with isn't it?"

I bent my head down.

"I knew it. But see. He loves me. He wanted me to run away with him. I bet she made him kiss her."

"How did the police find out?"

"I talked some sense into Roberto. I told him if he wasn't guilty, he had to be the first one to go to the police.

Maybe he could make a deal and not have to serve any time for breaking into those houses."

"You did that?" I guess at heart, Stephanie was honest and far brighter than I gave her credit for.

"Yes. I wasn't going to be plastered all over the post offices on one of those most wanted posters."

"You did good, Stephanie."

"Did he ever tell you where he was last night?"

"He did and he was so sweet. He said he was at home all night, but he didn't want to answer the phone because he would put me in danger. Isn't that so sweet?"

I smiled with relief. "Yes, Stephanie. It really is."

"Can I go? I told Roberto I'd come down to the station. Do you think Jack could represent him?"

"I don't think that will happen since he's representing Mr. Q. But, I'm no lawyer so I'll have him give you a call. I'm sure he can recommend someone."

Stephanie walked out the door in some sort of oddly confused looking state – a little bit of shock, mixed with euphoria, and dampened by a dose of reality that the man she loved was a criminal.

26

"I NOW PRONOUNCE YOU HUSBAND AND WIFE. You may kiss the bride," Judge Hart pronounced.

A single tear rolled down my cheek as Belinda bent down and gave Thomas Brackford a kiss.

The mid-morning wedding hadn't been an easy thing to pull off. With the debacle surrounding my life, I'd had to convince Belinda and Brackford to push their wedding to give me a couple of weeks to arrange everything.

"Congratulations!" I hugged Belinda and shook Brackford's hand.

"Aspen. I don't know how you did this, but it is absolutely perfect," Belinda said.

"I couldn't have done it without my friends. This is Mrs. Paddy. She's responsible for us snagging this location."

The private condominium was Mrs. Paddy's new residence. Junior had in fact sold her penthouse and it was too late to back out. I was helping her plan the move and when I'd mentioned the last minute wedding I was planning for a client, she'd stepped up and offered her new condominium. It was empty and a blank slate. I'd draped white silk fabric over the floor to ceiling windows. They framed an incredible view of the arch grounds.

"Thank you so much." Belinda went to shake Mrs. Paddy's hand.

"Oh no, Dear. Give me a hug."

Belinda obliged.

"And of course, Jack was responsible for getting his friend Judge Hart to officiate."

"He did a perfect job too. Where is Jack by the way?" Brackford said.

"He's over there talking to Mr. Quetzalcoatl."

I left the newlyweds and walked over to Jack. "Did you enjoy the wedding?"

"I'm going to talk to Thomas," Mr. Q said and walked off.

Jack put his arm around me. "More than I thought I would."

"So congratulations on getting Mr. Q released."

"It's the facts. Nothing more."

"What's the word on the street?" I asked.

"Did you really just say that?"

I laughed. "I'm curious. What did Bella say about her and Mr. Lott?"

What I really wanted to know was whether or not the police knew we'd left the two of them tied up in the Mark Twain forest.

"Evidently Bella spilled quite a bit before she asked for a lawyer. I think she was mad at Oliver Lott since he lawyered up the second the handcuffs were heading toward his wrists."

"I'm assuming Mr. Lott's lack of attention to his wife wasn't about his business, but about Bella, am I correct?" I asked.

"That's what I hear."

"Did Bella say why she killed Greg?"

"She thought he was Mr. Quetzalcoatl."

"But she was in Greg's house," I said. It was time to reinforce the position that Greg had been killed at his place.

"The paperwork she lifted from the office at the auction house in Denmark where she worked had Greg listed as Mr. Quetzalcoatl."

Thank goodness for Mr. Q's paranoia. Listing Greg as himself made it easier to believe that Greg was killed at his home. A case of mistaken identity. I looked around the room until I spotted Mr. Q, then lowered my voice. "Why'd she want to kill him?"

"A blue diamond. But she said it was an accident. She slipped him something in a glass of wine to get him to tell the truth. He told her he'd sold the diamond to Mr. Lott. But she didn't believe him and thought he needed more of the drug so she put more into his wine. Turns out the increased dosage caused Greg's throat to close up suffocating him."

Greg stole the diamond from Mr. Q. Some friend. It was falling into place. If Bella thought Mr. Lott had the diamond, it made sense she would try to get me to steal it by telling me she saw a blue diamond in the safe. And she probably started coming on to him after that too.

"So where is the diamond?" I asked.

"Time for brunch everyone." Albert, the caterer I'd met at the dog parade, motioned all of us to the table.

Jack walked toward the group of people milling about the dining area, leaving my question unanswered.

The bride and groom sat in the middle and the rest of us scattered around on either side. It was a small affair, which included Belinda's parents, Mr. Q as best man, me as the maid of honor, Mrs. Paddy, the judge, and Jack. Stephanie was holding down the office and Peter had flown out the night before to California.

Jack lifted his glass of champagne. "I'd like to make a toast to the bride and groom."

Normally the best man would make the toast, but Mr. Q had asked Jack to do it since all the hoopla over Greg's death had left him, in his own words, "weak."

Jack continued, "To trumpet your love with a wedding ring, shows commitment's a beautiful thing..."

Did I just hear those words coming from Jack's mouth? I sat alert, waiting for the rest of the toast.

"...Together you will share the loss, together you will share the gain, but only one can be the boss and that dear Thomas is your ball and chain."

Now that sounded more like the Jack I knew. His commitment phobia was shining bright. I smiled nervously at Jack.

The chuckles rippled through the guests seated at the table.

Jack smiled back at me, then added, "May you live well, laugh often, and love much."

The laughter slowed to a trickle as each guest raised their champagne glass and took a sip. After that the conversation slowed as everyone turned their attention to the food. Albert's brunch consisted of eggs benedict, lightly fried potatoes with rosemary, fresh fruit, and small blueberry muffins.

Mrs. Paddy banged her spoon against her water glass. "Everyone. I have a special announcement."

All eyes were on Mrs. Paddy.

"Today would have been my sixtieth wedding anniversary. My husband and I got married on the same day you got married." Mrs. Paddy looked at Brackford and Belinda.

"Really? That must mean our wedding day is lucky," Belinda said.

"As a matter of fact it is. When Aspen mentioned the day of the wedding I wanted to help make it special. So I had Aspen book you a honeymoon at the same place I had my honeymoon. St. Croix in the Virgin Islands. It's my gift to you." She raised her champagne glass.

The gasps were audible and everyone clapped.

———

"Thanks for being Brackford's best man," I said to Mr. Q as I dropped him off at his townhouse.

"Why are you thanking me? Thomas is my friend."

"I just want you to understand how much I appreciate you being his friend."

"Can you come inside for a moment?"

I was taken aback by his offer. Whatever he wanted must be important. Or perhaps today's event brought back sad memories of his friend Greg. "Sure for a few minutes then I need to get back to the office to relieve Stephanie. She doesn't usually work on Saturdays."

Mr. Q and I went into his place. After petting Mr. P, I followed Mr. Q into the kitchen.

"I apologize for not being honest with you about the Blue Monkey diamond," Mr. Q started, "but, I was nervous about who I could and could not trust. I didn't think I could trust you. But, now. Now, I know I can trust you. You are not only my personal concierge, but you have become my friend."

Sigh. I didn't want to officially be Mr. Q's friend. Too many friends made life too hard. The closer I got to people the harder things would be if I had to relocate again. It was bad enough that I had two men I cared about and a landlady I adored. Mrs. Paddy and now Mr. Q knocking on my friendship door was a little too much for my mind to process. "Thanks."

"I want you to know I have the Blue Monkey diamond."

"But I thought Greg stole the diamond from you and sold it?"

"I thought he did too, but he actually hid it."

If Greg had actually hidden the blue diamond then he'd given his life for his friend Mr. Q. Telling Bella he'd sold it to Mr. Lott, got Bella off Mr. Q's trail. "Where?"

"In here."

I watched Mr. Q open a hidden door on his kitchen wall. "What's this?"

"It's my secret room. I had it built so I could hide from intruders if I needed to. Greg knew about it. And now, you are the only one who knows."

"How did you find the diamond?"

"Greg left a note inside one of my comic books. He hid it in a box under the bottom shelf. He must have known I was in danger."

Mr. Q walked over to a shelf, bent down and removed a small box. He opened it and I caught my breath. It was so beautiful. I could see why so many people wanted the diamond.

"You are going to get it insured, aren't you?"

"Already done. I called Friday afternoon, the minute I found the diamond."

"I'm glad. And I'm glad you're safe. I better go now, but I will come by tomorrow to check on you."

"But I don't have any need for your services tomorrow."

"That's okay. I'm coming as a friend." The words rolled out of my mouth effortlessly. Whether I wanted to or not, I cared for quirky Mr. Q.

I picked up Mr. P and gave him a kiss goodbye. His soft fur made me want to run home and scoop PJ into my arms and snuggle up with him forever.

I texted Stephanie letting her know I was on my way. As I drove to the office, I felt relaxed for the first time in more than a month. When Monday rolled around, I was going to sign up for yoga classes so I'd be better prepared to handle stress when it came my way and it would come my way because that was my life.

Stephanie was sitting at the reception desk when I pulled up. "Thanks so much for staying at the office until I got here," I said as I entered.

"No problem. I don't have much to do now that Roberto is in jail. How was the wedding?"

"Charming. It's so nice to see Mr. Brackford and Belinda in love."

"Like Roberto and I?"

Right, except Mr. Brackford's not a criminal. "Yes."

"I miss him already," Stephanie said.

"Hopefully he will not serve much time."

"He can't serve any time. I don't know what I'll do without him. I wish Jack would represent him. Did you ask?"

"I'm not sure. It might be a confl—"

"But he's not representing Mr. Q any longer."

She had a point. I just wasn't sure I wanted Stephanie's relationship with Roberto inserted into my relationship with Jack. "But, I thin—"

"Please?"

"Okay. But, I can't promise anything. He's busy tonight, but he's going to call me tomorrow evening, so I'll ask then. In the meantime, I have something I wanted to talk to you about."

"Please don't fire me. I didn't know Roberto swiped information from our client files."

A few weeks ago I would have scooped up that information and used it to get rid of Stephanie, but she'd proven herself to be loyal and showed a glimmer of responsibility that I believed I could polish. "I'm not firing you Stephanie. I'm giving you a raise."

———

Stephanie had been elated about her raise. I hoped I was accurate about being able to make her an even better employee. I locked up the office and jumped in my car. There was one more thing I promised Stephanie and I planned to get that out of the way pronto. I dialed Jack.

We chatted for a while as I drove.

"I'm sorry about this, but I need to ask...hold on. I'm getting out of my car. Why don't I call you back when I'm inside my apartment?"

"But what are you sorry about?"

"I'll call you back in a minute," I said.

I made my way up to my apartment. I picked up PJ and sat him on the couch with me before calling Jack back.

"Hi. As I was saying. I sort of promised Stephanie I would ask you about whether you could represent Roberto,"

"I'm not sure I can."

"That's what I told her."

"But, I will confirm that with my firm."

"It's really okay if you can't." I didn't want to come right out and tell him not to represent Roberto, but I hoped he'd understand my silent wishes.

"I'll keep that in mind. Now, let's talk about our getaway to St. Croix."

Mrs. Paddy's announcement at Brackford and Belinda's wedding yesterday caused Jack to decide we too should go to St. Croix and experience what Mrs. Paddy experienced sixty years ago. Although I was pretty sure he just wanted to get me away from my work, so we could have uninterrupted sex-capades.

"I would love to go with you to St. Croix, but—"

"I knew there'd be a but."

"No. Now hear me out. I want to go, but—"

This time it wasn't Jack who interrupted, but call waiting. "Hold on a sec." I pulled my phone away from my ear so I could look at the screen. Peter was calling. I hit the ignore button, wanting to get back to my conversation with Jack, so we could get past the travel discussion and into the heart of our relationship.

"Before we set off—"

Peter called again. I hit the ignore button for the second time.

"Before we set off on our romantic getaway can we just write the first sentence of our relationship? I'm not expecting an ending, or anything about the future. I just want a first sentence," I said.

Peter called for the third time. I knew I could no longer ignore him.

"I'm sorry Jack. Don't hang up. I promise I'll be right back."

I swiped my finger across the screen effectively putting Jack on hold.

"Where's the fire?" I asked Peter.

"Aspen?"

"Peter. Where are you?"

"I'm at Lambert airport. It's Madeline. She—-"

"Oh my God, was there an accident? Is she in the hospital?"

"No. She—"

"Oh God, Peter, is she dead? I'm so sorry. I—"

"Aspen, no, she's not dead. She's married."

I couldn't believe it. Peter and Madeline had gotten married. I should have been happy for them, but I was sad. Sad that a man I wasn't sure was capable of true love was currently on hold while the man I believed I loved was permanently shutting the door on my heart. I squeaked out what I could, "Congratulations."

"What?"

"I said congratulations. But, I thought you all would have planned a big wedding."

He didn't respond and I thought we'd gotten disconnected. I was about to switch back to Jack when I heard something. "Peter? Are you crying?"

"You never gave me the chance to finish my sentence. I—"

"Well that's no reason to cry."

"Madeline married someone else."

My gasp was so loud I was sure even Jack could hear it while he was on hold. "Who?"

"Who cares? It was some guy she met on set. Six years. We spent the last six years of our lives together and she didn't even have the guts to tell me in person. I flew all the way out there and she wasn't home. I tried to call her and she responded with a text message. A text. Can you believe it?"

"I...I'm sorry Peter. I really am."

"Can you meet me for a drink?"

Peter was my best friend and no matter how hard it was on me, I had to be there for him. I had to let him cry on my shoulder without any thoughts of kissing him. I had to let him grieve the loss of Madeline. "I'll be there at the bar around the corner from our office in a half hour."

I switched back to Jack. "Hey, sorry about—"

"You want a first sentence, Aspen? Here it is. I'm scared to death because I'm falling in love with you."

THE END

ACKNOWLEDGEMENTS

Procrastination, you were there even when I insisted you were better off somewhere else. I don't thank you, but I accept you. Many others are more deserving and as always, my husband Bill is first. He sure does put up with a lot having me as his wife – so thank you!

When it comes to crafting, it is important to acknowledge the Ladysleuths. Ten years ago, I joined Lisa Bork, Teresa Inge, Shelley Shearer, and Kathy Whalen in an online critique group. It amazes me after all these years that they are still there to provide support and feedback.

Thank you to my beta readers, Pat Davis, Betsy Ninneman, and Karen Shaffer for your thoughtful feedback and quick turnaround. My appreciation to Steve Liskow for providing feedback and to the Guppies chapter of Sisters in Crime for their continued support of fledgling writers.

Finally, to my girlfriends, Karen Shaffer and Pam De Voe, thank you for your support, much needed coffee get togethers, continued encouragement, and for always making me feel like a best seller.

ABOUT THE AUTHOR

A geographic mutt, Kelly Cochran has lived on the East Coast, the West Coast, and many places in between. During her childhood, she attended thirteen different schools, in twelve years, all before going off to college at the age of seventeen. To her surprise, she turned out somewhat normal and went on to have a 20-year career in information technology.

Currently she lives in Austin, Texas with her husband and three dogs. Her son lives in the Washington, D.C. area where he never tires of Kelly's efforts to get him to move closer.

When she isn't writing, she divides her time between managing Internet-based retail businesses, talking to her mother, and playing Monkey Wrench and Candy Crush on her mini iPad all the while wondering why she doesn't have enough time to finish writing her next novel.

Kelly is a member of Sisters in Crime. Find out more at www.KellyCochran.com